RHIANNON

Margarita Felices

Margarita Felices

For Mum.

Who taught me that we all have a little magic inside of us.

Margarita Felices

Excerpt from Rhiannon

"Burn her!" screamed Elizabeth as she stepped forward. "Burn her now!" She reached out for a lit torch and stood at the base of the stacked wood. She looked up at Rhiannon. "I don't care what you are. You took my Evan. You took my hopes of our own child and for that, I will never forgive you. You will burn in hell tonight, witch." She lowered the torch as Rhiannon screamed and then she withdrew it without lighting anything.

Elizabeth looked up at Rhiannon with a smile, "Your pretty face will no longer look upon my husband," she said and tipped the torch forward, lighting the first section of the pyre. "Evan isn't here to watch you burn and your devil child will certainly be dead by now." And then Elizabeth threw the torch into the rest of it and lit the second pyre. "I made sure they left it out there for the wolves to feast on."

Welsh translation (and my thanks) - Cymen Cyf. Caernarfon. Wales.

Copyright

Rhiannon
Copyright © Margarita Felices 2020

Books to Go Now Publication
http://www.bookstogonow.com
Cover Design by Romance Novel Covers Now
http://www.romancenovelcoversnow.com/

First Paperback Edition January 2020
ISBN: 9781658042918

Warning: the unauthorized reproduction or distribution of this copyrighted work is illegal. Criminal copyright infringement, including infringement without monetary gain, is investigated by the FBI and is punishable by up to 5 years in prison and a fine of $250,000. All rights reserved. No part of this book may be reproduced or transmitted in any form without written permission from the publisher, except by a reviewer who may quote brief passages for review purposes.

This book is a work of fiction and any resemblance to any person, living or dead, any place, events or occurrences, is purely coincidental. The characters and story lines are created from the author's imagination and are used fictitiously.

If you are interested in purchasing more works of this nature, please stop by www.bookstogonow.com

OTHER STORIES BY MARGARITA FELICES

Judgement of Souls 1: Origin
Judgement of Souls 2: Call of The Righteous
Judgement of Souls 3: Kiss at Dawn
The Psychic
Story of My Heart
A Christmas Embrace
Ordinary Wins
The Decoys
Trancers

Passage from RHIANNON...

The Welsh mountains are not a place to venture out in the winter months. It's dark, cold and the winds scream like demon banshees through them. The wild nature of the area will drive any mortal to despair and it has been responsible for the deaths of many lonely travelers who veered off the pathways.

A mile away from the mountain base of Cadair Idris, Rhiannon slipped as she hurried along the wet fields. She had to get away, but the child she carried wasn't going to wait. Another kick made Rhiannon scream and drop to the floor on all fours. It was too early, she still had at least a month. She struggled to get up and looked behind her. The lights from the torches were closer and coming toward her. If she was going to deliver her child, she would have to work through the pain and reach the mountains before it was too late. She stumbled back a step and held onto her stomach. "Hush, my precious child. You must wait until we are safe." The pain subsided slightly and Rhiannon quickened her pace. She could see the light from the farmer's cottage in the distance and knew that the mountain path was just beyond it.

"Where are you in a rush to get to?" A voice coming from the near darkness startled her.

"The mountains...I have to get to the mountains."

"I can see the light from torches, the villagers are after you. What have you done?"

"They accuse me of being a witch and they want my child."

"And are you? Are you a witch?"

"Do I look like one to you?" asked Rhiannon. "I have to keep going," she pleaded.

The voice came closer and Rhiannon saw that it was the farmer who lived in the house near the foothills. "I think you have run far enough. They won't hurt you while you are with child."

"I wish I could be so sure…please, I have to get to the mountains. I'm safe there."

Rhiannon left the farmer behind as she stumbled toward the pathway. She looked behind her again and saw the lights were even closer. No time to lose. She stumbled with a few more steps and doubled over in pain sending her to her knees. Her child was ready to birth now, but she could hardly move as she continued to crawl on all fours. Each move more painful than the last until she couldn't bear it any longer and turned to lie on her back. She lifted up her skirt and pushed. Warm liquid flowed out from her body as the pain came again and she pushed harder. She screamed as she was lifted up to stand on her own two feet. The men from the village surrounded her as she shouted out, "My child is coming!"

"Bring her," said one of the men, "and tie her hands so that she cannot curse any of you with them." And then they pulled hard on the ropes to walk her away.

Rhiannon stumbled as she screamed, "I'm giving birth, let me be, let my child be free!"

The villagers pulled harder on the ropes and ignored her pleas until she stopped and screamed out again. Within seconds, a newborn fell to the ground and even though still attached to her, the villagers pulled at her once more to carry on walking. Her child dragged on the ground beneath her, still tethered to its mother as Rhiannon gazed down in horror, begging for them to stop. "Please help my child, please help."

One of the villagers took out a knife and cut the cord. The child lay on the wet ground and began to cry out as each man stepped over it and carried on walking, not looking, not caring.

"My child!" screamed Rhiannon. "Please help, please bring it with you."

The head of the villagers stood in front of her and tugged at her hair to turn her head around.

"Take a look at your demon child, witch. Tomorrow the wolves will have had a small feast."

Rhiannon's eyes widened. "No...you cannot. My child is an innocent."

As they dragged her away, Rhiannon could hear her child's cry as they walked farther and farther away from it.

****

The village of Treharne lay two miles from the highest mountain range, Cadair Idris, in the northern part of Wales. The astonishing route through the treacherous Llanberis Pass goes from the southeast to Treharne between the incredible mountains of Snowdon and Glyderau, supplying any walker with elevations and incredible scenery. The surrounding community is made up of sheep and cattle farmers with a few fields dedicated to wheat and barley, but the village itself is a thriving community. It's made up of small white stone cottages with thatched roofs and wood shack shops, two inns, a chapel, a school, a physician and also a midwife.

In the summer the quiet village is a gentle paradise. Flowers grow around the perimeter of the boundaries and the sweet smell of violets, gardenias and hyacinths coat each and every person with a scent that would rival any French perfume.

But in the winter the terrain makes it a harsh place to visit and live. Many a year the village remained cut-off from its neighbours and had to survive on the produce grown that year. Heavy snows would last from early December to mid-February, with the occasional glimpse of the sun around Christmas time and then the grey snowy skies continued for the rest of the time.

CHAPTER ONE

In a cottage just far enough away from the centre of the village, lived an elderly woman. She'd lived in the village for over forty years and had arrived as a young woman one summer with a cart full of belongings and settled into a ramshackle stone cottage. She kept to herself and very rarely integrated with anyone else, except perhaps to get things from the local stores or maybe at the village market where she would sell some of her garden vegetables. No longer that young woman, she was now nothing more than a harmless old spinster to the others in the village, that they knew little about, and who they weren't really that interested in getting to know either.

It was January and it had started to snow heavily again as it did each year, cutting off the village and her home from visitors for at least two months. If you were to ask when the young woman had arrived, none of the villagers could tell you. Like the thaws that happened in early March, one day they opened their doors to the melted snow and she was there.

So, when the elderly woman heard a knock on her door late one evening, she was surprised to see a young woman standing half frozen on her doorstep wearing nothing but a grey woollen dress and a long black and red velvet hooded cape. Although the door was open, she seemed reluctant to enter.

"Come in," said the older woman softly. "You look half frozen."

"Are you inviting me into your home?" asked the visitor.

"Yes of course I am. Come in. I have a large fire that you are welcome to warm yourself next to. Child, why are you out in such weather? Have you lost your way?"

The woman lowered the hood of her cloak and the elder woman saw her for the first time. A beautiful pale-faced woman with blue eyes and long dark lashes. Her lips were full and a deep pink. Long wavy hair fell down her back and was the deepest black that could be deemed possible. She smiled as she entered the house and made her way to the fire.

The elder woman returned to her stove and stirred a pot of stew that bubbled away. She reached over to the small bowl that she'd previously placed there for herself, scooped up a ladle full of vegetables and small chunks of beef. Then she took it over to the younger woman. "Here, you must be starving too. It's not much, but it's warm and will fill your belly for a while. Why are you out in the snow? The mountains are dangerous at this time of the season. Were you lost?"

"My name is Rhiannon," the young woman said quietly, not answering her questions.

"How do you do, Rhiannon? I am Mother Tydfil."

"Mother?"

"A name I came by so long ago by the villagers here, I don't even remember how or when it happened. It just did."

Rhiannon shrugged, and appeared not to care about the reason. Then she sighed deeply.

"What is it child?" asked Mother Tydfil. "What troubles you?"

"You're pretending to be one thing and yet I know who you really are." Rhiannon said, raising an eyebrow.

Mother Tydfil felt confused. "What is it that you think I really am?"

Rhiannon smiled slightly. "You are a child of nature," she said confidently, "a witch, just like me. Isn't that right?"

Mother Tydfil hesitated. "Why do you say that? Of course, I'm not. I'm simply a spinster who—"

Rhiannon interrupted. "But you are. You can't fool another who is the same as you. Mother Tydfil, what is your true name? You are sister to Ferch Ellis."

"I have no sister. I am alone," insisted Mother Tydfil.

Rhiannon smiled coyly. "Your sisters cry out to you, can you not hear them? I can. I can hear their anguish. I know of you and I know what you can do. And I know what you have done. I sensed your aura as I came down the mountain and it drew me here to you."

Mother Tydfil took a moment to answer. "I do not practice the old ways. I left that life a long time ago." She sat back in her chair. "These days it is too dangerous to let the powers glow, even for a second."

Rhiannon raised an eyebrow. "Dangerous? Out here? You are far from any eyes that would protest against you."

"If we attempt to use our power, others will see it and we will be hunted. Fear has replaced the need for us and there have already been stories of others of our kin who have met a most terrible fate. I use my spells sparingly, perhaps to grow my garden when it appears slow, maybe to help a little around the cottage, but I do it in private, because if the villagers saw us for what we are... well, I would hate to think what they would do."

"They can't stop us," Rhiannon said and smiled "With a wave of the finger we can control them all."

"That would take a great amount of spell casting that we cannot use. Only another witch of a greater power can command such a thing. Don't underestimate these mortals, there is a great danger using the craft these days and no amount of powers can stop the hangings." Mother Tydfil saw the change in Rhiannon's face. "Yes, even here in this remote area, I hear of the hangings. I hear the cries of my sisters and their pain and I cower in fear that I will someday be discovered too."

"A witch like you has all those powers," said Rhiannon quickly.

"Perhaps once, but now I choose not to use them. The people around here are gentle souls and they do not need such enchantments."

"You sound as though you are afraid of them."

"I am afraid of what they can do. Gentle or not, fear would rule what they did if we were ever found. You think we are truly invincible? We are not. The other sisters who have been captured even with all of their magic, could not set themselves free. I am not taking any chances, so I live here alone and carry on the mortal way." She nervously smiled at Rhiannon.

Rhiannon leaned over the arm of the chair, getting closer to Mother Tydfil. "You shouldn't be afraid of letting them know who is in control."

"I don't need control, I need peace and I am content living as I am." Mother Tydfil stared back into Rhiannon's eyes. "Is control what you tried to do in your last village? I can sense a fear in your very soul. I can sense that you have run away from where you were. You were frightened, and you fled. You feared you had been discovered and into the night you ran. You have been running for a while now. And if you choose to show them your powers in this village, the same will happen."

Rhiannon looked away and closed her eyes, as though shocked at the revelation.

"Yes," continued Mother Tydfil. "You barely escaped with your life. What did you do? Did you expose your magic, hoping it would control them with fear? Or, did you think they would greet you with open arms, the saviour to all of their woes, when you showed them what you could do?"

Rhiannon stayed silent.

"Yes, yes," continued Mother Tydfil. "I see your aura now. You are frightened and you are trying to shut me out from what's in your heart, but you won't. You are a young witch, your powers are not yet used to their potential. And you come here preaching about controlling others? Do you believe that you are the first to come here? Do you think you will challenge me? I think not."

Rhiannon licked her lips, tilted her head slightly to the side and spoke quietly. "Perhaps what you have seen is true. That shows me your powers...which were truly great."

"Were?" questioned Mother Tydfil. "They found your true self, did they not?"

"You have not practiced in a long while." Rhiannon sighed. "Even the most powerful witch needs to still use them, even if it is every now and again. But you know what I don't really understand?"

Mother Tydfil shrugged.

"Why you are so old, why did you let yourself get so"—she looked at Mother Tydfil, gazing at her from her feet to her head—"old?" she asked with a smile

Open-mouthed because of the disrespect, Mother Tydfil waved a finger at Rhiannon. "There's no need to be rude."

Rhiannon smiled. "Oh, but there is. We are strong. We are able to live beyond the normal years of humans, so why do you choose to be old? You can revive yourself with one simple task, one simple offering to Mother Morrighan. Yet I can see that you enjoy this time. You're going to die this way. Your skin is already wrinkled and it's grey like your hair."

Mother Tydfil wasn't happy listening to Rhiannon. In a dismissive way she said, "I've lived long enough." She looked at Rhiannon who was staring back into the fireplace. "I'm tired of it all and I have no reason to stay on this earth any longer than is necessary. I will leave as a spirit and join my sisters in the wind."

Rhiannon sighed and then said in a matter-of-fact voice, "Did you know that you can possess another's powers when they pass on? If you were to die for example, your powers can go to another..." she paused and chose her word, "witch."

"Of course, I know that!" Mother Tydfil said angrily. "I have taken away enough from others. But I don't intend to pass mine on or give any of them away. My powers will die with me, so forget trying to persuade me that I should pass them onto you. They have already done enough harm and have seen and spilt enough blood."

"Ah yes, the stories," Rhiannon said with glee. "The tales of Beatrice Tydfil and her coven of darkness. The village and the villagers that you wiped out with a single flick of the hand and the souls that you then possessed." Then she paused and asked, "Just where are the ones that you have collected, by the way? If you are old, then you haven't used them all."

"Hidden," replied Mother Tydfil. "Hidden and buried where no mortal or... witch... will ever find them."

"Those souls can give you back your youth and your powers if you keep them close. Even if you say you don't want to use them, there's always the chance you'd change your mind for some reason. So they must be here somewhere or you wouldn't do your little 'garden' spells. You can still possess the life that they have left before they died."

"I told you, I have no interest in living my life again. I do not fully use my powers so that nothing can give me away to the others. I live a quiet and simple life away from the village and its people. I no longer raise my hand to cast against another mortal and I never will again." Mother Tydfil walked to the stove, spooned out some of her stew and walked back toward Rhiannon.

Rhiannon stayed silent. She accepted a second bowl of food with a nod and a smile, and then looked around the cottage. "This is a nice cottage."

"Yes, it is," replied Mother Tydfil, relieved that the conversation had changed so quickly. "I came here almost forty years ago." She sighed deeply as she stared out through the window. "The garden though, these days, needs a helping hand, and even if I do, on occasions, cast a small simple spell, it's still too much. I've grown too weak to do a lot of the digging myself anymore and no help will come here."

"Do you think they fear you, the peasants from the village?"

"I don't know why they would fear me. I've given them no call to. They have no suspicions as to what I am. I have never cast anything to make them suspect."

"Wouldn't your garden grow faster with a little magic, though?"

"Would you cast in these dangerous times? I will not give myself away like that."

Rhiannon looked out of the window again and then scanned the room with her eyes. "I've been looking for a place like this. I would be happy here." said Rhiannon changing the subject again.

Mother Tydfil felt bemused and a little confused at what she'd just said. Perhaps Rhiannon had been affected by the cold after all? "Child, you are a strange one." she said and smiled, shaking her head slowly.

"Do you have family, people who visit you often?" asked Rhiannon.

"No, I am unmarried. And I live far enough out of the village to avoid visitors." Mother Tydfil frowned and pouted.

"Good." Rhiannon said and smiled.

"Good?" Mother Tydfil was again taken aback by her rudeness. "Why do you say that? I have invited you into my home and you've repaid me by being rude at least three times already."

Rhiannon stared into the fire again and without looking up said, "That was one of your first mistakes." She smiled broadly and then lifted her head to look at Mother Tydfil.

"Mistakes? What do you mean? What was one of my first mistakes?" asked Mother Tydfil.

"You invited me into your home. That was your first mistake."

"I don't understand. What are you saying?"

Rhiannon continued, "Your second mistake, of course, was telling me that no one will come to call on you. Because that means that no one will miss you when you die." She took out a small bottle from her dress pocket and stood up. Rhiannon then loosened her cloak fully and let it drop to the floor. "Your third mistake was not using your magic to look deeper into why I was really here."

"What are you doing?" asked Mother Tydfil.

"If you won't give it willingly, then I will take it." Rhiannon's eyes turned black as she stared at Mother Tydfil and spoke the words. *"Gad i'th enaid gael ei fwrw i'r cysgodion. Ei gipio am dragwyddoldeb. Gad i'th ysbryd oleuo'r sawl sy'n ei gymell o'th gorff. Gad i'th ffurf ddiflannu."* Let thine soul be cast to shadow. Captured for all time. Let thy spirit enlighten the one that calls it from thine body. Let thine form be gone.

Rhiannon watched as Mother Tydfil stepped back and tried to run, but her frail body didn't even make it to the door. Her body shook, her head tilted upwards and her arms outstretched to her sides, her hands seemed paralysed as a bright white light shot out of her opened mouth and entered the bottle. Rhiannon closed it quickly with a cork before the bright white glow that was inside could escape.

But she saw that Mother Tydfil's body continued to shake. A bright blue aura surrounded her and seconds later it was at Rhiannon's side, surrounding her, wrapping itself around her and beginning to absorb into her.

Mother Tydfil's body turned black, like a charcoal statue that began to flake and shed and fall into a pile of ash on the floor. Rhiannon looked at the broom in the corner. She walked over to it and began to sweep the ash pile toward the front door. She opened it and swept the powdered remains of Mother Tydfil out the door and then closed it.

Then she smiled as she looked around her new home. Yes, this would do nicely for a while.

Margarita Felices

CHAPTER TWO

A few days later Rhiannon - the newest member of the small Welsh community - walked out of her newly acquired cottage and along the snow-covered paths toward the village and the local produce shop. The walk wasn't as far a distance from her little cottage at the edge of the village as she'd thought. In a long green woollen dress and a thick black woollen hooded cape, she wrapped herself from the cold until she arrived outside the shop where she let the large hood float down her back.

Rhiannon walked in and looked around. It was the kind of shop that carried anything and everything a person could ever need, from cotton threads to ploughs. They had anything that a small community could ever want, all tied up in one shop. Two men, one very much older than the other stood behind the counter and she tilted her head slightly to hear the elder man who was in the middle of chastising his young assistant. He stopped and turned around quickly when he felt the cold wind from outside enter the shop as the door opened and he looked over to who had entered. The shopkeeper gasped as he stared at her. Even his assistant stopped what he was doing and let two tins fall to the floor from his hands.

The coldness from outside could not spoil her flawless pale skin and cheeks coloured with a hint of pastel pink. Her eyes large and wide and a brilliant sapphire blue with the longest and deepest black lashes framing them. Her lips were full and pouty with a shade that was a mix of light red and pink. Just over five feet six inches tall and even under her cloak you could tell that her attributes could be likened to any statue of a Greek goddess.

The shopkeeper almost fell over the young man in his rush to serve her. "Good morning, miss," he said almost too enthusiastically. "Is there something you are looking for?"

Rhiannon smiled as she tipped her head down slightly in a polite bow. "Yes, thank you, I find I have no tinder for the fire and no food to make a broth."

"I have plenty of it all." He smiled broadly.

"Thank you, yes. My name is Rhiannon Turner. My elderly aunt owned the cottage beyond the stream and in her passing she willed it to me."

"I'm sorry, I hadn't heard of her passing," said the shopkeeper. "I am Ivor Griffiths and that gangly lad over there is my nephew, Lloyd. I remember your aunt very well. We called her Mother Tydfil in the village. A fine woman, but she kept to herself. I never knew she even had family."

"She was my mother's cousin and it was sudden. I came to visit her and found her unwell. Would you make sure to include plenty of root vegetables and perhaps a small cut of meat?" Rhiannon asked, changing the subject. She took out her purse and placed two small silver coins into Mr. Griffiths' trembling hand. "I would be most grateful if you would have your shop boy deliver them for me."

Mr. Griffiths bowed. "He will deliver it all to you this afternoon."

Rhiannon turned to leave and bumped into a man who was part of a couple standing behind her. She dropped her purse onto the floor.

He bent down and picked it up at the same time as Rhiannon. As he rose, the man gazed at Rhiannon. "My apologies," he said without taking his eyes off her. The man stood a little taller than her, his hair was mid-brown. His eyes, also brown, were opened wide. And he had a smile that she couldn't stop staring at.

Rhiannon took the purse from his hand. "Sir, it is I who should apologise."

The man coughed. "You're new to the village?"

"Yes," said Rhiannon. But before she could get another word out, the woman stepped between them.

The woman was not smiling. She wore a brown dress with gold edging that made her face look pale and washed out. Her blonde hair was tied back in a tight bun and her green eyes gave Rhiannon a disapproving stare.

"I am Elizabeth Harding. This is my husband, Evan Harding, and you are…"

"Rhiannon Turner," she said quickly and extended her hand to greet the woman."

Elizabeth Harding looked down at Rhiannon's hand and then to her husband who was still staring at Rhiannon. "Evan?"

With a jump he snapped out of his stare.

"Tell Mr. Griffiths why we have come and let's get back to our warm home," said Elizabeth. "I'm cold and I want to go back quickly." She promptly walked past Rhiannon. Not accepting her handshake or even acknowledging her presence any longer, she walked up to the shop counter.

Evan bowed his head with a smile and walked over to his wife. "Did you have to be so rude?" he said sharply.

Rhiannon smiled as she overheard his reprimand.

Elizabeth looked back at Rhiannon who had covered her head with the hood again and stood by the door, getting ready to leave. "Yes," she said with a sneer. "Yes, I did have to."

Rhiannon opened the door and stepped back into the cold air, maybe this village had other perks too.

****

Mr. Griffiths was standing behind the counter and faced her. "She's moved into old Mother Tydfil's house. She's her niece. She arrived just before Mother Tydfil died."

"That old hag didn't have any family," hissed Elizabeth.

"Elizabeth! Please," Evan scolded and seemed clearly embarrassed by her rudeness in front of Mr. Griffiths. "We have no idea about her family."

"How long ago did she arrive?" asked Elizabeth.

Mr. Griffiths touched his chin and thought for a moment. "Well, she didn't actually tell me. But it can't have been that long ago because she has used up all the supplies in the cottage. I distinctly remember sending the boy out with a few extra supplies before the snow got worse."

"What! She came to the village in this weather where no one else can pass?" queried Elizabeth. "With a horse and cart?"

"Well maybe she has a good horse," answered Mr. Griffiths, smiling.

Evan stifled a small laugh.

"Over the pass and also the mountain. Really?" Elizabeth sighed and rolled her eyes upwards. "You know, I don't even remember holding a service for her aunt. It was as if she was here one day and gone the next. Don't you think it's funny a niece turning up just before she dies?"

"There's nothing funny about it at all," said Evan in an irritated voice. "The woman came to see her aunt, only to have her die while she was here. I'd say it was quite tragic. She didn't know anyone here or where she should go to summon anyone. She was virtually cut off from the village with no-one to help her. She is most likely still mourning her aunt's death and you have shown a very un-Christian like manner toward our new neighbour, Lizzie. Now let's get what we came here for—which, I may add, were things that you said couldn't wait until tomorrow to have—and go home."

CHAPTER THREE

It was a modest little stone-built cottage. There were two bedrooms, with a big enough cupboard in the main bedroom to place dresses and cloaks. Rhiannon took great amusement when she opened up the trunks that were in Mother Tydfil's bedroom. They were filled with the most wonderful dresses made of velvet, another of linen and cotton and some even edged with silk and delicate lace. Also, two white aprons and a long blue cotton nightdress, all unused. There were two white cotton smocks decorated with handmade cotton lace and a beautifully embroidered brown bodice with hand stitched colourful flowers over the shoulders. In a smaller box and rolled up neatly, there were wide and thin ribbons of several colours placed side by side. And in another trunk, she found three pairs of shoes decorated with small beads and loose buckles. *From her younger days, no doubt,* thought Rhiannon. She took out a wonderfully rich red velvet dress and placed it against her. It appeared to be an almost perfect fit. She placed it against her body and twirled around the room.

The outside of the cottage was painted white with two black window frames at each end of the wall, but it had seen better days and was in need of new paint. She would fix that soon enough. The roof was thatched and inside, the wooden beams added to the warmth of the house. It accommodated a large ceiling that also provided an extra room in the top half of the house where Mother Tydfil had stored a few more old wooden boxes.

The living area was one large room with a kitchen, a larder, a huge fireplace with a very comfortable armchair right next to it and a small kitchen table and two chairs in the middle of the room. Rhiannon was happy that Mother Tydfil had made the fireplace bigger to accommodate a larger cauldron. The covers over the chairs were a dark brown with large green flowers.

Rhiannon sighed. Some things needed to change. She pointed and waved her finger. *"Troi'n las tywyll a gwyrdd"* 'change to dark blue and green' she said and the covers magically changed to a deep blue with green flowers. The curtains in the kitchen window were a very unsightly brown colour with loose threads from the bottom. With another wave of her hand, they changed to a brighter blue. The four walls were bare and old, paint flaked from the alcoves. Rhiannon fixed that with another wave, and the paint was restored to a deep shade of beige and then she repaired the broken tiles next to the fireplace.

The larder was big enough to accommodate hanging meat as well as vegetables and anything else that needed to go in there. Behind the cottage there was a deep well with fresh water from the mountains and enough land around the whole place to grow vegetables and to have a small sized chicken coop and still leave enough room for flowers and herbs. There was a forest nearby where she could gather firewood and in some areas find a good selection of mushrooms and a small orchard.

Rhiannon stared out into the garden. She thought back to Mother Tydfil and to the souls that she'd collected and hidden. Where would a frail old woman like that hide such things? They had to be close. Perhaps digging up the garden might have to be her first task. But to use her magic outside, what if someone was passing by and saw her? Perhaps she should adhere to what Mother Tydfil had said until she knew more about the people of the village. After all, she couldn't risk what could happen, not this time. Yes, she would look for the souls in the garden first.

Rhiannon made a wonderful beef and vegetable soup that evening. The smell alone would have tempted any traveler passing by and she was happy that she'd made enough for the next few days. She baked bread and ate that evening as if she hadn't eaten in a long time. But she felt more rundown than she had done in a long time. Settling into her new life had taken more energy than she'd hoped and she thought that she'd have had more time before starting what she was about to do. She walked over to a large blue patchwork and embroidered throw cover and pulled at it to reveal a large wooden trunk underneath. She opened it and took out a large book. The red leather-bound cover was embossed with several small scroll design brass markings and had a lock that Rhiannon snapped open. She took it back to her armchair and rested the book on her lap. She flicked through a few pages, stopped at one and guided her finger over the words. She stared up to the ceiling, then closed her eyes and whispered, *"Hed yr ysbryd i enaid y sawl a gododd ei law heddiw. Tyrd â'r bywyd i mi ond gad anadl. Ychwanega'r blynyddoedd at fy enaid a'm cadw rhag marwolaeth."* 'Spirit flies to the soul of that who raised his hand today. Bring me the life but leave a breath. Add those years to my soul and spare my death.'

The fire glowed in the darkness as Rhiannon stared deeply into the fire, closed her eyes and slumped back into the chair. Seconds later, an almost translucent Rhiannon floated out of her body and through the walls of the house. High above the ground over the fields and past the horses that bolted in different directions while in the presence of the spirit. The clear skies turned dark as the moon fell behind a cloud and Rhiannon flew overhead toward the village.

She circled and entered the house of a man that was known to locals for mistreating his wife. Rhiannon had seen him raise his hand to his wife in the street that very day. Dafydd Hughes was not a pleasant man. His drunken temper had been the talk of the village for months and he seemed to get worse as the weeks passed. His wife made light of it when Rhiannon went to help her off the ground where his last punch sent her right in front of the shop that morning. But her visible bruising told another story of past beatings.

Dafydd was deep in his dreams as Rhiannon hung overhead and then settled on top of him. He smiled and moaned in pleasure as Rhiannon stroked his head and kissed him. He opened his eyes and stared out to her as she whispered, "I offer myself to you Dafydd Hughes. Do you want this body? These lips?" Dafydd didn't speak, he was unable to. Paralysed by Rhiannon, he merely grunted. His wife woke, gave him an elbow to the side. Then she turned over and fell back to sleep.

She smiled as Dafydd's face changed. He appeared in the throes of an orgasm as Rhiannon rubbed her pelvis over his crotch. But then his eyes widened in terror. He tried to take a breath but could not. He couldn't move at all as Rhiannon moved down his body just stopping short of his crotch and sliding back up so that she was face to face with him. From his chest, a shadow rose up as though the very life was being sucked out of him.

Rhiannon's hand opened to reveal a small bottle. Inside, a yellow light glowed brightly as it danced. Rhiannon placed a stopper on the neck of the bottle and trapped the light. Dafydd's chest rose up once more and then it collapsed again. Rhiannon's spirit emerged and left him. He took a few small gulps of air, clutched at his chest, trying to gather enough strength to wake his wife…and then stopped breathing.

****

Rhiannon stepped outside of her cottage and leaned up against the frame of the doorway. She had a small glass of wine in her hand and she sipped it slowly devouring each drop. She could smell the berries and spices that had been fermented with it and it coated the inside of her mouth. The moon was full and bright again and it illuminated her garden and shone on her face. She closed her eyes as she let the glow of it engulf her and smiled. Could life get any better right now?

CHAPTER FOUR

The next day Rhiannon woke up with a new vigour. She felt regenerated, full of life and energy. She was going to put her dream catchers and Ogham stones just beyond the orchard so that her sacrifices to Mother Morrighan would be welcomed and most importantly, not found. And then she was going to start her search for those lost souls that Mother Tydfil had hidden away as well as tackle that huge tree trunk in the middle of her flower garden. She wasn't going to let a little hard work beat her or let that stupid old woman's mind taunts get to her.

But she'd thought about what Mother Tydfil had said to her for a few days. Perhaps, using her magic right now was not a good idea. She barely got out of the last village alive once they realised she had the craft and she would need to be a little more cautious here. So, her new garden may have gotten a little overgrown in places over the years, but it was going to be the most beautiful she'd ever had. There would be no use of any magic spells to help her with it this time —well, not too much. She had a plan. She knew where every seed, every bulb would go and where each vegetable, herb and flower would go. She tried to imagine where Mother Tydfil had buried those souls and finding them while she planted. Her only problem was the huge tree trunk that wasn't going anywhere. She tugged and pulled, she'd tied a rope around it and secured it to her horse to pull, but it made no difference. She'd found out the day before that even taking an axe to it wouldn't work. The chop vibrated so hard from the impact that it sent her flying backwards. With little patience, she was about to point and cast a spell to help remove it, when she heard a voice from behind. It was Evan, the man that she'd bumped into in the shop a few weeks before. He was on his horse and dismounted before she uttered a word.

"You're having some trouble," he said with a smile. "And I can see that you've got the rope tied up all wrong. Your horse will never be able to pull it that way. You'll do it more of an injury and it will still not move."

"And how else should it be tied?" she asked impatiently.

Evan walked over to her horse and took off the rope. "Well, to start with, if you don't want to decapitate your horse, I would refrain from tying the rope around his neck. It is much better to tie it to your saddle and lead him away from that which you would like him to pull." He tied the rope to the saddle. "And now you simply lead your horse away without hurting it."

Rhiannon pouted as she looked at her horse. *Men always liked to take the lead,* she thought raising an eyebrow, but any help right now was appreciated. It didn't matter where she was, men would always think they could do better than she could. "Shouldn't you be running errands for your wife?" she asked giving him a half smile, half sneer.

"Just pull the reins of the horse," he replied. "I'm sure my wife would be just as helpful as I am, were she here."

"And somehow I doubt that very much." Rhiannon tutted and folded her arms.

It took three heavy pulls with both the horse and Evan pulling together for the trunk to even move, but it did. Rhiannon jumped up and down clapping her hands. "Look, it's moving. It's working!"

Evan smiled as he pulled harder on the rope, even more when Rhiannon joined him and helped pull. "Just a few more times!" he cried out.

Slowly, the trunk began to lift. Evan took a shovel and forced it under a section of root and soon half of the trunk was on its side. Rhiannon pulled the rope again while Evan continued to dig. Then her horse took a large step forward and the trunk was dragged across the garden.

"We did it!" shouted Rhiannon. "At last. Oh, it has been bothering me since I came here." She looked over to Evan who was still digging up roots and then looked away. It was just a kind gesture from a passing neighbour, she told herself. Don't think any more of it.

Evan appeared more pleased with himself than perhaps he should have. His boots were muddy and his white shirt had specks of dirt thrown up from the roots as they parted with the earth. He wiped the dirt from his hands and from wherever he could and walked over to his horse. Turning back to Rhiannon he asked, "Are there any other trees you want lifted from your land? Or perhaps there are rocks you want moved from one side of your garden to the other?" He raised his hand and pointed from one side of the garden to the other and then laughed.

Rhiannon curtsied as she spoke up, "No, not unless you can move the mountains closer?"

Evan mounted. "Perhaps someday someone will move the heavens for you. Until then, I have done the only thing this mortal can do." He tipped his head and bowed in respect, "Good day, Mistress Turner," he said and rode off.

Rhiannon looked at the empty ground and jumped up again. It was the ideal spot for her lilies and one place less to look for soul bottles.

Margarita Felices

CHAPTER FIVE

That evening, after eating the remainder of her broth, Rhiannon opened the grimoire again. Skimming through the pages while picking away at the rest of her bread, she looked toward the open fire and then back at the book. Deep in thought she uttered, *"Ysbryd, hed i mewn i enaid. Dyn sydd wedi byw,* a'i enaid yn hen. Tyrd â'i enaid i mi. Gad ynddo ddigon o fywyd i gydio ynddo." Spirit fly into a soul. A man who has lived, whose soul is old. Bring his soul unto me. Leave him life enough to hold" and watched as her spirit rose from within her, hovered in the air, disappeared through the closed window and floated upwards.

Mathias Eliot had lost his wife three years earlier. They'd had no children and he lived alone on a farm on the farthest part of the village. He hardly ever ventured into the village, much preferring his own company. As he sat in the darkened room with just the light from the open fire and an oil lamp on the table next to him, he looked up from his book. A noise disturbed him, a low hum that suddenly engulfed the whole room. Rhiannon's spirit passed through the light making him stand up. She stood in front of him completely naked and walked slowly toward him. Breathe to breathe they stared into each other's eyes. "Do I not please you?" she asked. "Do you not want this body, Mathias Eliot? Do you want it to come closer so that you can touch this soft skin and then love this body?" Before Mathias could answer, Rhiannon insisted, "You must want it Mathias, for me to come closer."

"Yes," Mathias whispered. "I do want it. I have missed the touch of a woman."

The flame of his oil lamp rose high casting bigger shadows around the room as Rhiannon stepped closer. Her hand rose up as she touched his chest and drew out his soul and then she took a step back from him. Mathias took a further two short breaths and then slumped to the floor and died.

At the same time in her cottage, Rhiannon inhaled deeply, opened her eyes again and smiled. She flicked her hair back, licked her lips and waited for her spirit to return. As soon as it joined her again, she was able to get up and go to bed.

CHAPTER SIX

The half stone, half-timber built chapel in the centre of Treharne was where some of the more affluent ladies of the community congregated to gossip or complain about their husbands and their children. It was also the place to discuss matters relating to the village—or anything else they could find to ridicule—or to belittle certain members of the village. It included a small graveyard to the side and to the back and had been built two hundred years previous.

Elizabeth Harding walked into the chapel in the middle of a conversation between four other women. Two of the women, Ellen and Lowri Edwards, were sisters and the owners of the two inns locally. The others were Mari Thomas, the wife of the physician and Anna Johnson, who was the wife of the pastor of the chapel. It was almost time for their annual flower service where they gave thanks to the Lord for the beauty surrounding them. They were oblivious to Elizabeth who'd sat down in the back of the chapel and was listening to them all talking.

Anna, the pastor's wife, was paying attention as the two middle-aged spinster sisters, Ellen and Lowri, spoke enthusiastically about a newcomer. "I have no idea really," said Ellen. "All I know is that the men who come into the inn talk about her often." She looked at the other women as her sister, Lowri spoke up,

"It's been nonstop since she arrived. And that's just it. No one really knows when she arrived. Isn't that strange?"

The physician's wife, Mari, nodded and eye rolled at the stories. "What do we know about her?" she asked. "Except that she walks about the village baring her shoulders and without a wrap. To me, it seems we all know what type of woman that is."

The women all looked at each other and nodded.

"We have all seen it," Lowri continued. "The way she walks to the village and smiles at everyone— especially at the men. Ellen? Didn't you complain just last month about the men watching as she walked and how she is often mentioned regardless of your presence in the inn? You were most severe in your talk of her. And Anna? Have you not scolded your husband who stopped to stare while walking with you?"

Each woman fell silent.

Elizabeth wanted to say something then. She wanted to join in with the gossip and let them know what her feelings were. But instead, she sat silently.

"There is something about that woman." Anna said tugging at a flower leaf. "But then she does appear to be very gentile," she continued. "And she keeps herself to herself."

"Gentile?" Mari raised her voice slightly. "Let's see how gentile you think she is when she is with any of your husbands!"

All the women gasped as Mari continued, "Not with mine. But I have heard that Evan Harding spends time at her cottage. Elizabeth tells me that he is a good neighbour helping another." She winked at the ladies. "Even today, he is in her garden planting vegetables."

All the women raised an eyebrow, all understanding the meaning of the last comment.

"I don't know how Elizabeth can stand it," continued Mari. "It's the talk of the village. Mark my words, nothing good will come from this woman and I hope that Elizabeth exposes her for what she is."

Elizabeth watched the women for a few more minutes and then got up quietly and left.

In her study Elizabeth called out to Evan when he arrived back home. "Evan? Can we speak for a moment?"

Evan hung up his coat and stamped his feet on a small mat so as not to trample dirt into her study. "What is it Lizzie? I've had a long day."

"How hard can it be tending to a garden for a neighbour?" she called out.

"I haven't just been there," he said, entering the room. "Do you not remember the crop failure in the top fields? I have been there too. And the merchant from Towyn was here today to see about buying some of the sheep."

"Yes, but you spent less time with farming duties and more time with that woman. You have a duty to our small holding, not to our new neighbour."

"And I fulfil that duty every day. While you lie in bed, I am up and tending to the farmhands. I am paying the merchants, receiving and also selling our cattle and wheat to—"

"I want you to stop visiting her." insisted Elizabeth quickly.

"You want me to what?" asked Evan.

"Rhiannon. You must stop going to help her."

"And why should I do that?"

"She doesn't need it. Her garden must be in some sort of order by now the amount of hours you have put into it. It takes you away from here."

"Is that the only reason?" asked Evan. "You think I neglect my duties?"

"I just think you've helped her enough."

Evan huffed loudly. "Oh Lizzie, listen to yourself. Have you forgotten your compassion for those less fortunate?"

"No of course I haven't. I just have for her."

****

Elizabeth was right in a way. Rhiannon's garden had begun to take shape. The land surrounding the cottage had given her enough space to plant vegetables for the winter, herbs for all year and enough space for colourful flowers – now that the tree trunk was gone.

It also uncovered nothing.

Mother Tydfil had buried the souls somewhere else, she must have. They may not have even been near the cottage. And lately, it didn't feel as though they were as important as they had been when she first moved there.

Evan had spent only a few days that month helping in the garden. It was true that the other men of the village had stopped by, but they had tended to her chicken coop or to the roof that needed thatching and she never invited them to stay. It seemed that in some way, they had all made their presence known to her. But Rhiannon, always seemed to feel happiest when Evan was helping in her garden.

The sweet smell of the violets greeted her when she walked out of the cottage late that morning and she was surprised that Evan had already made a start digging in the farthest corner for her roses.

"Evan?" she greeted him slightly shocked. "I was not aware that you had arrived." *Lucky, he hadn't entered the house moments before*, she thought, *when she carelessly evoked a spell to clean the kitchen.*

He was already sweating and had removed his shirt. His body glistening in the sunlight made Rhiannon stop and stare at her helper. There was something about the male torso that made her catch a breath, and when it was one as fine as this, she couldn't help but admire it.

Evan was crouched over picking up large stones and tossing them aside and stood up straight when she spoke. "You wanted the roses planted before it got too warm for them to take root."

"Yes, but I did not want to take you away from your own chores at home."

"There's nothing for me to do there. The farmhands tend to my land and Elizabeth insists on tending to the garden herself. I find most of my day is spent, either meeting with other merchants or in the stables brushing my horse and riding to the outer fields. Or I sit and read or... well let's just say, I spend little time at home."

"Doesn't Elizabeth miss you when you're away?"

"I scarce say that she does. At least she will not admit it to me. Besides, she is busy with the chapel preparations. This year it will be holding most of our garden in it as it prepares for the festival, so I'm surprised she even knows I'm gone."

"I'm sorry Evan," Rhiannon said sympathetically.

"Sorry? Why?"

"That my garden takes you away from your home... and from your wife."

Evan stared at Rhiannon and looked as though he was about to speak but must have decided against it. "I think the sooner we plant your roses the happier we will all be."

Rhiannon went back inside and fetched the foot-long root that had already started to spring other stems. She hoped they were the white roses she'd seen growing on the other side of the forest to the back of her cottage. They were her favourites. But either way, these particular roses she would love more and tend each day, as a reminder of the man who helped plant them.

Evan forced the spade into the ground and started to dig away, picking up small stones and rocks as the dirt lifted easily around them. And then the spade hit a solid mound and virtually vibrated off it. Rhiannon stared down at the ground as Evan grabbed hold and pulled, and pulled and then quickly yanked his hand away with a small cry. Blood poured from a wound and Rhiannon rushed over lifting her apron to stop the blood loss. Evan winced as she pressed hard against it. "Come inside, I'll bathe it in a lotion I have before it gets infected."

"It's all right," said Evan staring into her face. "I'll just bathe it in the pail of water by the well and it'll be fine."

"It will not be fine," scolded Rhiannon. "It might get infected and what kind of a friend would I be if I let that happen?"

Rhiannon poured a green liquid into a bowl and heated up some water. When it was near boiling, she poured the water into a smaller bowl, stirred some of the mixture into it and placed it on the table. "Sit here and let me see how deep the wound is."

Evan did as she asked and she took his hand. Carefully, she cupped it in hers and with her other hand, sprinkled the mixture over his hand. Evan tried to pull his hand away when the liquid touched the open wound, but Rhiannon held it tight. "I'm sorry," she said looking up at him. "It will be better soon, this does work. I've used it on open wounds before."

"It feels better already." He smiled.

Rhiannon reached over to a shelf and picked up a witch hazel leaf and then placed it on his hand. "It feels good, right?" she asked.

He nodded.

Rhiannon grabbed a clean bandage and wrapped it on top of the leaf.

"This will keep the wound clean and help it heal. Don't take it off until the leaf dies," she instructed. Rhiannon blushed when she noticed that Evan's eyes followed her around the kitchen. "What is it?" she asked him, "Why do you stare at me?"

"I know nothing about you," he said. "I don't know where you came from, whether you have family...nothing. We've never spoken about anything outside of this village and your garden."

"There isn't much to tell," Rhiannon said with a smile. She sat next to him. "What do you wish to know?"

"Where are you from?" asked Evan.

Rhiannon paused for a moment. Should she tell him the truth or a lie? Lie it was. "Afonwen," she replied quickly. "I was born in Afonwen, but my parents were labourers so they moved around Wales a lot. I came back after my parents died two years ago. My father died of an illness that made him cough blood. My mother nursed him until his death and then she joined him shortly afterwards. She couldn't live without my father and she just faded away. My aunt, her sister, sent for me, but when I arrived, she was ill too. I couldn't get to the village when she died so I buried her past the orchard. That was the last thing she asked of me. She told me that the cottage was mine and to do what I wanted with it. I've never had a real home."

"Afonwen?" said Evan. "I think I have merchants from there."

"Well, they won't remember my little family. We didn't see much of the village people. Our house was quite a way away from the village."

"Like this cottage is?" asked Evan.

"Farther still. At least I can walk to the village if I need to from here," said Rhiannon.

"And you have no other family?"

"Perhaps cousins somewhere, but not close by and I have never met them. When I came here, I thought I would at least have my aunt to care for, but then I was alone again." She gazed at Evan. "Until now."

Evan looked into her eyes and Rhiannon savoured the glance until he suddenly pulled away. "I have to go," he said sharply. "Elizabeth will be expecting me home." And with that, he abruptly got up and walked out of the door.

Rhiannon smiled. Wife or no wife, she was going to take him.

CHAPTER SEVEN

Evan arrived home and made his way toward the study. He could see that Elizabeth was sitting in the room alone. He took off his jacket and placed it over the arm of a chair as he bent over to kiss her.

"What's that?" asked Elizabeth pointing at his hand.

"I cut my hand. Rhiannon placed a potion on it and wrapped a witch hazel leaf around it to heal the cut."

"Witch hazel?" asked Elizabeth. Her lips were pinched, she wasn't happy. "Take it off. I won't have any of that in this house."

"It's just a leaf to bind the wound from infection."

"Witch hazel is not used by decent Christian folk to heal. Take it off and let me use a clean bandage."

"Elizabeth, I despair. She is a kind and godly woman who wants to fit in with you all here. She has kept to herself and asks only that you become her friend. She always asks about you and speaks very highly of you."

"I will dance with the devil before I befriend that woman. I would ask you to do the same, but I know you will not." She sat back in her armchair, not looking at him. "I am a laughingstock among the good people of this village because you feel the need to befriend her. People are talking, Evan, and I don't like what they are saying."

"It's nothing but foolish talk," said Evan dismissing the claim. "And you should pay no attention to it. We are married and I abide by our vows and our promise and if you cannot see how thoughtless your accusations are—"

"It may be thoughtless to you." interrupted Elizabeth sitting up. "But foolish talk will get you into trouble. And it will shame our family." She gestured for him to get closer and continued to wrap the bandage around his hand.

"Family?" asked Evan quickly. "Elizabeth are you…?"

"No, I am not. You know that I am not." Elizabeth tied the bandage up tight, got up and walked out of the room to leave him standing.

****

Elizabeth decided she was not going to discuss this harlot with him any longer, it seemed pointless. But there had to be a way of removing this person from their life. She looked down at the witch hazel leaf that she'd put in her pocket and smiled. An idea had suddenly settled in her head. Perhaps there was a way, not a full-blown open accusation of course, just the odd small talk now and again within the circle of ladies. Plant a seed and watch it grow. Perhaps witch hazel wasn't such a bad plant after all.

****

Elizabeth Harding, Mari Thomas and the two spinster sisters, Ellen and Lowri Edwards stopped to talk on the corner of the main street and were in the middle of some chat when Rhiannon noticed and walked over to them.

"Hello Elizabeth," said Rhiannon with a smile. "Good day ladies. Isn't it a beautiful day?"

Elizabeth looked for a second. Her thin lips and widened eyes said it all. And then she looked away to carry on her conversation, leaving Rhiannon to realise the displeasure of all the women, but she wasn't giving up. "Isn't it glorious that it is March and the sun has brightened up the skies and made the days warmer? It is a delight as we can now venture out and meet neighbours."

The women continued their snub.

Rhiannon took in a breath and then nodded. She'd been slighted by better and by considerably more elegant ladies in the past. And if it wasn't because of the talk she'd had with Mother Tydfil about using her magic in public when she first arrived, she would have happily turned them all into bugs or some beast of burden. She smiled as she left them all and entered the village shop.

The women's eyes followed her until she was no longer in sight and returned to their chat. Ella huffed loudly, "Did you see what she was wearing? The shame of it. That neckline is far too low and she's showing her shoulders again like that. Doesn't she own a shawl?"

"Apparently not," said Elizabeth.

"Your Evan spends a lot of time at her cottage," said Lowri with a wry smile, and the other ladies looked at Elizabeth, appearing eager for her answer.

"He feels sorry for her," she began. "He thinks that as she's alone, we should be Christian and neighbourly."

"Really?" asked Mari. "Neighbourly?"

"Yes, you, of all people, with your husband being our pastor, should know all about Christian charity," Elizabeth said sternly. "And I'd thank you all for not spreading vicious gossip about my kindly husband. All he's doing is helping a neighbour as he does with many, many others. You should tend to your own husbands and their lack of being charitable to our new neighbours."

"I meant nothing but—" Ellen began.

"Yes, you did!" snapped Elizabeth, interrupting. "You all meant each and every word. I will not have you gossip about my Evan. If you are to seek any truths, you should start with her." Elizabeth pointed toward the shop. "Strange things have been happening since she arrived."

"What things?" asked Mari. "I've not noticed anything strange."

"I don't want to say too much right now. But you mark my words, there is a dark air about this village now, I can feel it."

****

Ellen and Lowri Edwards had inherited the inn from their parents. It wasn't a very big building and had been in their family for generations. The two spinsters would turn a blind eye if any of the local men would bring company that wasn't the man's wife. They also made a lot of the alcohol that they served, often after hours, in the cellar, even though the law had prohibited such a practice.

The bar in the inn was made from old oak with a few hand carvings that were very much worn in places through the years of its clientele leaning up against it. The walls had long lost the paint that had once adorned them and the pictures were old and faded with broken frames. Some had been taken down, leaving nothing but the outline of a picture that was once there. Tables and chairs also filled the room and it wasn't strange to some days see one of its regulars slouched over them asleep.

It was full of male laughter most days, drunken fights on weekends and stories about neighbours or other people in the village, being discussed over a pint.

The man who demanded she pour him his fourth ale was a gruff and boorish specimen. He drank his first tankard in one go, not taking a breath and immediately demanded another, not by asking, but by grunting and pointing, insisting she hurry. Ellen poured him another and he snatched it from her. He threw two copper coins on the counter before finishing that one off too. Then he stared at the group of men nearby having a noisy and sometimes riotous conversation, before joining in.

"She's a fine wench that's all I can say," said one of the men.

"I would ride that filly so hard," said the drunken man, joining the conversation and spilling a little ale onto the floor.

"Oi Gethin!" shouted Ellen from behind the bar. "I just cleaned that floor. Watch it or you can drink outside!"

The men huddled around each other in a circle. One of them leaned in closer and in a whispered voice said, "She lives all alone in that cottage, but I hear Evan Harding has had the pleasure of her company on more than one occasion." He laughed boorishly nudging the man next to him.

"Evan Harding?" asked one of the other men a little too loudly.

Ellen heard the familiar name and began to listen in.

"I hear he visits to help with her, um, garden." And all the men began to laugh again. "But we all know what bush he's helping to prune!" The men laughed again.

"Well if he is, he's a lucky man," said another. "I wouldn't mind visiting her garden. I have a long rake that would work on that garden." And the laughter continued.

"I'd happily prune her bush too." laughed another of the men.

And the band of men all roared in laughter again.

Ellen looked on in distaste. "What's the matter?" said a voice from behind her. Her sister Lowri had joined her.

"Well, Gethin Tegau started to talk about the woman who's taken over Mother Tydfil's cottage."

"What did he say?"

"Terrible things."

"Such as?"

"Well, Steffan Morris implied that Evan Harding is doing more than just gardening at that cottage. And then they all laughed."

"Anything else?"

"More, much more about what they would like to do with her…" She raised her eyebrows. "You know…" and she rubbed her breasts. "What they'd like to be touching on her."

"And who could blame them?" insisted Lowri. "The way she comes into the village and flaunts herself. Let alone what she's doing to poor Elizabeth."

"To Elizabeth? What is she doing to Elizabeth?"

"It's shameful. He's a married man and she is luring him with the pretense of helping her. But a woman like that, she's a husband stealer if ever I've seen one. I tell you, nothing good will come of his charitable actions. Poor Elizabeth, I can tell that she's in such despair."

****

The eerie silence of the night was broken in the small cottage by Rhiannon summoning her spirit again. *"Ysbryd yn hedfan i mewn i enaid. Dyn sy'n byw, pwy yw enaid yn hen. Dewch â'i anadl ataf. Gadewch ef ddigon o fywyd i'w ddal."* Spirit fly into a soul. A man who has lived, whose soul is old. Bring his soul unto me. Leave him life enough to hold.

Just as before, Rhiannon fell into a deathly sleep as her spirit-self left the house and made its way through the village and over to the other side of the valley to the home of Ieuen and Derwena Jones. Ieuen Jones rode past Rhiannon's cottage and stopped to talk, mainly about himself and how he wished his wife hadn't lost her shape after having the children, while he gave Rhiannon the look of a man who wanted to be invited inside.

Ieuen sat in his armchair near the fire while his family busied themselves with chores in other rooms and were oblivious to Rhiannon's ghostly image and who had emerged into their cottage. Ieuen stared widely at Rhiannon as she came close and untied her blouse, letting the sides fall around her shoulders and exposing her ample and perfect breasts. He looked around at the empty room not fully understanding why, but that he seemed to be the only one who could see her. Just as he was about to speak out, she knelt down in front of him and placed her hand on his crotch. "Do you want me to touch you more Ieuen? Did you not wish to be inside me and reach your ecstasy?"

Enjoying her touch, Ieuen nodded and then groaned yes as she massaged him again. Closer she came until her breast pressed up against his chest and their lips began to touch and she kissed him. She took in a breath to suck the very life out of him, to empty his body of his very soul. His fingers stretched out on his hands, his face convulsed as she continued to gather whatever energy the man had left. When she broke free from him, he inhaled deeply and then coughed as Rhiannon shot out of the open window having taken what she came there for.

Ieuen's son walked over to him. "Tad? Father" he said softly, shaking his arm. Ieuen turned his head to look at him, his eyes wide and black, vacant until he took a desperate last attempt at a breath and his body slumped down further into the chair—dead.

CHAPTER EIGHT

Evan arrived at Rhiannon's gate mid-morning only to find she'd already started on the herb garden they'd talked about earlier in the week. He couldn't help but admire her independence. It took all of his willpower to stop the lingering and lustful thoughts he'd had, especially as Elizabeth was so distant from him these days. Sometimes Rhiannon would spot him staring at her and he just wanted to share everything with her —every thought, every emotion, and every desire.

She wore a dark grey dress and it was already covered in earth and ash. She'd managed to dig quite a decent size trench by the time he stepped into the garden. "You started without me?" he asked and she jumped.

"Oh Evan, you're here. I woke up early, and I wasn't going to wait until almost mid- morning for you to arrive." She raised an eyebrow and smiled. "But now you're here you can carry on digging while I plant these seeds and cover them. I'm hoping some of these might even start to grow by next month."

"I doubt that will happen," said Evan. "The soil here isn't good for growing things too quickly."

Rhiannon looked at the ground and smiled. "Oh, you never know, I might be lucky."

Evan grabbed the spade from her and started to dig the trench a little wider. "What are you planting here?"

"I'm not sure yet," said Rhiannon. "This far away from the cottage it'll have to be some sort of berry, I think."

"Fruit? I thought you wanted the herb garden planted next?"

"I do but I don't want the entire garden just for herbs and vegetables. It doesn't need to be very big, a few berry bushes will be ideal. The herbs that I'll plant will grow in the patch over there." She looked toward the cottage. She pointed just right of it, "I want to plant lavender over there and sweet pea next to it. When the sun rises in the morning it will send a sweet scent into the cottage."

"You're making me dig again so your cottage can smell sweet?"

"No, I'm making you dig because I want to have things to cook with and to use for healing. Just over there"—she pointed to the other side of the cottage—"I have planted chamomile. It makes a great tea and I will also use it for illnesses of the stomach. Then next to it, neem and garlic that can help with the pox and with rashes—especially with children—and they can be added to food too, so it's not totally wasted. Next to that I have tea tree and maybe some yarrow. I can use that for any wounds. It helps them heal quickly."

"Do you intend to heal the world?" Evan asked and smiled.

"Maybe someday," said Rhiannon shrugging. "If asked... and if I feel the need to help."

Evan nodded. "OK... and the vegetables? Have you thought of a place for actual food?"

"Potatoes there." She pointed to a spot not far from her front door. "Beans alongside, the cabbages are already sprouting over there, they were the first things I planted when the snows thawed, and over there I have leeks and onions."

"You've planned it all very well. I have never known vegetables to grow so quickly after planting."

Rhiannon's eyed widened and she shrugged her shoulders. Then quickly she added, "I believe my aunt may have had some planted there already. Perhaps they have grown from what was there last year?"

"Yes." Evan nodded in agreement. "That's most likely."

"When the snows come again," said Rhiannon quickly, "I don't want to have to walk to the village to get food and where they are planted, means I don't have to venture too far out in the cold. I don't feel too welcome in the village and I feel no help will come my way as it does to the others."

"You just don't know them very well, that's all. I'm sure if you were in need they would come."

"Your wife doesn't seem agreeable to me when I pass her. I've been here three months already and not a kind word from her to me. Or from the other ladies she acquaints with even though I bow and politely ask if their day is well."

"Elizabeth is a loyal and caring woman. She sometimes doesn't see people for what they are."

"Is she agreeable that you spend so much time here?"

"It bothers her of late yes, of course, but she has to realise that my helping you is no different than when I help others in the village. It's a good and Christian thing to do. She will come round soon enough. Just give her a little more time to adjust to you."

"Adjust to me?" Rhiannon faced Evan. "Why does she have to 'adjust' to me? I have done nothing wrong to make her this way."

"I'm here." said Evan, digging, "I'm here with you and she is afraid."

"Afraid of what?"

Evan looked at her and then carried on digging. He didn't want to answer. He knew she would be upset and make him stop and he didn't want that. "It doesn't matter," he mumbled.

"I'm certain it is she who spreads stories about me to the other women." Rhiannon continued, "And each time I go into the village I feel those eyes upon me."

"I know what she does," Evan replied not looking at her. "It's hard for me to believe that it's her." He stopped and mopped his brow with the back of his hand, "I've spoken to her about her vicious tongue. But I suggest that perhaps it's best for now that you do avoid her."

Rhiannon dropped the trowel she was working with and walked over to Evan. Face to face she looked into his eyes and asked, "Will you avoid me too when she asks you to? When she insists?"

"She won't ask," he replied. "She knows better than to ask."

"But she will and you will choose her. You will choose her because she is your wife and it's the right thing to do." She looked down to the ground. It was obvious that she was unhappy of what she feared was going to happen and her body slumped in defeat or in grief.

Evan placed his hand under her chin and gently lifted her head. All logic aside, the thoughts and desires that he arrived with were now to the forefront. "No one will ever stop me coming here, Rhiannon," he said and he kissed her. As he broke away from her lips, he added, "Not even Elizabeth." He picked her up in his arms and carried her down the path into the cottage with Rhiannon kissing his neck over and over.

Rhiannon opened her eyes from the most wonderful dream she'd ever had and looked at Evan. It had been a long time since she'd been in bed with a man. It felt good to have his warm breath over her body, his hands over her, caressing each inch of her skin. She loved the feeling of him inside her. She needed to feel loved. Even if because of his wife, it might be for a short time. She gazed out of the bedroom window and saw that the light was fading. "Evan." She nudged his shoulder. "It's getting late, you have to leave."

Evan opened his eyes and looked at her. "I don't want to leave you ever again." He stretched out and touched her face and sighed. "But I suppose Elizabeth will start to wonder why I am late."

"We can't let tongues wag more than they are," Rhiannon said with a wide grin. "Or she will stop you coming here."

"I've already said it will never happen." Evan smiled. Leaving her bed, he dressed quickly and blew her a kiss as he walked out of her room. Rhiannon lay back in her bed, and wondered if she could be any happier.

Margarita Felices

CHAPTER NINE

Derwena Jones sat alone in the darkened chapel and thought back through her life. She was born in the village and never left it and here she was now - middle aged and a widow. She'd married her husband Ieuen when she was sixteen and he was seventeen and had four sons within the first five years of their marriage. Their one and only daughter came several years later when both thought she had become barren and unable to have more children. And the biggest surprise to the couple was a few years after that when out popped another son. She never thought of herself as a great beauty, but Ieuen loved every curve on her body. She smiled when she thought of the time she'd complained about being a portly set woman with stringy dark hair that she always had to tie back. But Ieuen never let her think it. He always said she was beautiful. No one ever called her beautiful. She looked down at her wrinkled hands from exposure to the winds and the sun as she tended the fields adjacent to her farmhouse, they weren't beautiful anymore. No one would ever call her beautiful again.

She stared at the coffin. They had purposely closed the lid so that those who came to mourn or pay respects wouldn't be alarmed at the way he looked.

But Derwena couldn't get that image out of her head. Her husband Ieuen had been a good, strong man. The corpse lying in the box looked nothing like him. The corpse lying in the box had a grey shrunken face with bulging eyes and hollowed cheeks. The corpse lying in the box was thin and waif-like.

The vicar entered the chapel and seemed surprised to still see her sitting there. "Derwena? Why are you still here? I left you this morning and it's now evening. You should be home with your boys."

"My mother is with them," she said, not looking at him. Her eyes were still fixed on her husband. "What could have done that to him?" she said softly. "He wasn't sick. He was never sick, even when the boys had the pox or a cold and we all got sick, he did not. One day he was tending the fields and the next he is was nothing more than a corpse in a box."

"Who knows how these things happen?" The pastor sat next to her and stared at the coffin. "We are not to know if a sickness came over him quickly. God takes those we love, we can't question why."

"I'm not questioning God." Her voice began to rise slightly. "I'm questioning how a healthy man can wake up one morning, go to work and come back in the same health and then a few hours later, while he sleeps, he becomes... what he is in there."

The pastor shook his head. "I don't know."

"I do," said Derwena. She lifted her head and stared at the pastor. "I do. We have evil amongst us. Someone has cast an evil spell on this village. You know it, we all know it."

"Derwena! I cannot have you speak that way in this chapel."

"It's the truth. I've heard the whispers from the good Christians in this village. Even to my farm the news travels. Nothing like this has happened here until..."

"Until what?" the pastor asked in a concerned voice.

"Until that Turner woman arrived here."

The pastor shook his head. "Gossip, it's nothing but gossip. You are in grief and that is why you say this. No other reason."

"Then she has bewitched you too as she has done to many of the men in this village! Yes, I am in grief... and I am only in grief because of that woman. She is an evil being. There is talk in the village about her and I will not stop trying to convince others of it too. She killed my Ieuen." She wiped a tear from her eye and then said, "And she killed Dafydd Hughes too. Who's next? You mark my words, there'll be another soon enough. She's evil. She has the craft about her."

"Derwena, please! You have to stop saying those things—it will do you no good. They have died of a sickness that we do not know about. Please do not speak of the craft or of other things that you know nothing about. It was not long ago we heard of the hangings of Pendle. Would you see such a thing brought to our door?"

"I made no mention of the trials in Pendle, but I do think her like them. A witch?"

"No, that's not what I said."

"But you mentioned Pendle so you must also think it."

"No, I do not. It was an example of how not to let hysteria challenge your mind. You are in grief, Derwena, and must realise that."

Derwena looked back at her husband's coffin. "We shall see."

Margarita Felices

CHAPTER TEN

Rhiannon had held off sharing her potions for weeks not knowing how they would be received. She suspected they'd be skeptical of her potions mainly because she could already feel the poisonous tension each time she went into the village. None of the ladies there would speak to her. Not that she craved their company in particular, but it would have been nice to receive a "Good morning" or even a "Hello" as she passed and she did miss female chatter.

Then one day while picking up supplies from Mr. Griffiths' shop, she overheard two women talking about a distraught mother.

"Well, Mrs. Barratt is already talking to the pastor, but his father is having none of it," said one of the women.

"I went to see her last week and he's deathly. The poor soul, he's so young it's unfair. You can tell he's not going to last much longer," said the other woman.

"Coughed up blood, he did," said the first woman. "Right in front of me too. The doctor has all but said for her to prepare for the worst. What a sad event, and him not even ten years old."

That evening Rhiannon made up a potion that she knew would help and left her cottage early the following morning to go straight to the home of the Barratt family.

The woman who opened the door looked as though she hadn't slept for weeks. She looked pale and dishevelled and surprised when she saw Rhiannon standing there.

"Hello, good morning to you. My name is Rhiannon Turner. I live in a cottage just over the next ridge."

The woman gave a small curtsy and replied, "Good morning, I am Rowena Barratt." She looked back into the house. "I'm very sorry, but I cannot receive visitors. My boy isn't very well."

"I know," Rhiannon began. "I heard that your son was very ill and I think I can help." She looked at Rowena Barratt, took out a small vial from her cloak pocket and told her, "It's made from the herbs in my garden. I've used it for years when I've had the blood colic. It will help your son." Rhiannon saw that Rowena's face looked unsure of what was being offered but she smiled when she stretched out a trembling hand to take the small bottle and began to cautiously swirl it around. The green liquid seemed to change its density.

"Don't shake it too much," said Rhiannon. "Just a little movement will mix it all up."

Mrs. Barratt still looked unconvinced. "And you're sure it will work? He's been so ill for weeks and the physicians can't seem to cure it. I'm willing to try anything."

"It will work. Once in the morning at first light," said Rhiannon. "Then one more at the final sun."

"Why then?" asked Mrs. Barratt scrunching up her nose.

"The herbs inside the bottle will wake up in the first light to give him energy and then they prepare to sleep as the sun goes down, so it will help him sleep." said Rhiannon.

Rowena Barratt shrugged, "I'm sorry, I don't wish to be rude but I'm just so tired and so sick with worry, I get very little sleep these days."

"Just don't go telling too many people about my potions." Rhiannon said.

"Why not?"

"Because everyone will want some and I don't have much. I heard that your boy was sick and I wanted to help in any way that I could."

"I am grateful," said Mrs. Barratt looking behind her. Her son lay in a small bed with a cloth over his forehead, "Can I give him some now?"

"No," said Rhiannon. "Give him the first spoonful this evening, as I said, just before the sun sets. By morning you will see a small change and then at first light give him another and he will be happier."

Rowena nodded.

"Perhaps I will return in a few days, just to see how he is and I may bring a tonic for you. You also have to keep your strength up."

****

They were lying in her comfortable bed, the afternoon sun warming their bare skin, when Rhiannon, out of the blue, started to laugh.

"What makes you laugh?" asked Evan.

"Oh, I was thinking of those women in the village who look at me as though I was about to steal their husbands."

"And why is that funny?"

"Because I have stolen one." She winked and smiled as she leaned in closer and kissed his chest again.

Evan wrapped his arms around her and turned her over while he entered her again. He lifted her leg higher and pumped her harder and deeper than before. Rhiannon's pleasured moans aroused him and he increased his momentum like a magnificent musical symphony. Until the moment had come and they both slumped back down to catch their breath.

"You can do that to me as many times as you like." Rhiannon said catching her breath.

Evan looked out of the window at the blue skies and then back at her face. "I will, my love. I will."

****

Elizabeth listened very attentively to Derwena as she described her feelings and suspicions about Rhiannon. She didn't want to appear too eager in agreeing with her findings, but was happy to think that her little hints had raised enough suspicions to get tongues wagging. Both women sat in Elizabeth's parlour drinking herbal tea, when Derwena spoke again. "I don't know, Lizzie, do you think maybe it's all just a coincidence? Maybe the pastor was right. I was overcome with grief. I didn't know what I was saying."

"You spoke with your heart Derwena. Something must have given you those ideas. They weren't just plucked from the air. All of a sudden, we have deaths in the village. I have been suspicious about it for weeks."

"Well, I suppose it could have happened anyway, even without her here. Ieuen wasn't so sick that he couldn't go and work, but he hadn't been well for a few weeks. I thought it was a stomach cold. He'd had them before you see and he couldn't be sick at this time. It's lambing season and well... he needed to tend to all of that," Derwena said submissively. "But then he'd heard from Mr. Griffiths that she'd given him a stomach potion when he ate that bad pork and it cleared it straight away, so he asked her to make him a potion."

"He took one of her potions?" asked Elizabeth.

"Yes, he took one a few days before and... well... it all happened around the same time and maybe I just didn't see things right."

"You don't sound very convinced now, even though it was you who voiced your suspicions about her. Are you telling me now that you were wrong?" asked Elizabeth.

"No, I'm not saying that... just that he wasn't himself for a few days and it 'could' have been that."

"I think you've said enough things to me now to get a constable interested."

"A constable? But why?"

"You have accused her of poisoning."

"I have not!" exclaimed Derwena.

"Didn't you say, only five minutes ago, that your husband drank one of her potions and then he was dead?"

"Yes, but he was feeling sick already."

"That's not what you just said."

"I-I-I don't think I was thinking it through straight," stuttered Derwena.

"Let's look at it all since she came here. Her aunt conveniently dies when she arrives. We have had four other people die in this village of some illness that our physician cannot understand or find cures for. She has prepared 'potions' that miraculously stops a fever."

"But our grandmothers have used the same herbs. She just practices the old ways."

"I know what she practices, but no one will believe me," Elizabeth said with a sneer.

Derwena took a sharp breath. "What are you saying?"

Elizabeth looked away and then back to Derwena. "I'm saying that she has such a mystery about her."

Derwena was quick to answer her back. "Between you and me I've had my suspicions all along. No one knows anything about her. How can we be sure she hasn't come to us from Pendle?"

"What?" Elizabeth asked. "Pendle? Oh Derwena, I was merely stating that she was a harlot, a husband-stealer, but you are saying she's a ..."

"A witch! That's what I'm saying, Lizzie. That woman has bewitched us all with her airs and graces. With her potions. She's a witch, Lizzie."

"Pendle though? Oh Derwena, you can't say such things. What if someone hears you?"

"I don't care! Witchcraft," insisted Derwena. "We all know about the witch Gwen Ferch Ellis, what if she's like her? She had sisters you know, well so they say."

"No! Derwena, please don't say another word." Elizabeth started to panic, this was too much. "This is the grief over you that's all."

"Oh, stop it, Lizzie. You thought it too before I came to see you. You didn't think she was a whore. You only wanted someone else to come out and say it because you're all just afraid of what will have to happen to anyone who accused her. But I'm not afraid. You want this woman out of this village as much as the others do, more I'd say seeing as we all know where your husband is today."

Elizabeth pretended not to let that last comment upset her and she took a sip of her tea, nodding slightly at Derwena.

"Well, I'm going to watch her every move and if anything else happens in this village," said Derwena defiantly, "let's just say I'll know what to do."

****

As soon as the sun had gone and the night sky took over, Rhiannon walked through her garden with a small oil lamp, carrying her magic book. At the start of the orchard she veered left and continued through until she came to an old tree and then stopped. She knelt down in front of a small altar she had made and placed the oil lamp next to the hand-painted Ogham stones— some of the few things that she'd brought with her when she first arrived. She began to chant, "Blessed Mother Morrighan, tonight I offer you these souls as a sacrifice to your goodness and for your protection." Rhiannon opened the book *"Ysbryd yn hedfan i mewn i enaid. Dyn sy'n byw, pwy yw enaid yn hen. Dewch â'i anadl ataf. Gadewch ef ddigon o fywyd i'w ddal.* Spirit fly into a soul. A man who has lived, whose soul is old. Bring his soul unto me. Leave him life enough to hold." Rhiannon sat on the ground, motionless, as her spirit flew out once more into the night.

She flew to the next farm along from hers where she'd heard that Lyr Edmond hadn't been seen for a while as he'd caught a heavy cold a few weeks before and it was starting to affect his weakened heart. Rhiannon remembered the conversation she'd had when his sister-in-law walked by her cottage and had stopped to talk to her.

"Lost his appetite he has" the woman began. "He don't look too long for this blessed world, my poor sister, too young to be a widow." she added. "Pale as death he is."

When Rhiannon's aura found him, he was lying in bed, half asleep. It wasn't strange for him to go to bed so early these days and his family thought it best he got the rest. Lyr opened his eyes and looked up at the apparition of a beautiful young woman that hovered above him completely naked, her long black hair blowing around her and her bright blue eyes sparkling as they looked down at

Lyr. "Are you an angel come to take me?" he asked awaiting her response.

Rhiannon's spectre hesitated for a few seconds. "I am whoever you want me to be. Do you want me to comfort you?"

Lyr didn't answer. He just looked up at the spirit above him.

Rhiannon asked again, a little more impatiently. "I cannot come to you unless I am asked."

"I do," said Lyr finally. "If you are a dream, then you are a most willing one. Lately they have been dark and I fear them."

Rhiannon smiled as she came close. Her spectre entered him through his mouth and nostrils making him close his eyes. Lyr began to convulse for a few seconds and then he soon settled. His eyes shot open, they were black as they gazed upwards. His skin colour changed to a deathly ashen white and his lips shrivelled to a light grey. At the same time the door began to open and Rhiannon shot out from within him and through the open window.

A small girl quietly entered the room carrying a hot drink on a small plate. "Da?" she whispered. "Are you asleep?" The girl came closer but he wasn't breathing. His eyes though were still open and staring upwards. The girl dropped the plate with the drink to the ground, shattering and sending hot milk all over the floor. She ran out of the room screaming, "Mam! Mam, come quickly."

****

The spirit returned to the orchard and entered Rhiannon. She opened a small bottle and then closed her eyes. When she opened them again they were both black.

A shining orange entity shot out of her mouth and entered the bottle. As with the others, the spirit of Lyr Edmond had now joined the souls of Dafydd Hughes, Mathias Eliot and the countless others that she had collected before arriving at the village. An orange glow shone as the soul entered it and Rhiannon closed it tight. She parted a few rocks and began to dig a hole with her hands. Once it was deep enough, she placed the bottle inside and covered it back up. She kissed one of the Ogham stones and placed it on top of the small mound. "Mother Morrighan, I am sending these souls to you. Please accept them as my gift in the hopes that you grant your servant the life that was yet to come to them and grant those years to her when she asks for it." She closed the book, picked up the lamp and walked back to the cottage.

Margarita Felices

CHAPTER ELEVEN

Owain Barratt was ten years old and had been afflicted with all sorts of illnesses in his short life. The last time he was so poorly that the physician had already told his mother Rowena to prepare for the worst. It was lucky that Rhiannon had heard such a sad discussion in the store one day because she would never have taken pity on the family and given them her potion that cured him.

So, one sunny morning, Owain woke up early and without prompting, walked to the meadow just behind his house and hand-picked a large bunch of the prettiest blue, red, pink and yellow wildflowers he could find. He tied a delightful blue ribbon around them, which he had stolen from his sister, and then returned home to tell his mother he was off to thank the lady who had helped make him all better.

Rhiannon stood in the doorway when Owain presented his bouquet to her. She accepted it with a small hug and a kiss to his cheek that made him blush. "I wanted to say thank you," he said churlishly. "My mam said that if you hadn't given me your medicine, I would be in Heaven now."

"I'm happy to see you are fully recovered, Master Barratt. And I am very honoured to receive your gift. They will be placed in my finest pot and placed on my kitchen table so that my house can be filled with their beautiful fragrance."

"My mam has told all the ladies that you saved me. She shouted at Mrs. Johnson, who said you were a harlot."

"A what?" asked a shocked Rhiannon.

"I don't know what that is, but my mam said it was very bad and that I should never ever use the word," said Owain, "but my mam, she told her to wash her mouth out with soap and to mind her own busybody nose and that maybe she should take a potion to get rid of her ugly nose warts."

Rhiannon stifled a laugh.

"Well I have to get home. I hope you like the flowers. I might bring you some more if my mam lets me come back."

"Well, you are very welcome."

The little boy smiled as he turned away. "I will tell my mam that I think you are beautiful too." And with that, he skipped down the path passing Evan who had also come to call.

"Do I have a rival for your affections?" he asked and smiled.

Rhiannon took another smell of the flowers and with a wide, broad smile, she said, "If he keeps bringing me such beautiful flowers, then perhaps you might."

CHAPTER TWELVE

It was the parish weekly meeting in the council town chambers where six of the village's most well-to-do women and the pastor sat around a table in a small room surrounded by religious figures and books, to discuss the upcoming winter harvest.

Elizabeth sat silently next to two other women and half-listened to the committee. But her head just wasn't taking in the discussions. The day before, she'd gone to see the midwife because she wasn't feeling very well and thought she was finally pregnant. But it was a falsehood and the news hadn't sat well with her—especially as her husband had left her bed early that morning on the pretence that he was visiting the outer fields, but she knew he'd gone to help Rhiannon again.

"Elizabeth, do you not think it would be a good idea to use some of the carvings the children have made in school at the harvest?" asked the pastor.

"What?" asked Elizabeth, "I'm sorry, I-I just can't—I..." Elizabeth rose from her chair and left the chamber.

****

In the chapel next door, Elizabeth sat in one of the pews in front of the altar with her head in her hands. "What's the matter?" asked a voice from behind her. It was Mari, the pastor's wife.

Elizabeth didn't even look up when she said quietly, "Nothing. I just have a lot on my mind."

Two more women from the committee joined them, Sian Roberts, who tended to her own farm with her husband and family, and also Mary Lloyd, a widow who made her living as a seamstress.

"I have some news," said Mary excitedly, as she approached them. She looked around as though to make sure they were all alone and then blurted out, "I hear that Mistress Megan, the daughter of Farmer Davies, is with child."

"Why is that worthy talk?" asked Elizabeth scornfully.

"But she is without a husband," said Sian.

"I know," said Mary almost shrieking with laughter, "such a scandal."

Elizabeth, less than pleased with the news, said sadly, "I thought I was with child, but the midwife says I am not."

It cut the conversations dead.

"Oh Elizabeth," said Mary, "I'm so sorry. I know it's something you want very much."

Elizabeth nodded. "I don't know how long we can pretend that it's going to work for us." She was about to burst into tears, but pinched herself to stop. "So, what else is there to tell? What other news is there?"

The women fell silent until Sian said, "Well, it looks as though your friend Mistress Rhiannon has been in favour with the villagers."

"She is not my friend." Elizabeth said in a slightly raised voice, not happy. "In favour how, may I ask?"

"Well, she has been making potions and giving them to anyone who is sick. She makes them herself."

"Have there been many who have asked for her potions?" Elizabeth was suddenly interested.

"A few," said Mary with a nervous smile and a nod. "I was thinking that perhaps she might be able to help you."

"Help me with what?"

"Well, maybe she has a tonic that can help you…you know, with getting…with child?" Mary said, looking as though she wished she hadn't asked.

"I don't want her help!" Elizabeth snapped. Under her breath she muttered, "She is already helping herself to my husband."

"Forgive me, I didn't hear you," said Mary.

"It's nothing," said Elizabeth. "Tell me something else about her."

"She cured Mrs. Barratt's little boy, Owain."

"But how? Wasn't he very sick? How did she do that?" asked Elizabeth. "Rowena was all but getting his coffin made."

"All I know is that she made a potion from the herbs and flowers around her cottage which she brought to Rowena's cottage for little Owain, and he was soon well. The physician tried everything to help him and nothing. She gave him her mixture and he began to recover the very next day."

Elizabeth suddenly was paying attention. "Well, that is very interesting," Elizabeth said. After her discussion with Derwena, maybe a few gentle and innocent remarks wouldn't really hurt. "See, this is what I've been thinking to myself," said Elizabeth quickly. "You tell me, is that normal behaviour? The way she walks into the village–I swear she has every man's eyes upon her and she enjoys every stare. And then peddling her herbs so that we trust her enough to accept her and then one day she poisons us all."

"Oh, I doubt that will happen," said Mary.

"Well she certainly has bewitched the men here," Sian said quickly.

"I agree with that," Lowri added immediately.

Elizabeth inhaled deeply and then asked, "Do you not think it strange that she can make up a simple potion from flowers and then suddenly a boy who was close to death is suddenly well?"

"What are you saying?" asked Anna.

"I am saying that there is more to her than we know. I am saying that no one can make a potion that can cure so quickly unless they are..." and she stopped before saying the word.

"Are what, Lizzie?" asked Sian.

Elizabeth turned and faced all three women. "Unless they are using... you know."

"Using what?" asked two of the women at the same time.

"Oh no, I can't, it's just too terrible to even think about. I shouldn't have even said anything. It was only something that Derwena mentioned to me when she came to see me. But I think she was still grieving and didn't know what she was saying," Elizabeth lied.

"Please tell, Elizabeth," Sian insisted. "What did Derwena say about her?"

Lowri waited for a second before she softly mouthed, "the craft?" And then placed her hand over her mouth as though she'd exposed a secret. Taking it away, she repeated, "Unless she was using the craft. She told me the same thing, but I thought it was grief too. But I have to admit..." She raised an eyebrow and shrugged.

"I didn't say that of course," said Elizabeth, "that's only what Derwena mentioned. She insisted on it and even now I'm starting to believe... you know."

The women gasped. But Elizabeth knew she had already planted that same idea into their minds too. Just as Derwena had 'sort of' done to her, even though she had been goaded by Elizabeth and didn't realise it until it was said.

All she had to do now was to wait on those stories to circulate and for the accusations to begin.

CHAPTER THIRTEEN

The whispers from the village could be heard as far as Rhiannon's cottage. She had become many things over the past few weeks. She was known as the woman who made 'strange' potions and for anyone too sick for the doctors to heal, her potions made them well again. She was also the 'harlot' who spent far too much time in the company of a married man and showed no remorse for doing so. And she was the woman who 'dared' to wear dresses that bared her shoulders when coming into the village. Rhiannon didn't care. For the first time in centuries, she had found a place where she didn't have to be frightened. She could put up with their petty jealousies. She had endured worse—much worse—so it was a small price to pay. She found that she didn't even need her magic—well, not for a lot of her usual daily things. A simple life that she found pleasing to accept now. She finally understood why Mother Tydfil had loved it there so much and had decided against using her own magic. If only it had become this clear when she first arrived, it may have been nice to have had an elder witch to learn from.

But one thing she had surpassed everything else—Evan. She was happy, really happy for the first time in centuries and she didn't even have to snare him with her magic. She might actually be in love and she knew that he was in love with her.

Her garden was stunning too. The weeks of working on the land proved successful. She had even stopped looking for the souls that Mother Tydfil had hidden. They seemed unimportant to her now and the offering to Mother Morrighan was still under the shrine for whenever she did need it. The fruit trees were full of the juiciest apples, plums, pears and cherries that would see her through the cold winters once she'd cooked them. The vegetables were big and seemed to ripen whenever she had the slightest thought of wanting to pick them. The lavender around the cottage pleased her most. Each day, she would wake up to the glorious smell that lingered throughout the cottage until the sun went down. And then, it was replaced by the honeysuckle and roses that grew nearby.

But not everything was perfect. Evan had decided to cut down his visits because he didn't want Elizabeth to be so critical of him still going to visit Rhiannon now that the garden was finished. But each time he did visit her, it would always end the same way. Not that she had any complaints to lying in her bed naked with a man that she loved. It was much more than she could ever have wished for.

That morning, Rhiannon had woken up as she had done so for the past few weeks - running to the open window and being sick out of it. She couldn't understand what was wrong with her. She hadn't eaten anything that should upset her stomach as much as it did. And even her own potions of ginger and mint weren't working. In fact, they just made her feel worse. Had she been poisoned? Perhaps it was time to walk to the village and see the physician.

"I'm just not myself," Rhiannon said to the physician. "Each morning, I have to rush to the window and be sick. I'm off my food even though I know the food I have is good."

The physician looked at her palms and then her eyes. "Let me see inside your mouth... open it wide."

Rhiannon did as asked.

"Have you eaten any Dyer's Greenweed? I know that you tend to use herbs for a lot of things these days," he said in a sarcastic tone. "Perhaps one of your 'potions' has gone bad?"

"No." Rhiannon thought back and then said. "Well, perhaps weeks ago there were some that I had to cut down, but I burnt it. I would never use it in any potions. It doesn't sit well with other herbs."

"Are you feeling tired, more so than before?"

"Yes, but I'm doing a lot of work at the cottage. My aunt was old and there is so much to do to make the place ready for the winter. That has made me more tired some days."

"You are occasionally off your food, or just in the mornings? How about your appetite later in the day?"

"I am sometimes very ravenous. I crave the strangest mixtures."

The physician smiled, "I think, just to be certain, you should go and visit Mrs. Walters."

"Who's Mrs. Walters?" Rhiannon asked, puzzled.

"The midwife. Just to see if she concurs with my findings."

"Why, what do you think is wrong with me?"

The physician smiled. His thin lips almost disappeared into his face as he said matter-of-factly, "You could be pregnant." He looked down his narrow specs and added, "*Miss* Turner."

****

The walk to the midwife took minutes, but Rhiannon didn't focus her attention on where she was going. She felt as though someone had shaken her so violently that she couldn't get back to normal. What if the midwife confirmed that she was pregnant? What was she supposed to do? She'd never known a pregnant witch, what would happen to her? And then as if by 'magic,' she found herself outside a small cottage where a woman swept the porch.

"Hello," said the woman, "can I help you?"

****

Later in the afternoon, Rhiannon bounced around her cottage with an abundance of energy. It was the most incredible news that she knew would only bind Evan's love for her even more. She wanted to go to him straight away, but stopped herself. Elizabeth would be there and they would have to plan what was going to happen very carefully. After all, he was a respected man in the village. What if they had to leave it? What if they were made to leave everything? Her heart began to race, with so many things to consider.

She put on a loose-fitting red velvet dress and sat down near the open window. She knew he would arrive soon. She'd willed it in her heart for it to happen. When she saw his horse stop outside her fence and then watched as he walked down the path, she was ready. When he walked in through the door, she couldn't wait. Rhiannon ran across the room and threw her arms around him. As they embraced, she whispered, "I have some wonderful news."

He was smiling as she looked up. "You seem different today. What's the matter?"

"Evan, come and sit next to me. I need to tell you my— our—news." She took a breath. "For a few weeks I've not felt right." Evan started to speak, but Rhiannon raised her hand to silence him, "I'm well, but not—"

"Rhiannon, please," interrupted Evan, "what is wrong with you? Are you ill? Do you need the physician to visit you? I can pay for him to—"

"No! Listen to me," she said quickly, "I don't need the physician, I've seen him already and I know what's wrong with me." She held his hands tightly and smiled. "What is the one thing that you have always wanted but could never have?"

"A destrier horse?" said Evan, appearing confused.

"Well, you can always get one of those, Evan. No, not that. What have you always wanted to happen?"

Evan smiled broadly. "You are always teasing me. Rhiannon, just tell me what's going on, I don't have time for—"

Before he could finish Rhiannon interrupted him. "I'm pregnant."

Evan's smile disappeared. "What?"

"I'm pregnant! I wondered why my dresses were a little snug these days. Now I know. Three months at least, said the midwife, maybe a little more. We're having a child. Evan, this is what you've always wanted."

"Yes, but..."

Rhiannon was a little taken aback; she was waiting to be swept up into his arms and for him to make such a fuss. She couldn't quite believe that he hadn't done so yet. "But what? What do you mean 'but'? You look angry."

Evan remained speechless.

"Are you angry that we are having this child?"

"No... I'm just..."

"You're in shock, I know. So was I when I learnt of it. I suspected something, but now I know." She patted her stomach.

"The physician told you?"

"Haven't you been listening? I went to him first and he sent me to see the midwife. She told me this morning. At least three months, maybe even four." Rhiannon raised her eyebrows and crossed her arms. "Evan, you don't look very happy. In fact, you look very angry."

He inhaled deeply and looked at her. "Of course, I'm happy. It's just that—"

"Elizabeth? You're worried about Elizabeth and what she will say or do? But you needn't worry. I'm sure she will understand that we love each other and that even though you are leaving her, it is not the end of her world."

"Somehow I don't think she will see it like that. And why do you say 'leave her'? I never promised to leave my wife and I don't think I ever would. I love her."

"You love me!" Rhiannon raised her voice. "You have said it many times. Have you been lying to me?"

"Not lied…"

"Did you only say it to get into my bed?"

But his face showed a different side to him. "It's the scandal, Rhiannon! You cannot understand what this is going to do. It will ruin me. I-I'm a man of business. No one will deal with me if this comes out."

"But this is what you've always wanted."

"For Elizabeth and me, yes."

"Well it's for you and me instead. You will have a good life, Evan, with me. I will make you a good wife and I will be a good mother."

But Evan didn't answer.

Rhiannon was stunned at his cold reaction. "So… you have deceived everyone. First of all, your wife and now, me."

Evan started to speak but Rhiannon interrupted him. "I hope you realise that I can raise this child alone if I have to."

"I'm a Christian. I wouldn't leave the child or you alone. I will provide you with whatever is needed."

"Christian?" said Rhiannon in a huff. She took a step back and looked at Evan from head to toe. "You, with all your pompous sermons, but I see every man in that village wish he was with me in my bed, and in-between my open legs at night. And I see every woman wish that she looked like me or pray that I do not come to take their husbands. Christians? You are all not worthy of walking on this earth. Are you really a good Christian? You, who has lied to his wife and who bedded me."

"Rhiannon, please."

"No Evan, you have made your choice." She raised her palm in front of his face. "I hope your faith helps you overcome your greatest sin. And I hope that your wife realises such a man that she has married. But I will not be shamed in this village. I have nothing to be shamed for. But you?"

"That's enough!" shouted Evan. "You gave me the eye the minute we met in the store. Don't play your innocent games with me. Your looks, your touches, your laughs—all there to tempt me and I was foolish enough to take them all. I was flattered, like any other man that such a beauty would look at me with any sort of affection. But you became nothing more than a distraction when I needed it and nothing more."

"Get out!" screamed Rhiannon. "A distraction, was I? I will entertain you no more in this cottage. You will attend only to this child. You will pay for the midwife and when the child is born, you will care for it and it will have your name and all that is due to it from its birth right."

"And if I refuse?"

"Then I will rain nothing but hate for you."

Evan shrugged. "You won't be the first and I dare say the last. I am going home to my good wife now. Tonight, I will love her in our bed and I shall not remember our time together."

"Get out!" Rhiannon screamed again. "The devil take you, get out!"

Evan picked up his jacket and left the house, leaving the door wide open. Rhiannon walked over to it, slammed it shut and then burst into tears.

****

Rhiannon's tears continued to fall over the flowered blanket that she removed from the top of a large, wood carved chest. She unclipped the locks and raised the lid. Under an old blue quilt, two round bulb bottles lay perfectly protected. She picked up one bottle, gave it a little shake and it came to life. The silver glow from inside woke up the other bottle and they both illuminated her face. "Do you wish to be free, soul?" she whispered to the bottle. "I wish to be free from this pain." She sobbed again. Her moist lips almost touched the glass as she brought it near. "The goddess will be pleased to receive extra souls this Winter Solstice. I saved you for a reason. And she will reward me as she has always done." She placed the bottle gently back where she'd taken it from and brushed her hand over the other. "All of you will play an important part in the new magic that I will possess." She replaced the quilt, closed the trunk and locked it. "I will make them all suffer, and as their village falls around them, I will leave it forever."

CHAPTER FOURTEEN

Evan tied his horse up in the stables and thought about what he was going to say to Elizabeth. Rhiannon's revelation still rang in his ears and he couldn't believe the mess he was in now. He stood at the front door unsure whether he should enter or not. He could hear Elizabeth in the parlour. He hung his head and took a deep breath. She'd been a good and faithful wife, but now he was going to break her heart and which she didn't deserve. He walked up the path and saw her in the window. He stopped just before he entered the parlour and took a breath, as he stepped into the room, he saw her still standing near the window. She'd been watching him as he rode in and then as he entered the stables and then as he walked up the path towards the house.

"Lizzie, I need to speak to you," Evan said softly. He wanted to turn away and not see the look on her face once he'd told her.

"You're leaving me, aren't you?" she said quickly.

"What? I-I..."

"I know about you both. The whole village knows about you both. I've kept my vows and I turned away but I'm the laughingstock of—"

"She's pregnant," interrupted Evan sharply. "She's pregnant."

Elizabeth was silent for a moment. And then she began to cry.

"I'm sorry," said Evan. "I'm sorry I've hurt you."

Elizabeth finally spoke. "When are you leaving here?"

"I'm not." He walked over to Elizabeth and put his arms around her. But she shrugged them off and stepped away.

"Do you love her?" she stifled a cry as she spoke.

"I love you," he began and placed his hand on her shoulder. "I'm sorry for the pain I am causing you. I have told Rhiannon that I will not be leaving you, but I will help her with the child."

Elizabeth pulled away angrily and just before she was too far away from him, she stopped and slapped Evan hard across the face. "If you loved me, you wouldn't have done this. You wouldn't have taken her to your bed. You wouldn't have even been tempted."

"I know. And I have no excuses to tell you. I don't even know how it started. I meant only to be a good Christian to her, to help as a neighbour and welcome her to our village... but... I-I can't explain any of it."

"She captivated you the first moment you saw her. I saw it. I saw your eyes light up the way they used to for me."

"They still light up for you too."

"No Evan, they haven't for a long time. And now I know why."

"I will do anything for you to forgive me... anything. Just name it and I shall fall at your feet for forgiveness."

"Tell your harlot that she should not show her face in the village."

"Elizabeth, you can hardly ask that of her."

"I can ask it of her and I will. I will go to her and tell her that she may have lain down with my husband but she will never have him."

"Lizzie... you mustn't—"

"Mustn't what?" Elizabeth interrupted. "I hate her! I hated her when I first saw her and now, I hate her even more. I knew she had taken your love from me that first day, but I didn't want to accept it. I allowed you to help her, knowing how much it ate away inside me."

"Allowed?" asked Evan, surprised.

"I should have put a stop to it from the start. But I allowed it so that you thought of me as an understanding wife. A good-natured wife, who trusted her husband not to bed the first whore who took his fancy."

"Don't call her that. It is as much my fault as it is hers."

"Oh yes, I will lay blame on you both. But I will make her life a misery and she will beg for my forgiveness. Decent people, Evan—decent and married people—do not behave like this. I am a laughingstock."

"You are a laughingstock? Elizabeth, it's not always about you."

"But it is, Evan. You have deceived me and lied against our marriage vows." Elizabeth brushed past him and headed for the door. "The devil take you, your whore and your bastard child. This is not over, not over by a long shot."

Elizabeth left the room and Evan stood shocked in the room alone. He wasn't going to leave Elizabeth, but what could he do about Rhiannon? Part of him did love her, but was it her beauty and her character that he loved more? Was it her beauty that had drawn him to her the most, like a moth to the brightest light? What was there left to do but pray that Elizabeth forgave him and not throw him out of their home?

****

Elizabeth wiped her tears with her shawl and walked out of the house. She ignored the greetings from people in the street. All she could think about were the words 'she's pregnant' over and over. She was the one who should be pregnant—she was his wife, not some whore who'd used her body to seduce Elizabeth's husband. Before she even realised it, she was walking down a path, kicking stones away as she walked. Elizabeth looked down and saw a scattering of holey stones on the sides of the path, marking the path. She bent down, picked one up and gazed at it. What a strange stone to have outside a cottage like this, thought Elizabeth. Her mother had always said such things were used as hexes and that if you found the right one, you would see Fae folk. Superstitions and stories to scare children, but she never forgot the poem her mother used to sing to her when she was a child.

Holey stones, break your bones, witches only grind them.

Throw them in the burning fire and let them burn around you.

The cottage had changed a lot since she passed there many months earlier, not since Mother Tydfil lived there. No doubt because of Evan's good work in transforming the place. Elizabeth knocked on the door and a minute later Rhiannon stood at the doorway.

Elizabeth couldn't speak when she saw Rhiannon. Her beauty was really beyond anything that she'd ever seen or could compare to. Her thick dark locks of black hair covered her shoulders with curls and ringlets and her ivory skin and bright blue eyes made Elizabeth know that she couldn't dismiss such an attraction.

"Hello Lizzie. You'd better come in," said Rhiannon.

"No," Elizabeth said sharply. "There is no need. My name to only close and good people is Elizabeth, but you are not good. My name to the likes of you is Mrs. Harding, and what I have to say can be said out here."

Rhiannon smiled. "As you wish..." She paused and then finished with a sarcastic, "Mrs. Harding."

"Evan tells me you are with child."

"That's right." Rhiannon stroked her stomach. "I am blessed with his child and he loves me now."

"Loves you?" Elizabeth mocked. "Does he act like he loves you?" She looked around, turning in a complete circle. "I don't see him here. If he loved you, he would be here with you, beside you. But at this very moment, he's at our home wondering what he can do to make up for betraying me with you." Elizabeth paused and softly said, "I know I cannot compete with you, Rhiannon, and I don't intend to. He is my husband and all I ask is that you keep your distance from him."

"I will not. And I cannot." Rhiannon brushed her stomach with her hand and smiled. "We are linked forever now, whether he comes to me or stays with you."

Elizabeth gave her a stern stare, "You know, I don't only blame him. Oh, he has a lot of the blame...but I mostly blame you."

"Two of us made this child. I didn't force him into my bed," said Rhiannon defiantly. "He was most willing to be in it."

"He's not going to leave me for you, child or not. You do know that, don't you?"

"We'll see. Right now, he is in shock and I understand that. But things have a way of changing when you least expect them to and he will see that when my belly grows and he feels his child move inside me. He will understand that he belongs here with us."

"No, he won't. He's already said he doesn't want to leave me."

"He will change once the child is here. He will want to have something to do with our child."

"Not necessarily. That's why I'm here. I'm giving you the option of doing something about it."

"What are you talking about?"

"I want you to leave the village. We have some money, you can have. Go find somewhere else to live and have your bastard, not here."

"I'm not leaving. I like this cottage. We have fixed it so that it will be warm in the winter and the gardens are very well stocked with what we will need. It will provide food for us, even during the winter. Evan, our child and I, will be very happy here."

Elizabeth was silent for a while. She looked down at the ground, almost defeated. "My heart breaks each time he calls your name in his sleep," she said. "He doesn't know he does it, but I hear the passion in his voice and I know if you don't leave him, he will leave me." Her voice was soft and her lips began to quiver. "I beg of you, please have nothing more to do with Evan. I cannot lose my husband. I have nothing else. You can make a good life in the next village. You can take a good bag of money with you, buy a new horse and cart. You can buy a bigger cottage, and more land."

Rhiannon shrugged. Elizabeth continued, "This will ruin him and you don't see it. The men of business he deals with out of this village with will not speak to him again if they learn of it and they will not do business with him. He will be poor. Is that what you want?"

"Is that really all you care about? You're standing in this community or the money that you have? There is plenty here for us to live our lives away from any of that. We won't ever need your money."

"Do you think he could stay away from my money or our business? Stay away from his place in this community and that respect from the merchants of the other towns that he has spent years in getting? I think not. The thought of living poor doesn't appeal to him. If you truly knew him you would know it's what he dreads the most. So, perhaps you don't know him as well as you think? You have this romantic vision of your life with him, but he would rather die than be poor."

"I know enough to know he's a decent man and he will not abandon us."

"He will not leave me, what part of that do you not understand? And I will make your life and the life of your child in this village, harder than you can ever imagine."

"Once our child is born, you won't stop Evan leaving you. This is what he's always wanted." She patted her stomach again and smiled.

"You are a cruel woman. You know that I have tried to give him a child over the years and God has not blessed us."

"God?" Rhiannon laughed. "He has nothing to do with this."

"So, you admit that your child is born from…" She stopped.

"From what?"

"I think Derwena is true in her thoughts. You have bewitched us all in this village, Rhiannon Turner, you and your potions. You heal the sick when the physician cannot? I know what those potions are. I know what you are and I will announce it before the council." She took out the holey stone from her pocket. "Only a certain kind of woman would have these stones line her doorway. Only a certain kind of…" She paused and then said, "Witch!"

Rhiannon took a moment before she answered. "You are being ridiculous. Who would believe such a story? And you would do well to not spread such gossip at this time. You are hurt and I understand."

"I can be very convincing... The deaths in this village began when you arrived, many people have said it already...and you have bewitched my Evan. You have a child inside you made from sorcery and I will convince the world of it. Who will believe you over me?"

"I have a child inside me made from love, not magic. And who would believe such a story? A witch? Me?" Rhiannon let out a laugh. "You think too highly of yourself, Mrs. Harding and you will lose everything—the respect of this village, your husband and eventually your mind. You are an empty, barren shell, whereas I am full of a new life." Rhiannon stepped backwards into the house. "Now, I am going back inside and you are going to go back to your home and take what little time you have left with your husband before he leaves you for me." Rhiannon closed the door leaving Elizabeth without the last word.

Elizabeth stood at the closed door for a few moments with Rhiannon's words still ringing in her ears. And then she smiled and nodded as she stared down at the holey stone. She had a plan - and it was fool proof.

****

Rhiannon felt her child move inside her and it made her cry at the thought of them being alone. Contrary to what she had led Elizabeth to believe, she couldn't forget that Evan didn't seem as happy as she did. But the last thing she was going to do was let Elizabeth know of their words before he left her that day. That he'd only used her and now he didn't want her. Rhiannon felt anger well up inside of her. She would make him sorry he left her, and she was going would make the whole village sorry for the alienation that she felt. She would make them all sorry. The memories of why she hated mortals so much, came flooding back. She had forgotten why she was there to begin with and why she had picked that village. Why had she been so foolish as to trust one of them?

Rhiannon walked over to her wooden chest and opened it. She took out her grimoire. She hadn't needed to use the book for a while. She hadn't felt the need to. The past few months had made her so happy, beyond anything that she'd experienced before. She flicked through the pages and stopped at a spell. What better revenge than to kill most the crops, lay waste to some of the animals and turn them all to dust? But first, she would conjure up a wind to flatten and break the stems from the cornfields, a few little mishaps that would not raise suspicion. That would teach them. Let them all go a little hungry for a while. She had enough for her, let them starve. Then she'd raise another storm to drown the rest of the fields later on. And then she'd move on to the livestock. As soon as they begged for some miracle, she'd leave them. She would take her child away from the miserable village and its heartless people. Away from Evan, the man she loved and trusted, because he couldn't be trusted.

Rhiannon took a breath and closed her eyes. She centred her mind and cleared her thoughts. When she opened them again, she looked down at the verses and began. *"O wyntoedd y dwyrain rwy'n galw eich bod yn cylchdroi ymylon y pentref hwn. Yr wyf yn eich galw i fynd â'u bwyta o faich a gwastraff gwag i'w cnydau. Yr wyf yn galw mor hapus na all y pentref oroesi mwyach."* From the winds of the east, I summon you do circle the reaches of this village. I summon you to take their beasts of burden and lay waste to their ripened crops. I summon such a hunger that the village will suffer.

She waited for the rush of the wind to sweep past her cottage on its way to the fields beyond.

And waited.

Nothing!

Had she summoned the correct spell? Had she cast it wrong? Why wasn't it working? She began to recite it again, *"O wyntoedd y dwyrain rwy'n galw eich bod yn cylchdroi ymylon y pentref hwn. Yr wyf yn eich galw i fynd â'u bwyta o faich a gwastraff gwag i'w cnydau. Yr wyf yn galw mor hapus na all y pentref oroesi mwyach."*

Again, nothing.

No sound, no lights, no magic.

Rhiannon picked up the book and sat by the fireplace. She flicked through the pages and stared at one chapter. A chapter that she had never stopped or needed to stop on before. One that was simply entitled, 'Bywyd newydd' New Life.'

Rhiannon's eyes widened as she read it. The pages displayed simply one verse: "Rhaid i wrach gyda phlentyn ddileu pob hud tan y lleuad llawn cyntaf ar ôl ei eni." A witch with child shall relinquish all magic until the first full moon after birth.

Rhiannon stared at the fire in horror. She was one of them, she was mortal.

CHAPTER FIFTEEN

It had been one of the hottest summers they'd known for a while. But when the autumn finally broke through the heat in early October, it brought a heavenly respite for the heavily pregnant Rhiannon.

All summer long the only thing she had been able to do was sit near a window and let the breeze cool her sweating brow. It did not improve her temper each time that Evan came to call. She would shout and scream to the point that she knew he couldn't wait to leave her. Then of course it would make her cry and her temperature to rise and start the whole hot cycle again.

Each morning as the sun rose in the sky, Rhiannon opened the grimoire in the hopes that reciting a spell would somehow work that day and help her. But each day, the spell failed. Undeterred, she tried it as the sun went down and whenever a full moon appeared, or a half moon or even just a glimmer of any part of a moon. She would wait for the evening before walking down the path to her goddess shrine to pray or beg for some help. Even for a reprieve from her constant mood swings or from the weight of carrying her child. But it always failed and then Rhiannon waddled down the path and back into her cottage, slamming the door behind her and opening all the windows again to let in the cool air.

The autumn made things more bearable. At least the heat was not as severe, her night sweats were at a minimum and her ankles looked like ankles again. By November, with just a few short weeks to go, Rhiannon was feeling more like her old self, happy and content.

Even when her mood swings appeared from time to time during the day.

Early one evening on one of Evan's daily visits, Rhiannon noticed how tired he looked. "It's because of me, isn't it?"

"What is because of you?" he asked.

"Why you look so tired."

"I'm up at dawn to tend to the fields and the workers. Then I have duties in the village and some days I have to travel into the other towns. I have to spend time with Elizabeth and then I come here."

"Yes, your wife must come before your child," Rhiannon snapped.

"She's my wife!"

"And I am carrying your child!"

Evan shook his head. "Is there anything that you want me to bring tomorrow?"

"No," said Rhiannon abruptly.

"Then I will be back tomorrow as always. And perhaps your mood will have improved again."

He walked out before she could answer.

****

The village council congregated every two months and was only called upon any earlier for extreme purposes only. Some of the council members lived out of the village and others lived in the village. It took several weeks for Elizabeth to plan what she was going to say and do and to call the men for this extraordinary meeting.

The meeting room, situated right next to the church, could pack in at least fifty people. It had been used for numerous council and village meetings and also for many trials, over the years. The last was two years prior, when a thief had raided the pastures and stolen some sheep stock. The penalty for rustling was death and on a quiet spot on the northeast side of the village, gallows were erected and the man was executed.

So, when in early November, Elizabeth Harding entered the room accompanied by Derwena Jones and Mary Hughes, she was excited to see that all of the council members had also turned up. Twelve men sat in front of her as she approached them—Tom Benant, Sion Evans, Alwyn Creu, Caradoc Enfys, James Clwyd, Steffan Morris, Cai Donal, Alun Donal, Emyr Roberts, Gethin Tegau, Glyn Griffiths and Llewellyn Madox. Elizabeth and the other two women stopped in front of two long tables and looked across the line at the members who sat there behind it.

"Mrs. Harding, you have asked the council to convene with some urgent news?" asked the council chairman, Emyr Roberts.

Elizabeth cleared her throat and began. "I am honoured that the council has seen fit to grant me an audience. Most of you know me as Elizabeth Harding. My father was Edgar Jones, the magistrate of these lands for many years up until his death five years ago. I am a trusted and good married woman of this parish." She turned to the first woman on her right. "This is Mary Hughes. Her family has been in this village since the first settlers and is of good character. Her husband died ten months ago of a most unexplainable illness." She turned to her left. "And this is Derwena Jones. Her husband, Ieuen, died nine months ago. The physician does not know what he died from either. He went to the fields to tend to his cattle and sheep and that evening just died. I'm sure Derwena will not mind me saying that he was a strong man. But on the night, he died, you would hardly recognise the corpse that lay on the bed, his face sunken and his eyes black." Derwena began to lightly weep.

Elizabeth placed her arm around her and looked at the council. "These deaths and the death of two others in this village – all the same – should not go unnoticed."

Tom Benant spoke up. "We are aware of the illness, but we cannot make a decision if our very own physician does not know what infected them."

"I know what infected them," Elizabeth said sharply. "Derwena here can tell you that she has suspicions about a certain person in this village over the past months and I too have seen and witnessed many 'odd' things."

"Such as?" asked Sion Evans.

"Farm crops turning to dust or infested with beetles. Milk turning sour overnight. The moon shines with a red cast down on us and on one such night, an infant in this village died."

"We have had these things happen in the past." said Sion, "It was seen as a passing of the seasons, milk often turns sour. The mother of the child was weak and struck with an illness while carrying. Her child died because of that."

"I can tell you that the child was born healthy, the midwife herself told me that. Then it just faded away and died. I profess that I blame a member of this village for all of the unnatural occurrences that have befallen this village." argued Elizabeth.

"Whom do you speak of this way?" asked Tom Benant.

"I speak of the woman who lives at old Mother Tydfil's cottage. She has made potions and given them to the villagers. One child had a fever and her potion cured his fever overnight! How is that possible? Even the physician has no explanations. He told the boy's mother to prepare for his death!"

"Who is this person? Name them," said Alwyn Creu.

"Rhiannon Turner. Since her arrival—almost twelve short months ago—we have had these strange deaths. This village has never suffered from such a disease. And she peddles her potions that-that cure so quickly."

"What do you accuse Rhiannon Turner of doing?" asked Tom Benant. "Surely all she peddles is a potion of herbs as our grandparents used to practice."

"If it were like that I wouldn't be standing here. I wouldn't speak out by accusing her of using her darkness against us... I accuse her of using the craft to imprison us all."

The council chambers filled with whispers for the few that had gathered to hear the meeting. Looks of concern changed the appearances of the council members.

Elizabeth continued with a satisfied grin, yes she could be very convincing. "I request that you send for the Chief Judge for his investigation. If she is innocent then I will revoke my accusation."

"Why do you choose to accuse her?" Cai Donal asked.

Before Elizabeth could answer he added, "We are aware of your husband and his friendship with this woman. Are you perhaps accusing her because of his infidelity?"

Elizabeth took a deep breath. She could feel the anger in her heart and with pinched lips at having been dealt such a painful and embarrassing statement, she looked to her left, "Derwena. Did you not tell me, not long after your husband died, that he took one of her potions and then he died? That was true?"

Derwena looked at her and then to the council, she took several breaths, her eyes widened, nervous of what her answer could do. Elizabeth looked at her, her lips mimed 'go on,' her eyes widened as she goaded Derwena into a response.

"Yes. It's true." She began. "My Ieuen was feeling tired all the time and I saw Rhiannon in the street outside the store. I'd asked Mr. Griffiths in the shop for some tonic, after the one that the physician had given him didn't work, and we couldn't afford another visit from him. Rhiannon was standing behind me and she followed me as I left. She said that she had something that would do what we wanted and that she didn't want any money for it. She said she was being a good neighbour. But my Ieuen died two nights after he took her potion. You didn't see what it did to him." She started to stutter and quicken her speech, "His eyes turned black and his face... his face was like that of a skeleton. He couldn't breathe. I tried to help him, but he couldn't move. I ran for the physician, but by the time we came back, it was too late. Her potion killed my Ieuen. She killed my husband. I'll swear it to our Holy Father himself, she killed him!" And she burst into tears again. "I swear she did," she said in-between sobs.

Elizabeth spoke up again. "You can see for yourselves the sorrow that this woman has brought right into the midst of our small village. If she is not a witch then let her deny it. More so, let her say it in the presence of Chief Judge Harris himself. Send for him. I demand it! Let him preside over this matter and if she is an innocent, then I will remove my testimony from the court and I can be punished. But if, as I suspect, this person be practising evil, the craft, then the council will see fit how to proceed."

Whispers filled the room. "The Chief Judge? Do we really need to go to such lengths? Why not just ask her?" inquired Sion Evans.

"Do you think that she will admit to it? To us, the very people that she has come to harm? Should I ask for the Witchfinder General himself to call on us instead?" asked Elizabeth. "He is only residing in Manchester Town, so I have heard, and I can send word for him to arrive here." She waited for a response, but none came. "I think not. We have evidence enough to ask the Chief Judge to come instead. We shall write to him with our council minutes and put it to him whether or not it is worthy of his court."

The court members looked at each other and nodded. The chairman of the council, Emyr Roberts spoke again. "So, it shall be, Mrs Harding. We shall today write to Chief Judge Harris and ask for his guidance. And if he agrees, then we will grant you all an audience with him."

Elizabeth smiled at the members and then at the other two women. This would teach her to leave Evan alone. The Chief Judge would come, he always did.

****

He didn't want to be seen.

Evan sat in the back of the hall, silent and motionless, trying to come to terms with why his wife would accuse Rhiannon of anything and certainly not of this. He could tell that each member of the council panel was taking Elizabeth seriously. Had she been bottling up so much hate for Rhiannon that she'd concocted this story? Her witnesses seemed to confirm it all too. Every accusation was followed up with some sort of proof. Or, it was explained in a way that incriminated her.

But it wasn't true.

Rhiannon wasn't a witch. He hadn't been put under any sort of spell. He did love her, though, however much he tried to deny it. And what was going to happen wasn't fair. Of course, Elizabeth was hurt, but this was the worst thing she could have accused her of. News and hysteria of witches had taken hold of the good folk in the whole country and now every person stood accused even for doing the simplest of things. It had gotten to the point where neighbour would accuse another neighbour simply so that they could claim lands, property—even family.

He listened intensely to the findings brought by Elizabeth and the other two women. There was only one thing that he could do. He had to warn Rhiannon to leave the village as soon as possible or face their justice. And the council would not rule in her favour. Not with the testimony that Elizabeth and the other two women would give, he could guarantee that much.

****

Even if Evan was upset that Rhiannon was pregnant, he couldn't believe the council would even consider the accusations that Elizabeth was casting. After the meeting ended, he saddled up his horse and rode as fast as he could to Rhiannon's cottage only to be greeted by a cold stare that couldn't be mistaken for anything other than pure hate.

"Rhiannon!" he shouted as he dismounted.

"If you've come to say sorry for your actions, Evan, it'd better be said on your knees."

"Listen... just listen." He was out of breath, trying to get the words needed for her to trust him again. "The council just held a meeting. They have spoken about you and your potions and said that it must be some kind of witchcraft and that the deaths in this village are down to you."

"What?" Rhiannon asked. "Who would make such an accusation?"

"It-it doesn't matter who, just that it has. They intend to summon the Chief Judge. So, you must leave the village today. Now! You have to pack whatever is needed and I will help you head toward the mountain."

Rhiannon looked at Evan. "Elizabeth, it was Elizabeth, right?"

Evan couldn't utter a word.

"Your wife hates me so much that she would do this?"

"You are carrying my child, Rhiannon. She always thought it would be her doing that. What part of that don't you understand? Of course, she hates you."

"Well, so what? The villagers won't believe her story."

"But the council do and as we speak, a messenger has been sent to Manchester where the Witchfinder General is conducting a trial with a request. He will send his Chief Judge to us, you can be sure of it. If you stay here when he arrives, you will be brought before him."

"I'm pregnant, Evan, in case you've forgotten. They won't hurt me. It'll all be blown over before you know it."

"No, it won't!" He walked around the room, rubbing his head. He was palpitating and unsure of what he should do next. "You might want to believe that, but I know different—you have to leave here. You would be wise to hear me when I tell you that I have heard the stories that plague these lands. There is a frenzy and it is all because of fear. They fear anyone who they think practices the craft—and Elizabeth has convinced them that you do too."

"It's very sweet that you still care, but really, if they are true to their Christian beliefs, they won't hurt a woman who is carrying a child." She smiled and lowered her head slightly, raised an eyebrow as she looked wide-eyed and winked back at him. "It's not the Christian way, right?"

It seemed that no sooner had Rhiannon convinced Evan it would all blow over and never happen, that a few days' later, three men turned up at her door, requesting she accompany them into the village.

Even with her objections, she knew that fighting it wouldn't go in her favour. She had to act as normal as possible for the sake of her child, and then once she'd given birth, she'd burn the ungrateful village down to the ground.

CHAPTER SIXTEEN

The Chief Judge that the village council had called upon to oversee the allegations was seated just above the other members of the courtroom. Chief Judge George Harris was in his late fifties and had presided over many cases that the Witchfinder General could not delegate with. He wasn't a pleasant looking man and his temperament was most displeasing to those who had to suffer under his ruling. His round face would turn red at the slightest increase in temperature or even when he had to raise his voice. Little beads of sweat would come down his bald head which he wiped away with a small white handkerchief. His teeth were yellow and his lips small and light pink. His voice was high-pitched at times which made some of the audience in the courtroom chuckle until he looked at them with his small round brown eyes and they then sat in silence for the remainder of the proceedings. He obviously suffered from gout. He limped into the courtroom and sat in the chair, not moving from start to finish. He wasn't the only judge to be appointed to this type of position either. In the whole of the country, there were fifteen men that were sent for to judge over in these types of matters that were now on the increase. Some were fair and listened, but some were more inclined to find guilt without a proper trial.

The village council members— Tom Benant, Sion Evans, Alwyn Creu, Caradoc Enfys, James Clwyd and Steffan Morris— sat to the right of the judge and Cai Donal, Alun Donal, Emyr Roberts, Gethin Tegau, Glyn Griffiths and Llewellyn Madox sat on the left. They sat upright and still as though afraid to move for fear of his wrath and stared out to the whole court. At least most of the village filled the court, not only from that village but also those who had heard of it and had travelled in from the next village.

The judge yelled out to the bailiff, "Bailiff, would you bring in the accused woman, Rhiannon Turner?"

As Rhiannon entered, she could hear whispers echoed in the room. She looked over at Elizabeth who fidgeted uneasily in her seat. She was sat in the front row with three other women. Both women stared at each other, until Elizabeth took a deep breath when she looked at Rhiannon's heavily pregnant and almost to term stomach.

The judge bellowed out to the court, "The accused, Rhiannon Turner, has been brought before us, accused with the dark ability of witchcraft. It is said that you had instigated in the harm of at least four men from this village"— he looked down and read from his papers— "Dafydd Hughes, Mathias Eliot, Lyr Edmond and Ieuen Jones, and have, in an unnatural way, aided in the recovery of several sicknesses here in the same village with your potions. Do you understand the charges made against you? Rhiannon Turner, you have heard the accusations made against you. Is it true that you are a witch?"

"No of course not," Rhiannon flippantly replied. "Can you not hear how ridiculous that sounds? The charges are false and have only been made because of an envious wife"—she looked over at Elizabeth— "and nothing more than that. Jealousy, because I carry her husband's child, whereas she remains empty, barren, scornful"—she ran her hands over her large stomach— "and alone."

"Have you conspired with the devil?" asked the Chief Judge.

"No, never!" replied Rhiannon.

The appointed Court Prosecutor, John Maddox-Hughes, stood up from his seat. "I will address the court before proceeding with my questioning. I am the Court Prosecutor for the Royal house that governs Wales and its borders and I have lived in the neighbouring town of Nantlle for most of my life. I was one of the witness prosecutors in the courts when the Ferch Elis sisters were tried and convicted." He stared at Rhiannon with a face that had already condemned her. "If you are not a witch, how do you explain curing the child, Owain Barratt?"

"Where is my defender?" asked Rhiannon. "You are accusing me of falsehood and you will question me, but I should have a defender too!"

"If you are innocent, then you don't need one to speak for you."

"Yet I have a prosecutor that speaks against me?"

"If you are in need of a defender, then one can be appointed, but you will remain in custody until one arrives."

"Even if I am innocent?"

"Or you can answer the questions and the learned men of the jury can give their verdict," said the judge.

Rhiannon scanned the panel. Would a defender even be of help anyway? Perhaps if she answered as honestly as she could and was careful, she might be freed. "Ask the questions and I will be truthful. I only hope that the jury be fair and honest and listen to my innocence. And then leave me to birth my child with no harm to either of us."

"Then you will answer this, Mistress Turner, why did you help Master Barratt?"

"Because he was sick and was going to die without some help."

"Your potion cured him when a physician, a man of medicine, a highly educated and respected man, could not. Explain yourself to us. Is that not the way of the craft?"

"No, it is the way of nature! As it has always been so."

The prosecutor adjusted his robes. "The defendant, Rhiannon Turner, is charged with committing acts of witchcraft by means of her potions, and also that she took the lives of four men by dark means. Council members, I will begin the proceedings by calling one who was given a potion, Master Owain Barratt."

The small boy wandered across the courtroom and sat in a specially adapted chair. Cushions and books were used to elevate him in the witness box.

"How old are you Master Barratt?" asked the prosecutor.

"I am almost nine years old, sir," Owain said quietly.

"Now Master Barratt, I am sure that your mother will bear witness that your voice is strong and loud, let us hear how loud as you answer my questions."

Owain answered, "Yes sir" in a loud voice.

"Do you know the defendant, Rhiannon Turner?" asked the prosecutor.

"Yes!" Owain shouted very loudly amidst laughter in the courtroom. His voice had indeed been heard that time.

"How do you know the woman over there, Rhiannon Turner?"

"I brought her flowers."

"Why did you bring her flowers?"

"Because I was very sick and she gave me medicine and I got better."

"The court has heard that he was given a potion," said the prosecutor. "If the court will permit it, I would like to bring the boy's mother to the stand to submit her account alongside her son."

The judge nodded.

"I call to the council, the mother of said child, Rowena Barratt," said the prosecutor.

Rowena Barratt slowly made her way to the front of the court. She'd been sitting a few rows back from Elizabeth and hardly raised her head until she was called. As she walked past they made eye contact, but not a word was spoken.

"Mrs Barratt," the prosecutor began. "You have been brought here to bear witness and to tell us all of the deathly illness that afflicted your son, Owain."

"Yes, he was very poorly," Rowena said.

"Did the fine physician of this village tell you of his fever and what you should do to help him?"

"Yes," she said quietly. "But he couldn't help him really and each day he just got weaker and weaker."

"Close to death?" asked the prosecutor.

"I don't wish to think of it."

"But he was close to death. The physician had all but told you to summon the pastor."

"He did." Rowena looked up and for the first time she spoke, she looked assertive. "And my boy would have died if it weren't for Rhiannon. I know what you've all been saying about her, but you're wrong! She is of a good nature. She's not a witch. She uses potions that our grandmothers used and theirs before them."

The judge hit a setting maul onto a small round stone and called the courtroom to order, "You will only answer the questions given by the prosecutor."

Rowena nodded. "I'm sorry."

"So, she came to you and gave your son a potion?" the prosecutor continued.

"No, she didn't give it to him, she gave it to me. She told me to give it to him in the evening."

"And did you?"

"Yes. Yes, I did."

"And what happened?"

"Well I gave him a little chicken broth and then I gave him a spoonful of the medicine."

"It wasn't medicine!" snapped the prosecutor. "That is something only given to you by your physician. You were given a potion."

"I don't care what you want to call it. It worked."

"He was well the next day?"

"No, but he was much better than he was the day before, his fever was less. He wasn't fully well... but when he woke up, he was hungry and that made me happy. My mother always said if a person still has their appetite, then there's hope. And hope was all I had." She smiled for the first time since being called to give her statement.

"Didn't you think it strange that Mistress Turner would give you something that worked so quickly, when the help given to you from your physician did not?"

"I didn't question it. She told me it was nothing more than blended herbs that her family used. Sometimes those old remedies work better than —"

The prosecutor interrupted her in mid-flow. "I thank you kindly, Mrs Barratt. You may take your son and go back to your seats again."

"No!" shouted Rowena. "You don't understand. He would have died, the physician couldn't cure him. He was spitting up blood. They told me to prepare myself for his death. My eight year old was going to die."

"Thank you Mrs Barratt, you are no longer needed to speak."

Rowena took Owain by the hand and they left the stand. As she walked back, she glared at Elizabeth as she passed. Just a few steps away, Rowena turned and leaned in close to her and uttered in her ear, "Do you know what it's like to watch your child almost at a point of his death and know that no one can help him? No of course you don't. You are a shameful woman, Elizabeth Harding." And then she sat down in her seat, holding Owain tightly by the hand.

Elizabeth didn't even look up at Rowena, but the look of betrayal that Elizabeth must have felt was obvious to see.

Rhiannon looked over at Rowena—who'd started to tear up as soon as she got back to her seat—and gave her a little smile. At least she had one person on her side in this village.

The prosecutor and soon presented another accusation. He picked up a sack cloth and emptied the contents onto the table in front of Rhiannon. "And what are these?"

Her colourful dream catchers lay tangled and broken. Six holey stones flew out and bounced on the table. Some fell to the floor.

Rhiannon looked at them and then she looked harshly at the court. "They are...or, these were my dream catchers. The stones are used for protection."

"Protection?" asked the prosecutor. "Against what?"

"Just protection against any evil that can come your way. They can be found in the mountains. They were scattered on the path near the cottage before I even got there. They are not truly mine. They belong to the cottage."

"If they were found on your dwelling, then they are yours. These trinkets are of a pagan religion. Paganism is forbidden under God's law," insisted the prosecutor.

"Not pagan," she snapped. "They are older than that. They are older than your God and they belong to the earth."

"Are they used as tools to summon your demons?" asked the prosecutor.

"No, of course they're not. How foolish to say that. They are to capture the spirits of the forests. To help when your thoughts are unclear and dark."

"Unclear and dark?" copied the prosecutor. "I say that you pray to that darkness and to false gods. That you hope to conjure up false images of your gods and that you pay sacrifice to your god."

Rhiannon rolled her eyes. "I do not pray to your versions of a god. Does that make me wrong? My prayers go to a much older god of this earth. She is one that protects our nature. We are all children of nature."

The court whispers were louder as the prosecutor grabbed two of her dream catchers and threw them at her feet. "They are to summon up the devil and I accuse you, Rhiannon Turner, of evil. I accuse you of using the craft as a witch. I accuse you of heresy herein witnessed in this very courtroom." He looked at the judge. "And those are my words for this court."

Voices filled the courthouse and the Chief Judge made notes in his book as he listened.

Rhiannon tutted, such fools. "And I accuse you of being ridiculous. I shouldn't even be here," Rhiannon insisted again. "I am a woman who came here because my aunt was sick. None of you went to her aid when she needed you and now because I have loved a man who has a wife, I stand before you accused of this ridiculous story."

"If you are innocent, you will be found that in this good court," continued the prosecutor.

"Really?" Rhiannon raised an eyebrow. "Then why have I a prosecutor and no defender to speak for me? Why has one not been appointed at the same time as a prosecutor? Why do I have to defend myself? What are you afraid of? Why am I not being questioned by the judge to make a ruling based on the findings of this court? Let me ask you this, how many women that are sent to courts like this, are later released without charge?"

Derwena stood up and interrupted the questioning. She pointed directly at Rhiannon. "You are a murderer!" she screamed. "You killed my husband, Ieuen, you killed Dafydd Hughes, you killed Mathias Eliot and Lyr Edmond. This court will find you guilty and you will die like the murderous witch that you are!"

"Silence!" Chief Judge Harris shouted at Derwena. "You will sit down and let us conduct our court as we see fit."

But Derwena insisted on shouting again. "You knew all of those men. I've seen you speak to Mathias and to Lyr many times in the street. All the men have died since you arrived and it will be proven that you had something to do with all of them dying!"

Rhiannon rolled her eyes. "She's nothing more than a hysterical widow full of grief who has been talking to another wife who is full of jealousy toward me."

Elizabeth prompted her to sit down and placed her hand on her shoulder to calm her down. Derwena never took her eyes off Rhiannon. "You were right about her, Lizzie, and I wasn't sure then," Derwena raised her voice so that most, including Rhiannon, could hear. "But

I'm sure now. That woman is a witch and I won't rest until she is gone!"

Elizabeth sat back in her chair and smiled.

****

The following day, court resumed and Rhiannon found herself back in the courtroom. Two men had been sent to stand guard outside her cottage to make sure that she didn't decide to leave in the night and so that she'd be brought back promptly to answer even more questions.

The judge yelled out to the bailiff, "Bailiff, bring in the accused, Rhiannon Turner."

From a door on the left side of the building Rhiannon walked, visibly uncomfortable, into the courtroom, accompanied by the two guards. She held on to the long table where the council members sat as she passed it, and guided herself to the chair that had been provided for her in front of the dock. As she sat, Rhiannon asked, "Were they really necessary?"

"Silence!" shouted the judge and banged the hammer. "Rhiannon Turner, you are hereby accused that in an unnatural way you did harm to the bodies of Ieuen Jones, Dafydd Hughes, Mathias Eliot and Lyr Edmond, for which by the law of God and that of this country, you deserve to be punished. Rhiannon Turner, you have heard the complaints made against you. I say again, is it true that you have conspired with that which is unholy, dark and demonic?"

Rhiannon tutted, "Of course not. I will say it again that I am only here on the ramblings of a jealous wife, and nothing more."

The prosecutor got out of his seat and walked around. He stroked his chin and looked deep in thought when he turned to face her. "Did you visit Ieuen Jones's farm?" he asked her.

"I did not," Rhiannon replied looking over at Derwena and Elizabeth.

"Liar!" shouted Derwena rising from her seat. "Liar! Your spirit must have visited him and then you killed him."

Rhiannon shook her head. "That indeed would have been something to see. Does such a thing happen often in these parts for you to have such a vivid imagination?"

The prosecutor continued, "How do you explain the deaths since your arrival?"

"Were there no deaths before I arrived? That would indeed be the work of the craft," Rhiannon said sarcastically

The prosecutor called out for another witness, "Please bring Mary Hughes forth."

Mary Hughes timidly walked to a chair and sat down. She was a petite woman with long brown hair tied into a double bun on top of her head. She looked down at the floor, avoiding any gazes from the court. She wore a deep burgundy dress and a white bonnet with the peak turned over, a double sided collar over her shoulders with ties attached and double-sided white cuffs. And she lived, until his death, with a man who beat her severely several times a week. Dafydd Hughes liked to drink and the more he drank, the more depressed he became. His only release was to beat his wife, regardless of where she might have been. The first time Rhiannon had seen them both, he'd slapped Mary hard across the face, making her fall. Rhiannon had guessed that it wasn't the first time he'd laid his hands on her.

"Mrs Hughes," the prosecutor started. "Is it true that your husband, Dafydd, had been well and strong the day of his death?"

"Yes, he was", Mary replied, her voice a little shaky.

"What had he been doing that day?"

"He got up for breakfast as always," Mary began. "Then he went to work at the blacksmiths and then later in the evening he came home."

"And you found nothing wrong with him, no illness?"

"No, nothing. He felt a little tired after his supper. He'd stopped at the inn before coming for supper and he often drank a few tankards of ale with his food too..." and she began to cry. "He was a loving husband and a good man."

Rhiannon sighed loudly. "Oh, he was not! Why lie? He was not a good man," she insisted. "Everyone in the village knew that he beat you. He beat you in the street in front of these good people who did nothing to help you! But I came to you as you were on your knees in the street. I helped you up. I gathered the food that was on the floor that had fallen from your basket. He was not a good man!" Rhiannon folded her arms and looked in Elizabeth's direction.

"He was a good man," Mary argued. "He just-just," Mary stuttered. "He had a way of expressing his ways that was all." She began to cry again.

"He had a way?" Rhiannon shrugged. "He had a way of beating you, that's what he had."

Mary looked over to Rhiannon. "You said to me that a woman didn't need to be treated like that. You said men like him shouldn't be around good people."

The prosecutor stood up quickly. "What did you mean by that, Mistress Turner? That he shouldn't be around good people?"

"I meant that men who beat their wives shouldn't be—"

"Alive?" interrupted the prosecutor. "Did you mean that he should die?"

"No, that's not what I meant. How ridiculous of you to even suggest it," insisted Rhiannon.

The judge banged his setting maul on the desk. "Mistress Turner, you will no longer speak when there is a witness giving testimony."

"Why?" asked Rhiannon, looking up at him. "Am I not allowed to even defend myself as you deemed it correct to not find me council?"

"Again, with this, Mistress Turner?" asked the judge. "We have told you we can stop all of this and wait for one to arrive, but you know the consequences."

Rhiannon bowed her head and then as she raised it, she said, "The man died." And then she shrugged and said, "Maybe it was just very bad ale?" She laughed, as did several members of the public listening from the balconies above them.

The judge banged the setting maul again and then pointed it at Rhiannon. "Mistress Turner, you lack any respect for the dead and now you will be silent."

"I don't think so. If I have to defend myself, I will shout my innocence as loud as I can." She looked at Mary Hughes. "Mrs Hughes, did he drink any of my potions?" Rhiannon asked. "Go on, answer that. Did he?"

Mary looked over to Rhiannon. "No, he did not."

"There you go," Rhiannon said, sitting back in her seat triumphantly. "You cannot accuse me of his death when I was nowhere near him."

"B-but he died so horribly." She stifled a sob and wiped her face with her hand. "He was alive and then dead. I-I couldn't recognise my Daf. His eyes were black. His face was grey and sunken, like an old corpse. My son found him and he still wakes up screaming in the night."

The whispers rose around the room. Elizabeth smiled as Rhiannon looked toward her again.

"I am an innocent," Rhiannon said. "And you are all making a big mistake."

****

Derwena was about to rise from her seat, but Elizabeth patted her knee. "Calm down, all will be well soon."

"How can you be so sure, Lizzie?"

"Each day she digs her own grave. The outer villages already speak of the witch from Treharne. If they let her go, there will be consequences. None on this council will want that and they are already aware of the talk." She smiled at Derwena. "Be patient, my good friend, just be patient."

CHAPTER SEVENTEEN

Rhiannon was exhausted. The trial had already lasted three full days and now it was about to go into a fourth. Her only respite was that she was able to stay in her cottage with guards outside, but at least she got to sleep in her own bed.

She sat in front of her roaring fire, eating a pork stew prepared many days before her 'arrest' and pouted. Every now and again she would glance over to the chest and wished she'd been able to use her grimoire just one more time. She wasn't even allowed to tend to her garden and she wanted to make an offering to Mother Morrighan which she hadn't been able to do for a few days.

Her sleep was restless. Regardless of her very flippant behaviour she was frightened. As much as she demanded that the accusations were false – they weren't really. And her biggest fear was that someone from a village further away would hear of this trial and come forward and recognise her. She had only just escaped with her life the last time and this time she could barely walk let alone run. Each time she closed her eyes she would hear the thud of a trapdoor opening and the snap of a neck as the rope pulled and the body would fall down it. The rope would tighten around her neck until she could feel her throat close… and then she would wake up.

That morning, Rhiannon watched the sun come up. It was a winter sun but the little warmth that bathed her face was a welcome comfort to the coldness that she would receive that day.

She made herself a small breakfast and cut up vegetables for a soup that she was going to make that evening. A knock at the door made her stop.

"Mistress Turner, it is time to leave."

Her two guards helped her onto a cart and they drove to the village. Inside, the crowds had gathered again and Rhiannon saw that all the seating areas were taken, even in the balcony and that many of them were standing at the back of the hall.

She walked over to her chair and prepared to start the whole thing again. Perhaps this day would be shorter than the last. She was tired, her head hurt, her legs and back ached and her child had been restless during the night, so she got little sleep.

The judge, council and prosecutor entered after she had arrived and a deadly hush fell onto the courtroom.

The prosecutor placed his papers on the table and then turned to Rhiannon. "I would like to turn our attention today to the many deaths that have occurred here. Can you explain why there have been so many deaths since you arrived?"

"Didn't you ask the same question yesterday and got my answer?" asked Rhiannon, sighing. "Did you think that today I would give you a different one?"

"Mistress Turner, you will answer the prosecutor," said the judge.

Rhiannon almost lost her temper again, but she nodded instead.

The prosecutor asked again, "The deaths? How do you explain them?"

"What is it that you want me to say to you? I don't know why or how they happened," Rhiannon answered flippantly. "Maybe they were poisoned by their own wives." She shot a look at the two widows and to Elizabeth who all in the same seats as before. "Maybe they took their own lives through unhappiness. Who truly knows?" Laughter rippled through the audience.

"The physician thinks it a most mysterious illness," explained the prosecutor to the others in the courthouse. "Fit and healthy men who had been afflicted reduced to near corpses."

"Physicians can't know all the illnesses that inflict a man," defended Rhiannon loudly. "This world changes and so does sickness."

"But they happened as soon as you arrived. Explain that to the court."

"I cannot," said Rhiannon, defiant. "You know I cannot. But you are accusing me of witchcraft based on nothing. A few herbal potions that have helped some people with a mild sickness? You have four men that have died from an illness that we cannot determine—if they indeed died of the same thing—which you cannot prove it was. Perhaps you'd do better to question the physician who could not cure them? And as for my part in any of this, the help that I gave, you reward me this way, by accusing me of the craft? You would use such a story to accuse any of the good people in this court." She looked at Elizabeth. "Even there"—she pointed at Elizabeth—"at a jealous wife!"

Elizabeth stood up. "Only a witch would accuse any of the good Christian people here of that. Has she not convinced you of her guilt with this pitiful act of innocence?"

The prosecutor shrugged. "We have no evidence that you, Rhiannon Turner, are not a witch."

"And you have no proof that I am one!" shouted Rhiannon. "Don't listen to those that gossip, their lips only lie to you."

"No further questions," said the prosecutor.

"Wait? What!" shouted Rhiannon. "Are you not going to ask about potions given to some of the other folk in the village who have not died? Are you not to ask other witnesses—"

"Members of the court," began the prosecutor. "You have heard overwhelming evidence that Rhiannon Turner is indeed a follower of the craft, if not a full witch, then a willing disciple. You have testimony from Derwena Jones and Mary Hughes and that of our good physician. She also stands accused of enslaving the husband of Elizabeth Harding into a lustful pact and now she carries the child made by that enchantment. Only the good Lord can let us know how to deal with such a child once it is on our good land. Heaven knows what this child will grow up to do."

Rhiannon felt her eyes widen as she held her stomach. "My child is an innocent. It will grow with love and not hate!" Rhiannon shouted.

"Silence!" the judge roared. "You will listen until the end of the closing argument and then if we desire, shall give you a brief turn."

Rhiannon glared at the judge but stayed silent.

The prosecutor continued, "My learned council members. You have heard the evidence of Master Owain Barratt and that of his mother, Rowena Barratt that bear witness to her potions and its unnatural affects. I fear for the safety of this village and even for the world if this woman is allowed to be set free. I proclaim her a witch and a heretic so powerful that she could possess the very life of other strong men. I fear that the evil child that she carries will unleash a hell on this godly earth. I can see their wickedness spread unless we stop it here, now! We must exorcise this evil from our lives, from our very existence." He bellowed for the whole courtroom to hear and those outside the doors straining to get any information from within, "Good people of the council, you must help rid the world of this creature." He glanced over to Elizabeth who appeared to be spurring him on. "I see no other way than finding this person, Rhiannon Turner, guilty of witchcraft and of heresy and I seek the most severe of sentences... her immediate execution."

The courtroom gasped. As he continued, he turned to stare at Rhiannon. She was shocked and beginning to tremble. "But I do not ask for the punishment by hanging. I ask for her soul to be cleansed and also that of her child. I ask for this witch to be burnt."

Derwena stood up, clapping her hands and shouting, "Yes, yes, yes!" as the courtroom filled with chatter.

Elizabeth didn't move. She continued to look toward Rhiannon, not saying a word.

Rhiannon screamed from her chair. She got up and walked a few steps, but her stomach cramped. She stopped to grab it and tried to catch her breath. "No no, you can't mean that. I am not a witch, I am not! You are condemning me over nothing." She gasped, "A physician inflicts worse on you. I help with herbs." She looked over at Elizabeth. "Elizabeth, you can stop this. You know it's not true, any of it! I know you hate me, but this? Tell them the truth. Elizabeth, tell them the truth."

Talk around the room made it impossible to carry on or to speak. The chief judge banged his setting maul onto the small round stone and called for the court to come to order. "I will have silence or I shall remove you all." He looked down at Rhiannon. "You will be taken to a holding cell to await our decision. Be advised, that if we find you guilty, the penalty will be severe."

The guards took Rhiannon's arms and dragged her away to the jail while she still screamed, "No you can't do this, I am innocent. Please Elizabeth, please make them see sense!"

****

Elizabeth couldn't help the grin that was on her face as she sipped a small glass of wine in the living room. She thought about what she was going to do and what she was going to say, when they asked her to testify against Rhiannon. She would make the tears fall from her heartbroken eyes. But then Evan walked in and disturbed her thoughts.

"You've gone too far this time, what have you done?" he snapped at her. "I hope you're satisfied with what you have started." His voice was raised in anger that made Elizabeth's lip quiver before she turned to face him. "Don't you realise that if they find her guilty she will be put to death?" he continued to shout.

"If?" snapped Elizabeth. "I will make sure of it. Your whore will pay for what she has done to us."

"Us? I have a part in this too, Elizabeth, are you to punish me too?"

"Oh, I will punish you."

"Then do it and be done with it," said Evan sharply. "Because what you are doing to Rhiannon is unacceptable."

Elizabeth pinched her lips, and widened her eyes as she neared Evan. "You will both know what it means to cross me. You have shamed our name and I will not rest until they burn that witch and I send her to Hell."

"Burn? What are you saying?"

"I don't think hanging is sufficient," Elizabeth said, shrugging her shoulders.

"The prosecutor has asked for the same sentence?" Evan asked. He placed his hand over his mouth at the revelation, and then pointed at her. "You have convinced him to bring that sentence forth?"

"Yes, I have. It needs the most severe of sentences for the crimes she has committed and I intend to make sure she is convicted of being a witch and that she burns. And I will call for it all to happen right in the village square for all to see, including you."

"Elizabeth, please. You must be reasonable! A witch? She isn't a witch and you know it. Those stories are nothing more than hysteria spread by peasants as an excuse. They are—"

Elizabeth interrupted him. "I will take the stand and I will convince them of her dark ways. I will let them know of her influence over you that had to have been an enchantment because of your devotion and love for me and I will be very convincing."

"And I will take the stand and accuse you of being false. And when they find her innocent, I will leave this village with her and you will be here alone to answer for your false accusations," said Evan.

But Elizabeth was having none of it. "You can defend her." Elizabeth came closer, her voice lower and full of hate. "But the more you do that, the more they will think that her spell over you is still with you. I will make her burn and take that bastard child within her to the devil where they both belong." With that Elizabeth threw her wine glass across the room, shattering it against a painting of them both. Walking away from Evan, she continued, "Yes, I will make her burn and you will watch her die."

Margarita Felices

CHAPTER EIGHTEEN

Rhiannon had seen bigger pig pens than the cell she'd be put into. It was musky and damp and hadn't been cleaned in such a long time. Up against the wall was a wooden bed with a large brown sack cloth to be used as a blanket, but no pillow. There was the luxury of a small bucket but from the lingering smell in the cell that came from it, some prisoners hadn't bothered to use it as intended and confirmed by the stains up the walls. She scrunched up her nose - the setting was far from ideal. Her legs and back ached from standing for such a long time and her head spun as she tried to think of what she could do next.

She'd argued her case all day and didn't feel as though she'd received an ounce of leniency from any of them. Perhaps there was a tell-tale sign that she had overlooked that gave the game away to them that she couldn't see – perhaps they had already decided that she really was a witch? The look on Elizabeth's face as she was being taken to the cell was one she would never forget. Rhiannon had never wanted to use her magic against someone so much. She sat on the bed and rubbed her legs, then leaned back against the wall and rubbed her stomach, her baby had been restless all afternoon too. "Ssssh little one, we'll be home soon." She lifted her legs onto the bed to lie down. She was so tired that it took less than a few minutes before she'd drifted off.

But a little while later, she woke to the sounds of tapping on the cell door. "What?" she shouted. "I'm tired. I cannot go back into that courtroom today."

"Rhiannon? It's me, come to the door." It was Evan.

Without getting up Rhiannon shouted, "What do you want! Hasn't your wife done enough damage to me or have you stupidly come to ask how I am or ask how I'm coping with this mess?"

"No, I've come to get you out."

Rhiannon raised her head and looked toward the door. She swung her legs over the bed and carefully got up. "And how are you going to do that?"

"It's near darkness outside. You can run to the mountains and hide yourself."

"Run? You foolish man, I can hardly walk!"

"Just come to the door Rhiannon," Evan pleaded.

"How do you intend to get this door open?"

"The key, of course. It's hanging on the wall right next to the door."

Rhiannon rolled her eyes. Could the people in this village be more stupid? "Then why are we talking? Open it and let me go."

Evan stood with his arms open, ready for Rhiannon to run right into them, but instead she ignored him and walked toward the entrance. "There are too many people out there for me to just walk out of here. I may have to wait a while."

Evan put his arm on her shoulder, but she flinched and shook it off. "Why don't you want me to touch you?" he asked.

"W-Why?" Rhiannon asked, astonished. "Why do you think? Let's see. Your wife has brought a judge, who just so happens to like hanging women, to this village and who has accused me of witchcraft. I'm spending time in this filthy putrid prison instead of spending it in comfort in my own cottage."

"B-But Rhiannon, I had no idea it would go this far. I have spoken to her and asked her to speak for you and admit that it was all a mistake. But she will not. She is pleading with the court to not use the normal punishment... she..."

"What punishment is she asking for?" Rhiannon asked quickly.

"The same one the prosecutor has asked for, she wants you sentenced to burn if you are found guilty."

Rhiannon stood shocked. "And you know that they will! You have to convince her she's mad," said Rhiannon quickly.

"It won't happen I'm sure. She doesn't have it in her heart to do that. She's angry right now, but soon she will realise that it is all a mistake. I know she will."

"It will be too late by then! You really do not know your wife at all, do you? She is a jealous woman and you're a fool, Evan Harding if you believe that she will stop this viciousness..." Rhiannon walked away from the door and then turned back. "And I curse the day we ever met!"

Evan stood silent for a moment. "I know you don't mean that."

"I do," Rhiannon said, raising an eyebrow. "I will be found guilty. You know that. No woman ever accused has been set free."

"They won't harm you while you are carrying your child."

"Y-Your child?" She stood, open-mouthed. "Our child, Evan, get used to it,"

"Well, they won't harm you."

"Yes, they will." Rhiannon was unconvinced at Evan's disclosure. "Witches are hung Evan, child or not, they will find me guilty and we will both hang... or if she gets her way burn. Do you want that? Your child and I will burn."

Rhiannon looked out again. Five men were walking toward the cells. "They are coming for me, now? Why are they doing that?" She looked around. "Distract them. You must distract them"

"No, they won't be coming for you yet, not until tomorrow at least."

"Tell that to those men outside. You have to make time for me to escape."

"How will I do that?" asked Evan, "I shouldn't even be in here. How am I going to explain being here?"

"For once Evan, be a decent man. Think of someone else. If it weren't for your wife, I would be free. There is another door at the back, keep them here and I will be gone."

Rhiannon rushed past Evan, unlocked the bolted door in the back and closed it behind her. It was good to smell clean air again, away from the stale and putrid one she'd been inhaling all afternoon. Looking beyond the boundaries of the village the mountain loomed, but the movement in her belly meant that her time was short. She had no choice, belly or not, she had to run.

Rhiannon knew that the Welsh mountains were not a place to venture out in the winter months. It was dark, cold and the winds screamed like demon banshees through them. The wild nature of the area would drive any mortal to despair and she had heard stories of how they'd been responsible for the deaths of many lonely travellers who veered off the pathways. But she had no choice.

A mile away from the mountain base of Cadair Idris, Rhiannon slipped as she hurried along the wet fields. She had to get away, but the child she carried wasn't going to wait. Another kick made Rhiannon scream and drop to the floor on all fours. It was too early, she still had at least a month. She struggled to get up and looked behind her. The lights from the torches were closer and coming toward her. If she was going to deliver her child, she would have to work through the pain and reach the mountains before it was too late. She stumbled back a step and held onto her stomach. "Hush, my precious child. You must wait until we are safe." The pain subsided slightly and Rhiannon quickened her pace. She could see the light from the farmer's cottage in the distance and knew that the mountain path was just beyond it.

"Where are you in a rush to get to?" A voice coming from the near darkness startled her.

"The mountains...I have to get to the mountain."

"I can see the light from torches, the villagers are after you. What have you done?"

"They accuse me of being a witch and they want my child."

"And are you? Are you a witch?"

"Do I look like one to you?" pleaded Rhiannon. "I have to keep going."

The voice came closer and Rhiannon saw that it was the farmer who lived in the house near the foothills. "I think you have run far enough. They won't hurt you while you are with child."

"I wish I could be so sure… please, I have to get to the mountains. I'm safe there."

Rhiannon left the farmer behind as she stumbled toward the pathway. She looked behind her again and saw the lights were even closer. No time to lose. She stumbled with a few more steps and doubled over in pain, sending her to her knees. Her child was ready to birth now, but she could hardly move as she continued to crawl on all fours. Each move was more painful than the last until she couldn't bear it any longer and turned to lie on her back. She lifted up her skirt and pushed. Warm liquid flowed out from her body as the pain came again and she pushed harder. Rhiannon screamed as she was lifted up to stand on her own two feet. The men from the village surrounded her as she shouted out, "My child is coming!"

"Bring her," said one of the men, "and tie her hands so that she cannot curse any of you with them." And then they pulled hard on the ropes to walk her away.

Rhiannon stumbled as she screamed, "I'm giving birth! Let me be. Let my child be free."

The villagers pulled harder on the ropes and ignored her pleas until she stopped and screamed out again. Within seconds, a newborn fell to the ground and even though still attached to her, the villagers pulled at her once more to carry on walking. Her child dragged on the ground beneath her, still tethered to its mother as Rhiannon gazed down in horror begging for them to stop. "Please help my child, please help."

One of the villagers took out a knife and cut the cord. The child lay on the wet ground and began to cry out as each man stepped over it and carried on walking, not looking, not caring.

"My child!" screamed Rhiannon. "Please help, please bring it with you."

The head of the villagers stood in front of her and tugged at her hair to turn her head around.

"Take a look at your demon child, witch. Tomorrow, the wolves will have had a small feast."

Rhiannon's eyes widened. "No... you cannot. My child is an innocent."

As they dragged her away, Rhiannon could hear her child's cry as they walked farther and farther away from it.

****

Elizabeth sat in the courthouse listening to four of the council members, the judge and the prosecutor, deliberate over what they'd heard that day.

"I just feel that we may be judging her on rumours and not real evidence," said James Clwyd.

Emyr Roberts argued, "What about those potions of hers? Don't you believe that is the work of the craft? You've heard and seen that she can cure the sick and the dying just by drinking them? And let's not forget the men who have died. We have never had such an illness in our lifetime here. And soon after she arrives, we have many deaths—"

"Mr. Maddox-Hughes have you ever tried a case like this before?" the judge interrupted.

"I have not, your worship, but I have sat at the trial of the sisters not more than a few weeks ago. It was very similar, although there had been more proof of them using the craft than Mistress Turner. No one has actually witnessed her putting hexes on anyone. The ferch Elis sisters did on many occasions. But yes, some of the similarities are there. These are such strange goings on for such a peaceful town. There was so much evidence on those sisters that the trial lasted several weeks and the outcome provided a peace in the district on the same day they were hanged."

"Do you believe Mistress Turner a witch then?" asked the judge.

"I confess that the evidence and the charms that have come from her house do prove that she does not follow a Christian way. Do I believe that she has turned to devil worship? I'm not sure, but there is a fear in this village and she will have to be punished if you want to keep the peace, not just here, but in the surrounding areas too."

"Do you believe her guilty of the deaths in this village?"

The prosecutor sighed for a moment, stepped back and walked around the table. "This trial has attracted attention from other towns and if we do not conduct ourselves with the truth, the people may think that we are in favour with her too. But do I think that she was responsible for the deaths of Ieuen Jones, Dafydd Hughes, Mathias Eliot and Lyr Edmond? I cannot say. Whether they died through witchcraft or some other way, her association with the men and then their deaths shortly afterwards? It does tend to make one think that, yes, she is guilty."

The judge sighed. "Perhaps a long prison sentence in one of the bigger prisons in a town?"

He was just about to give a ruling when Elizabeth stood up. "If it pleases the council. may I come forward and speak?"

The judge looked surprised when he saw Elizabeth walk forward, "Mrs Harding, I didn't see you there. We had cleared the court for our review on the sentence."

"Your worship, I wish to give evidence and I believe that it would be better done in the privacy of this courtroom, even though I do see that some of the members are not present. Perhaps after I tell you my side, you will acknowledge and consider your sentence accordingly."

The prosecutor walked toward Elizabeth holding a Bible. Elizabeth placed her hand on it and raised the other. "Mrs Elizabeth Harding, do you swear to tell the truth in these proceedings, pledging your allegiance to the Lord himself that you will be truthful?"

"I swear." Elizabeth replied.

Elizabeth sat in Rhiannon's chair. "When my husband, Evan, began to visit Miss Turner, I was happy that my charitable husband would go and help out our new neighbour. But soon after a few short visits to her cottage, I began to notice a great change in him."

"Explain," said the judge. "What kind of change?" he asked.

"He neglected his chores. We have a small, but profitable farm, a small holding, with workers and fields of corn and barley and also sheep and some cattle. Men of business from nearby towns would visit to be paid or to buy from us and Evan was nowhere to be seen. His feelings toward me changed too. A loving, caring, dutiful husband, would now…" she paused, "would now not visit our marital bed." She began to weep. "And when he did, he would whisper her name in his sleep and some nights his movements in bed would be so violent that it was almost demonic, like his precious soul was fighting to escape and be free. I knew right then that something wasn't right."

"Demonic?" asked Emyr Roberts.

"He would toss and turn and moan and some nights scream out into the darkness, in a language that I could not recognise. Does that not sound like a man possessed?"

The council members whispered to each other.

"And you noticed all of this since your husband began to visit Miss Turner?" asked the judge.

"On days that he didn't go, he was Evan again. Smiling, teasing me in the most loving way, but on the days he would visit her?" She shrugged her shoulders. "I believe that she has enchanted him. Maybe one of her potions given in his drink when he worked so hard in her garden had an effect on him. He is bewitched and I can't bring him back. I believe that he is dying inside, his soul is dying and I know it! I must save my husband from the same fate as those other poor men."

The council members stood up and surrounded the judge and began to whisper to each other. Elizabeth tried to listen but could only hear the odd few words here and there. When they finally turned back to face her, the prosecutor asked, "Mrs Harding, do you believe that Miss Turner is a threat to this village?"

"I believe her to be, yes, but I also believe her to be a threat to our religious beliefs. If she is a witch, then she will be a powerful one and the bastard she carries inside her could be just as powerful. Do you all want there to be such a force in our presence? Can you imagine what evil they will unleash on us all?"

"Isn't the bastard she carries, that of your husband?" asked James Clwyd.

Elizabeth bowed her head. "I believe so," she said, not looking up. She lifted her head. "A child made from one who was enchanted? Tell me, would that be a pure soul or a possessed one? Isn't that something we should all fear?"

The judge took a breath. "Witches hang," he said. "And I can see no defence in this case. I shall suggest to you all that Rhiannon Turner is guilty of witchcraft. What sayeth my council?"

Just as they were about to reply, Elizabeth stood up and quickly shouted, "No! Not hang, she should burn as the prosecutor has requested! Burn her so that her soul cannot come back to enchant others in this village. Burn her so that the devil inside her dies too. You must burn her!"

****

Elizabeth Harding stood on the outskirts of the village and watched as the torchlights became more distant. She couldn't believe that Rhiannon had escaped and was even more surprised to learn that Evan had been caught in the prison. But they would catch up to that husband-stealing whore soon enough and bring her back to hear her sentence. The council had determined that she was responsible for the deaths, for enchanting Evan and guilty for having pagan idols that were found around her garden and inside her house so that she could summon spirits. Therefore, she'd been condemned not only as a witch, but also as a heretic.

Rhiannon was going to burn, whether she was giving birth to her husband's bastard or not.

CHAPTER NINETEEN

Rhiannon felt so weak and disorientated when she was dragged through the village that all she could see were angry faces and flames from the torches. She was pushed, pulled and punched from every direction. A smaller crowd circled around and she was pushed to the ground. She got to her feet and looked around. She just wanted to see one friendly face. She just wanted to see Evan.

The chanting began quietly at first, only a few of the women toward the back of the crowds. But it quickly spread into the rest of the crowd. "Witch! Witch! Witch!" Someone threw dirt at her and it hit her in the back.

Rhiannon turned quickly to see what was going on and saw the wooden structure behind them. She saw the stake, she saw the rows of dry wood and cut trees. Her eyes widened. "No, you can't do that!" She pointed and screamed. Another hard hit from behind. This time it was old food—a rotten cabbage, or a turnip perhaps? She shouted out into the crowd, "I have a trial. I have the right to speak my piece!"

The chanting only got louder, fingers pointed at her. "Witch! Witch!" All eyes were on her as she was pushed toward the assembled council members.

The long table and chairs where the judge and the council sat in the courthouse had been brought outside and now they all sat staring over at Rhiannon. The court had been moved and resumed outside. Their gazes had condemned her already as she was dragged in front of them. The crowds then surrounded them all, villagers from the next village along who'd also come as spectators and who were now getting a ringside view.

Rhiannon sighed with relief. "You must allow me to make my defence," she pleaded. "I can show you proof that I am not a witch and must be set free. I am innocent. Many here will bear witness to me helping them with their illness."

"Silence!" shouted the judge above the crowds who booed and called out her name alongside the accusations.

Then silence as the prosecutor made his way through the crowds to stand in front of her. The council members looked on while he unfolded and then read out a proclamation. "It has been deemed that tonight the heretic and witch, Rhiannon Turner, shall pay for her crimes of murder by the craft and shall be burnt at the stake. You have been found guilty by a jury of good people and of good character, of the murders of Ieuen Jones, Dafydd Hughes, Mathias Eliot and Lyr Edmond, by means of the craft. You are a witch, Rhiannon Turner. You are also charged as a heretic and that you built an altar to a pagan god. For these crimes, your punishment is death." He rolled his proclamation back up.

Rhiannon screamed, "No! It's not true."

The judge banged his hammer to silence the noise from the crowd once more. "Rhiannon Turner, thou shall be taken to yonder place where you shall be shackled to the stake and burnt for your crimes. Your guilt was proven to this court who sought a more lenient sentence until you escaped from your cell and fled to the mountains. After your death, your ashes will be gathered and thrown into a waste pit where you shall spend eternity in torment, your spirit unblessed by the Holy Scriptures and never to be remembered again. Take her and tie her to the stake."

Rhiannon tried hard to fight them off as they held her and pulled her arms behind her, but she was still too weak. She kicked and scratched as hard as she could, but with her hands tied, she couldn't do much else to fend them off her. Then, she was slapped so hard that she fell to the ground again. The pole was lowered, Rhiannon was tied by her feet, legs and arms, and then the pole was raised again. She watched in horror as the wood was piled around her in a circle and then closed off. The villagers gathered around smiling and excited.

Rhiannon looked out over the crowds as Elizabeth and the council members stood at the front.

Pastor Joseph Johnson pushed past the crowds to stand in front of them all and face the council. "I must beg you all to stop. This is not how Christians must solve this." The crowds yelled and shouted as he was pulled away. "This is not the way. You have to stop this madness," he continued to shout. He looked back over to Rhiannon and then shook his head as he was pushed away from the courtyard. The crowds closed the circle leaving him on the outside of it.

Rhiannon stared down at Elizabeth who was watching with some of the women from the village. "Stop them, Elizabeth, you can stop them. I know you hate me, but this is wrong. Where's Evan? I want him to tell them I'm not a witch, I'm innocent. Our child has been born early, please find it, please go and help it. They left it out there and tonight it's cold. Tell them the truth, Elizabeth, and I promise to leave here and never come back." She looked up at the skies. They were almost clear, but the moon was still too hidden by the clouds. Then she screamed out into the night, "Evan! If you loved me at all, go and find your child! Evan, please, I beg you!"

"Burn her!" screamed Elizabeth as she stepped forward. "Burn her now!" She reached out for a lit torch and stood at the base of the stacked wood. She looked up at Rhiannon. "I don't care what you are. You took my Evan. You took my hopes of our own child and for that, I will never forgive you. You will burn in hell tonight, witch." She lowered the torch as Rhiannon screamed and then she withdrew it without lighting anything. Elizabeth looked up at Rhiannon with a smile, "Your pretty face will no longer look upon my husband," she said and tipped the torch forward, lighting the first section of the pyre. "Evan isn't here to watch you burn and your devil child will certainly be dead by now." And then Elizabeth threw the torch into the rest of it and lit the second pyre. "I made sure they left it out there for the wolves to feast on."

As the flames spread to the kindle and dry wood and then took hold, Rhiannon panicked. She tried to get out of the ropes, but they just got tighter. The fire was doing all the work as the flames grew closer and she began to feel the heat. She could hardly breathe from the smoke that was coming toward her from the dry wood as it burnt. A breeze started to gather in the courtyard and although it gave her respite at times, it also changed directions and only helped to fan the flames even more, setting other parts of the kindling on fire. Her lungs wheezed as the smoke began to enter them and the taste was bitter on her tongue. The flames began to nip at her toes. She couldn't move them back any farther and soon her ankles were alight and her dress was on fire. She looked up at the skies as the moon finally made its entrance and with the final moments of her last breath, she looked down on the villagers.

Then, through the flames, she saw Evan on the other side of the courtyard. He was crying, on his knees shouting, but she couldn't hear what he was saying. He looked inconsolable and yet he wasn't doing anything to help her. She screamed out to him, "Evan!" But all he did was collapse farther down onto the ground, shielding his ears from her screams.

Then with the little of her breath that remained, she didn't scream his name again. Instead, she screamed her last words at the villagers who were still there watching and to Elizabeth. "I may be weak, but the moon shines bright and my child is no longer within me. With my last breath, I curse you, Elizabeth Harding. I curse you to die in such a pain as I will tonight. I will my soul to someday return to this village and to those who condemned me. I will end all of your sires. I will..." Before she could finish, a torch thrown from within the crowd hit Rhiannon in the chest and it ignited the rest of her clothing. It merged with the flames that had risen up around her. She screamed as she continued to burn. At first, the sensation was like small needles being pushed against her feet and then the nerve endings began to react to the fire as her dress continued to burn higher. The first layer of her epidermis began to peel away and she prayed to the Goddess to take her quickly. The awareness became deeper and a thicker layer of skin began to peel away and split open and the fat began to leak out of the muscle. But it took a half hour of agonising pain and screams before her prayers were finally answered and Rhiannon's spirit was taken by the Goddess.

****

The women from the village that stood alongside Elizabeth could watch it no longer. They urged her to leave, but she would not. Elizabeth stood expressionless, as she watched Rhiannon's beautiful long black hair catch fire and her beautiful face be totally obscured by the flames. With a final roar, the flames shot upwards, the fiery liquid of fat and blood poured out from her body sending sparks out to the villagers who had already started to leave and it made Elizabeth, for the first time, to take a few steps back. The smell of burning flesh replaced the smell of the surrounding farmland and charred pieces of cloth fell in burning strands to the ground and some flew upwards into the air, taken by the breeze that had remained.

But Elizabeth's gaze never left the burning mass of black flesh which was now all that was left of Rhiannon. Totally engulfed by the fire, Rhiannon's body could no longer be seen, the screams from within the fire had already subsided some time before.

Then the whole bonfire imploded and Rhiannon was gone.

Elizabeth made sure to stay until the fire was well and truly out. The sun began to rise and even though several hours had passed and she was alone, she couldn't leave until she was sure that Rhiannon's body was nothing more than a blackened pile of bone and ash.

CHAPTER TWENTY

The blackened embers of the previous night stained the courtyard and even though the ash was collected and placed in a sack, the charred stain could not be removed however many times the spot was cleaned and scrubbed.

Pastor Joseph Johnson knelt down in front of the cross in the chapel, deep in prayer, when the doors opened behind him and four members of the council entered. Sion Evans, Emyr Roberts, Alwyn Creu and James Clwyd walked down the aisle toward him. He took a deep breath; his feelings were mixed with what they had done.

"Can I help you gentlemen?"

The men looked at each other as Sion Evans held out his arm. He was holding the remains of Rhiannon in the bag. "The witch put a curse on this village."

"And what do you want me to do?" asked Pastor Johnson. "I told you all what you were doing was wrong. I want no part in this."

"It wasn't wrong that we burnt the witch," said Emyr Roberts. "We need to keep the ashes here."

"Why? Weren't you going to toss her into the waste pit?"

"Yes, but that was before she cursed us. We need to make sure that she doesn't come back. That's why we're here," Sion Evans replied. His hand trembled as he still held onto the bag with Rhiannon's bones and ashes.

Pastor Johnson looked confused. "She's dead. Your superstitions have murdered an innocent woman.

Even if, and I doubt she was what you accused her of, she's dead."

"But they are magical creatures. What if her soul possesses another?" asked Sion.

"Wha-what?" asked Pastor Johnson. "Are you believing the fables that are told to children to frighten them?"

"We want you to bind her soul. So, it can't be free and kill us all," Sion continued.

"I don't know how to do that," Pastor Johnson said aghast. "That is not what I am here for."

"The Chief Judge left us a prayer that he has used to bind other witches. It was given to the Witchfinder General himself by the Pope in Rome and we should use it. But only a pastor can do the ceremony and in a holy house. Here," insisted Sion Evans

Emyr Roberts handed the pastor two sheets of paper. On it, a Latin verse was written. "I don't read Latin," said Pastor Johnson handing it back to Emyr. "You will have to summon another pastor, perhaps even a bishop?"

"No, you can do it. You can practice. It must be performed before a week passes from her death and in here. It must be performed in here. Her bones must lie on consecrated ground in this chapel until then. A Buckley jar is being brought here in two days. She will be placed inside it and you will speak those words. We will then bury her high in the mountains, inside a cave and she will be hidden for all time."

"I don't understand why you want to do all of this. A simple prayer and burial here in the churchyard might lay her soul to rest. Why perform a ritual like this at all?"

"Because her curse is among us, that's why." said Emyr abruptly. "If we don't do this only the good Lord knows what will happen to this village or to us. You heard her. And her curse has begun already. The skies are turning dark and the milk this morning was sour and green. If we do not do this ritual, our village is dead."

"Well, after it is done, I will wash my hands from this whole thing," Pastor Johnson insisted.

"You needn't worry," said Emyr. "As a child, my father would take me shooting up the mountain. There is a cavern that you can only reach by descending into it. My father took me to it several times, but I never really liked going in there. It is high enough to be away from anyone wishing to call back this creature."

****

A few days later, Pastor Joseph Johnson stood in his holy robes at the altar and blessed the bag with the remains of Rhiannon. He placed them in the Buckley jar and began the prayer:

"Hoc enim abjecti infernalis adversarii. Hoc igitur maledictus pythonissam propulsamus tibi. Creatura diaboli hostis hac sancta. Et humiliare sub potenti manu anima tua, et projiciamus a nobis Dominum Deum nostrum corpus tuum. Anima tua occultam esse a mundo salus est ad nos, et nos cedamus amori in Deum. O Domine, libera nos ab hac creatura suo, et populo terræ. O Domine libera animam meam hanc se ipso die rogamus vos. Animabus nostris custodire ab hoc malo et salvum satanas. Nos rogamus te per Deum. Nos rogamus vos in sanctis est. Nos te rogamus ac tenebras. Domine exaudi orationem meam et ait ad illam ut in custodia."
We cast out this infernal adversary. This cursed witch we repel you. This creature of the devil, the enemy of this holy church. You will humble yourself under the mighty hand of our Lord our God and cast your soul from your

body. Thy soul to be kept hidden from the world until salvation is upon us and we be judged by God. O Lord, deliver this creature away from our earth and its people. O Lord deliver her soul this very day we beseech you. Keep our souls safe from this evil of Satan. We beseech you under God. We beseech you under his holy word. We beseech you to the darkness. Lord, we beg you hear our prayer that it may be answered with her imprisonment.

The same men—Sion Evans, Emyr Roberts, Alwyn Creu and James Clwyd—stood alongside him as he uttered the words and sealed the jar. Emyr Roberts placed it in a sack bag and carried it outside, followed closely by the other men. They walked away from the village and onto the mountain pass. On a small ledge, halfway up Heulwen's Pass, three of them sat down to rest, while Emyr walked to a nearby spot. Sion took out a knife and carved a triad with a line crossing its middle into the rock he sat on.

"What are you doing?" asked James.

"I'm leaving a warning so that no one will dare walk this way," Sion replied.

Alwyn shrugged. "Do you think anyone will walk this way again?"

"Better to be safe," Sion replied.

Emyr joined the others. "I have found the cavern," he said, out of breath. "My father lowered me inside it. We can tether the rope to the rocks here and go down into it one by one. It has a shaft at the start and then it opens up into a round cavern. We need to take torches. I will take a lit one down with me and you can throw down the others. I will light them as you all come down. The pastor gave me some sketches of the symbols we have to carve into the walls, so let's do this before it gets too dark and we have to stay up here. I do not wish to stay in the same room as the witch – dead or not – for any longer than I have to."

Inside the cavern chamber, each of the men took a piece of the drawings and carved them into the walls. They chiselled away and then created two smaller alcoves into the walls. One that would hide the witch's book, an unholy possession that would not burn when they set her cottage alight and another that would hold the Buckley jar with Rhiannon's remains, her soul blessed with the words of God.

The men looked around the cavern once they had finished. All that was left to do was just one thing more - they had been given one final piece of the prayer from the Witchfinder General. "Lord, bless this chamber that it may remain hidden for all time," Alwyn recited out loud and then splashed some holy water onto the walls where they had just carved in the symbols.

"Amen," replied Sion, James and Emyr.

"Amen," said Alwyn.

****

Treharne returned to its normal daily life and nothing was said again about the witch that had charmed a married man, except for the tales told to children to frighten them. Over the years, the stories were forgotten and the village grew into a prosperous developing town, never knowing the secret that was buried high in the mountains.

CHAPTER TWENTY-ONE

Present day 2019

Mari Lewis looked down in desperation at her blank dissertation paper due in three months. Unlike the other students at the University of Aberystwyth, she still didn't know what her main subject was to be about.

Mari had always taken an interest in the occult and folklore. She had a passion for the most obscure legends and she was one of the best of her class for researching each topic. When she finally did get a job at the British Museum, it was a boring assistant post away from anything exciting that was brought into the museum, so she left it and went back to school. When she heard about the new department that was due to open in a few months, she asked her boss for some time away from her job to do a course at the university so that she could study to give her a chance of a placement in it. But that just led to her boss telling her that it was either the course or the job she currently had. And after a short argument, Mari made her mind up and left. It was purely in the hopes that her new qualifications would entice that new department to eventually take her on.

The only course of its kind was at the Aberystwyth University, which made her feel as though she'd come full circle. She'd graduated in anthropology only five years previous, and since then had only participated in three foreign digs and helped some old professor write his book which she got no credit for doing so.

She studied the other students as they passed by her desk. She never did fit in, even when she was last there. Maybe she just looked a bit odd compared to the other trendy students. She was a little over five feet six tall. It didn't matter how much she stuffed her face—cakes, burgers, chips—she never put on weight. She didn't even exercise. She was a slim, dark-haired, dark-eyed girl with pale features who looked more at home during Halloween than in the bright summer sunshine outside. Where most of the female students wore pretty pastel-coloured clothes, Mari wore a colour occasionally, but it was mostly black and white, or just black with perhaps a touch of another dark colour.

If the other students just looked at her more closely, they would have seen a large-eyed beauty with full pink lips and sculptured cheekbones. Her slender figure may have disguised her curves, but she did have them. But Mari didn't really care. All she cared about was having no clue to what her research and paper was going to be about.

Her chair scraped along the floor of the large library making at least a dozen students look up from their concentration and frown. "Sorry," she whispered, raising her shoulders. "So sorry."

Thousands, if not tens of thousands of books were collected in the university library. It was one of the most comprehensive in the whole of the United Kingdom. But it was a maze of too much information that boggled the eyes and made it virtually impossible to find what you wanted to find, unless you actually knew what it was you wanted to find. Which Mari didn't.

"Is there a particular book you're looking for?" asked a voice behind her. The librarian stood nearby with a handful of books in her arms putting them back on the shelves around her.

"I'm not sure," said Mari.

"Have you started your research subject yet?"

"No, that's the trouble. I have no idea. None of these subjects are…" she stopped and scrunched up her shoulders and mouth, "gripping me right now."

"Well maybe something down in the basement might."

"Basement? We have a basement? With even more books?" asked Mari.

"Yes, that's right. There are some too old to bring up here. The light decays them, as well as chocolate and grease stains on the pages." She waved a small book at Mari. "I sometimes have to wipe down some books." And she placed it on the shelf behind Mari. "There are books on anthropology down there that you may not have read last time you were here."

"Oh, you remember me."

"Of course," said the librarian. "You were always in this room. But your mind wasn't this—"

"Empty?" interrupted Mari with a frown.

"Confused, I was going to say. But that as well." The librarian smiled. "Well, if you want the key, it's number 401 and you'll have to sign it out with my colleague over there. Tell her I said it was OK."

The basement was everything she thought it would be—dark, old, full of rotting pages and display cases with more obscure books inside them with white gloves on the side. But even though the smell was musky and damp, Mari was excited. She knew her subject was right there waiting for her to discover it.

She brushed her fingers lightly across some of the book binders on the first aisle and stopped every now and again if a title grabbed her attention or the book cover looked interesting. She wasn't even sure how long she'd been doing that, when one book caught her attention. Mainly because the cover was a little torn and it snared on her finger, almost cutting it. She pulled out the book and flicked through it. The story was about the witch trials and executions in Wales and the many legends that surrounded that time period. Mari was intrigued. She hadn't really known that there had been any in Wales, over the border into England yes, but Wales?

Mari sat down with the book and flicked through it. There had only been three executions in Wales in over a fifty year history of the 1600s, two of which happened in the south, but as the borders had changed since then, they had now been categorised as being committed in England and not Wales, and they'd been hanged. But one did happen in Wales and she was burnt at the stake, not too far from where she was studying. She smiled as she read more of the story and all of a sudden, an idea came into her head. Why not make her paper be about the only witch burnt in Wales? There had to be a lot of information around for her to discover. Mari put the book in her rucksack and headed back to her room at the bed and breakfast two miles from the university. At last, she had found a subject to write about.

CHAPTER TWENTY-TWO

Mari hadn't been able to put her book down since she took it (or stole it) out of the library. She stopped on the way home to get food, but scarcely touched it as she settled down on her sofa. Three women—sisters—in the mid-1600s and well before the infamous Salem trials had even taken place, had been tried and executed by hanging. But a fourth had been the only one to have been burnt at the stake a year later. Although the book had given in great detail how the sisters had conducted themselves before the trials and then afterwards with their sentence and eventual executions, there seemed very little about the fourth. The woman, only known as Rhiannon, had lived in a small village and had been accused of killing four men in the village and of bewitching another. But the details were sketchy. And she didn't know why, but this particular event had stirred up a curiosity that Mari knew only too well, and she began to eventually put pen to paper at last. Her outline was there. The research was to be the various witch trials of the century and why had the women not all suffered the same fate as others. Why was Rhiannon burnt instead of hanged or even drowned as others accused of witchcraft had been? What had she done that had been so terrible, that she suffered the worst death? Mari couldn't wait for the night to be over. Tomorrow, she was going straight back to the library to find out about Rhiannon, the last —and possibly the only witch—to be burnt in Wales.

****

But the library was a bust.

Nowhere was there any reference to Rhiannon. Even the three convicted sisters were barely mentioned, so Mari made her way to the librarian to ask for help.

"Hello," she said softly. "I was hoping you could help me with something."

The librarian looked up from her papers. Smiling she said, "Yes of course. Did you find anything after?" she asked.

"Yes," said an excited Mari. "But now I'm stuck."

"So soon?"

"I know. I'm not exactly proud of myself. But I picked up this book yesterday from downstairs." Mari placed the small book on the counter. "There's a reference in there to the last witches executed in Wales and there's not much more about them. I was hoping there were more books on the subject."

The librarian looked down at the book. "Well firstly, you were meant to just look in the basement and take notes, not take out any of the contents. And secondly"—she scanned the book sleeve—"I'm not sure we have anything else. We've got the trials of the Goodrich Four, but they were executed across the border in England, so I suppose that doesn't count." She walked to her computer "Let me just check the book out and see if anything else comes up."

Mari stood behind the librarian as she typed 'Occult and Welsh Mythological Beings' on her computer. "The author only wrote this book. And it's strange," said the librarian clicking on the computer keys, "because I have no record of this book even being in the archives. So, I'm wondering where it came from?"

Mari picked up the book and placed it in her holdall. "Well if you didn't even know the book was there then no one's going to complain if it's not downstairs. I promise to return it once I've finished with it. But maybe I need to read it again and get a bit more information. I can always try and get a few names from it and then try to trace that family line."

"I can help you with that too," said the librarian enthusiastically. "We have the census from the villages here in the north going back to the early 1500s. That's going to be a lot of research for you."

"That's not a problem," said Mari, relieved. "I'm very good at research and to be honest, I'm so behind on it all, it'll feel good to have finally started something."

"Who are you going to make your main focus? All of them or a particular one?" asked the librarian. "I can maybe help you look up the names to start you off properly."

"I think the last one," said Mari. "Yes, definitely the last one, Rhiannon. She was the only one burnt instead of hanged or drowned which is what they did to the others. And I want to find out why."

****

Mari looked at the map on her phone. According to the app, the town she wanted was at least an hour and a half drive from Aberystwyth and stood not too far from the River Llugwy, a lake in the Carneddau range of mountains in Snowdonia. Treharne had grown from a modest farming village back in the 1500s, to a large busy town with a spectacular backdrop of the Snowdonia mountain ranges.

When she reached the town, she searched for the local library and only found it after she had stopped at least two people for directions. It was hidden away in the older part of the town. It wasn't a huge building and it could certainly do with some renovations. It had peeling paint and a musty smell of mould coming from somewhere that Mari couldn't quite see. It had ten rows of bookshelves stacked five shelves high on both sides of the room and a reception desk with a surprised man standing behind it as she walked in.

"Do you have a computer I could use?" she asked the bemused man, and without a word he pointed to a solitary desk with a monitor that had seen better days. She switched it on and typed in "Rhiannon." A few options came to the screen—a song by a well-known band, the Mabinogion book, a poem of love to a seventeenth century girl—but nothing else. She typed in "Welsh witch." Up came the song again with a video of the woman singing it but no real information could be found. Mari sat back and thought about how else to search for it. Then she typed "Treharne 1684" and on the screen came up two references. One was to a terrible harvest and a disease that killed off livestock during one winter month just before Christmas. And the other was a small reference to a judge arriving to oversee the trial of a woman. But no other information was available. Mari sat back in her chair, frustrated. She'd come all this way for nothing. No mention of Rhiannon. No mention of anything happening in the village that could give her any more clues. Until she heard the chimes from a clock tower and walked over to the librarian behind the counter. "The church." she asked. "When was it built?"

The librarian looked up. "The chapel? I don't really know. It's always been here… I-I can't really say."

Mari returned to her computer and typed in "Treharne parish chapel." The information was glorious. The chapel had been built on the site of another from the 11th century that had burnt down. This chapel was then rebuilt later in the 12th century and would have been the main place of worship around the time that Rhiannon would have been there. Mari returned to the librarian. "Do you know if the chapel keeps its old records? You know, births, deaths and marriages... that sort of thing?"

"I don't know," said the librarian. "But if there are any, I don't know what state they'll be in. There was a flood in this area about two hundred years ago from the Llugwy, I do know that much. The pastor lives in the house next to it. He could tell you more than me."

Mari took seconds to pack up her things and almost ran to the chapel. A quant, small, traditionally built building of stone and red tiles. Outside it, and to the sides, were old gravestones. The grass had been cut short and was well-maintained. To the front of the building, there was one arched door that was split with one side open and the other closed—except for weddings or funerals, when both would be opened. The door was decorated with wrought iron strap hinges and a round iron door handle. She turned the handle and stepped inside. The chapel was like stepping back in time with stone walls and wooden panels. It had rows of wooden pews, tiled and stone floors with some crosses that marked where previous pastors had been buried and the usual crosses and pulpits. Stained glass and leaded windows let in colourful light. The whole place had the familiar religious smell of candles and spilt wax. And more importantly, at the bottom of the church near the altar, sat a pastor.

"Hello," said Mari in a voice in-between a shout and a high level whisper.

Her voice seemed to startle the pastor for a moment. *Perhaps he rarely had visitors to the chapel*, thought Mari.

"Hello," said the pastor standing and turning to face her. "I'm sorry, but there's no service today."

"That's OK," answered Mari. "I was hoping for some information, to be honest."

The pastor smiled. His face expressed a mild curiosity. Mari felt her cheeks start to get hot. The pastor wasn't much older than she was and quite attractive, not at all the cliché pastor-type she would envisage in such a chapel. He wasn't even wearing a dog collar, but wore jeans and a black shirt. He even wore trainers! His hair was shoulder-length, and he had slight facial hair. She wondered if this man was the actual pastor or not.

"I'm looking for information on a woman," she began. "She lived in these parts in the late 1600s. I can find a record of this town back then, but not much more, and I'm researching this for a paper at my university."

"Who was the woman?" the pastor asked.

Mari stepped closer. "Her name was Rhiannon. That's all I have. Back then, she was tried as a witch and burnt here in this town."

"And this is your subject? For your course?"

"It is. This woman was tried and burnt as a witch in Wales and I never knew that such a thing happened. You see, women who were accused of witchcraft were never burnt, they were hanged or drowned or just imprisoned. Burnings only first happened in America, at Salem, in the state of Massachusetts. It happened here much later, so it's unusual."

"It's a gruesome topic to be doing a paper on," the pastor commented. He seemed a little disturbed about what she was asking for.

"Perhaps, but all I need to see are any records that you may still have from that time. The librarian told me that you have records here."

"We have church records. Some do date back to the sixteenth century and beyond that. But we also had a flood almost two hundred years ago and it damaged a lot of the records that we have."

"I heard that as well, but whatever you do have, would you mind if I took a look at them? I may not get anything, but any little thing will help. Sometimes it only takes a name and the search can take you elsewhere."

"As well as the church records, we do have several gravestones of the villagers from back there too. I often walk among them, wondering what kind of people stood there before me. You may want to see those too."

"Wonderful," said Mari. "I'll definitely be doing that too."

"The cellars are very dirty. I can only apologise, but we don't have the luxury to display the books as we'd like. Some day we might, perhaps. But you are welcome to look at them. I would appreciate that they not be moved from here."

"Of course," said Mari. "Besides, whatever information I need, I can just scan with my phone and take it away. Is it this way?" She pointed to a side door.

"Yes," said the pastor, he walked in front of her and opened the door. "Let me make sure that the light is working first. I don't relish the thought of you falling down the stairs."

The cellar was a treasure trove of history. There were a few paintings of the chapel from various years and some of its pastors, faded sketches, wooden crosses, silver crosses and books. Big, wonderfully bound books covered in cobwebs and dust. Mari wiped away the dust, moss and small amounts of debris brought down from the room above her off the table top and carried over a metal chair that had been folded up against the wall. She looked at each book bound in old black leather and inscribed with different dates. She gazed at each one as though she'd discovered her very own ancient artefact and stopped at the book marked 1655 to 1885.

She carefully opened the fragile book as parts of its leather cover and inner pages came away. The faded words were impossible to read under the small light bulb that shone from above the table and she could just make out some of the writing. The pastor of the time, Joseph Johnson, had kept the books up-to-date with all the usual chapel activity, and several births, mostly around the same dates in May or June. There were two marriages in the summer and a number of deaths in the winter, which was the norm when the cold weather came. The entry for the year that Mari was interested in, was too faded to read, so she took out her phone and photographed the pages in the hopes that a contact of hers at the university could enhance it for her. She carefully turned over more pages and began to read a sort of journal, that the pastor had written...*'With the arrival of winter, the mountain road has proven to be an impassable task once more. Luckily, the harvests from the summer will keep our community strong and we will gather whatever we can, for those whose yield was not as great. The gentlemen of the community will visit various outer farms before the winter settles in and take whatever is needed to provide them with food until the thaw...'*

And then, at the bottom of the page, and what seemed to have been added a little later, Mari read on... *'It has come to our sad attention that one of our parishioners has taken on a great illness and has passed. It was God's will that in her final days, her niece had chosen that time to visit and cared for old Beatrice Tydfil, known to us in these parts as Mother Tydfil, a gentlewoman and much respected member of the community, until her death. She was buried with a prayer to the Lord in the plot near her own cottage just on the fringes of the Dewi orchard, by her very own niece, Rhi...'* The name had faded away.

Mari took a breath inwards. She turned over another page, but that had faded too, so she turned another. It was hopeless. The rest of the book was so old and had been damaged by time that it was illegible. She looked down at her phone and to the pictures of the pages she'd seen. She was hopeful that it could be enhanced, but at this moment with her luck, she wasn't holding her breath.

Just then, the pastor came into the room, "Any luck finding what you were looking for?"

The smell of a sweet cologne wafted through the doors. "Not really," she replied defeated. "I thought for one little moment that I had something. The pastor made a partial reference to, I'm hoping, 'Rhiannon,' but it's so faded out I can't be sure. He wrote about her arriving in the village to look after her aunt who was sick, but like I said, the pages are so worn that his writing is almost invisible."

"Why don't you read his journals?" he said, shrugging. "Pastors back then kept many journals. These books here are used mostly for noting the official gatherings at the chapel."

"Journals? He kept journals?"

"Yes," he said, looking around the room. "Let me see. I'm sure I saw them when I first moved here. We had to sort through some of the boxes. There was a very dodgy smell which I think was a not-so-invited fungus, and we threw out a lot that we couldn't salvage." He walked over to a few boxes that were stacked higher up on the shelves. "I think they're in here."

Mari got up to help. She lifted one of the boxes, dust splattered over her making her cough as she placed it on the table. Opening the lid, she gazed into a dozen or so books. Not leather bound as the others but simpler made, with a narrow black ribbon tied around each one. It didn't even look as though the flood waters or any of the fungus had even touched them. Carefully she took one out and opened it. Although the writing here was faded, it was much more legible and revealed the life and the times of the village. "Oh my God, these are perfect!" Mari looked up. "Oh, sorry reverend, no insult intended."

He smiled at her coyness. "It's OK, and I'm a pastor, not a reverend. You can call me John."

Mari smiled. "John, thank you. This is exactly what I'm looking for."

John stepped away and then stopped and turned back to her. "What are you hoping to find from the books?"

She looked up at him and paused for a moment. "I always thought the whole Salem witch trials and burnings never really spread around the world until after it happened there. But if I can prove that it started here…" She stopped talking and then said, "You see, women accused of being witches were always drowned or hanged or even imprisoned, but they were never burnt. So why did they burn Rhiannon? Why did they pick this solitary woman for such a punishment? I mean, what was it she did that was so terrible they changed their whole views on their sentencing? It means that the first documented official burning didn't happen in Salem as everyone thinks, it originated here."

"And that's important, why?"

"Because it rewrites history, of course."

"Then I'll leave you to study them. I've got a chapel meeting to attend. When you finish, just turn out the light and close the front door."

Mari nodded. "Yes, of course, and thanks for these."

The journals were just perfect. Mari got them into date order and began to read from them again, skipping forward over the irrelevant gossip of village life until she got to the information she needed.

11th November 1684.
'I here lay witness to the proceedings of our crime. My name is Joseph Johnson and I am the pastor of the village of Treharne. I pray that our souls be pardoned once we enter the Lord's paradise, for what I am about to recount has sent the fear of the Lord into our midst.

The accused, Rhiannon Turner, was brought before Chief Judge Harris, Court Prosecutor John Maddox-Hughes and twelve council members: Tom Benant, Sion Evans, Alwyn Creu, Caradoc Enfys, James Clwyd, Steffan Morris, Cai Donal, Alun Donal, Emyr Roberts, Gethin Tegau, Glyn Griffiths and Llewellyn Madox, to renege on the allegations made against her of witchcraft brought forward by three women of good character and social standing of this village, Mrs Elizabeth Harding, Mrs Derwena Jones and Mrs Mary Hughes. These ladies swore that they witnessed such magic coming from the potions that have been used to empower the sick. The accused is also alleged to have entered into immoral dealings with the husband of Elizabeth Harding, Evan Harding, and in their indiscretion produced a bastard child that grows in her belly.'

"Wow!" Mari exclaimed, putting the book down. At last, the name she was looking for, Rhiannon Turner. "This could end up being our very own Salem. And she was pregnant too?"

14th November 1684
'After a trial that has lasted only five days, Rhiannon Turner was to be summoned before the court to hear her fate. But before she was to be brought forward, the accused had freed herself from her bonds and prison and had absconded into the night. Hunted by the men of the village, her capture was marked by the birth and subsequent death of her child. Rhiannon Turner was condemned to be burnt for her crimes of witchcraft and heresy and her punishment was to be carried out that night.

On this night of the execution, witness that I, Joseph Johnson make these records known that I beseeched the judge, council and townspeople to reconsider, but they did not. I withdrew to my cowardly shame to this very chapel where I prayed over the soul of Rhiannon Turner. Witch or not, I prayed for her soul that night to find peace. From my chapel and in my shame, I did cover my ears to shield myself from her screams and cries into the night for mercy, but the stench of burning flesh as the flames rose around her clouded this village. Her voice cried out in the worst pain into the darkest of nights in which she then cursed the village with all the strength that she had left to give before her death.'

Mari hadn't even noticed that the pastor had left the room already when she looked up to ask him, "Can I just take this one with me? I promise to—" But she was alone. She stretched down and picked up her holdall. Closing the journal she placed it inside her bag and closed it. She was just going to borrow it, she told herself. She'd bring it back as soon as she was done.

Upstairs, she found the pastor lighting candles. "Have you found what you were looking for in those journals?" he asked Mari.

"If it's all right with you, can I come back in a few days and perhaps look at them again? I didn't quite finish reading them."

"Of course," replied the pastor.

"Thanks, I'll see you soon." Mari opened the door and walked out into the early evening air. She couldn't wait to get back to her room and read more of the journal. But for the time being, at least, she could fill in her official entry on the university syllabus, 'The Execution of Rhiannon Turner: The first witch to be burnt at the stake in Wales.'

Margarita Felices

CHAPTER TWENTY-THREE

Back in her room, Mari took of her coat and quickly settled into an armchair with a sandwich and a glass of wine. This book was just too important to leave for later. She took several gulps of wine and then opened the journal once more and began to read:

15th November 1684
'There is a ghostly silence throughout the village. A grey lingering fog hangs over the courtyard and no bird will dare pass nearby. The children cry out in their sleep at night in fear as if they sense a presence that is outside. Their cries echo from homes and into the night. There is a strange movement to the trees in the forest on the outside of the village but there is no wind to move them. There is nothing there. The birds fly overhead but do not land and their song is whispered. Perhaps they too sense the sadness that has taken hold of this village or perhaps they are part of her curse. They sense the change in the village.'

Mari took another sip of wine but scarcely took her eyes off the journal as she continued.

16th November 1684
'A good deal of the harvest has wilted and died overnight. The river that lay beyond the field has stopped running and its stillness has turned it stagnant. The fish have died and no others will swim towards it, animals turn away and will not drink from it. Any fish taken from the river is rancid to the taste. Where the river forks

further upstream, the fish take the other path, it will not follow to our river. Even the otters and mink have moved away from the rivers nearby and have gone to the other valleys.

It has not even been a week since the accused witch Rhiannon Turner, laid her curse upon this village. I am not saying that what she said has anything to do with this, but the people are frightened. The crops diminish and the livestock are sick and dying. Cows do not produce milk but a green sour liquid. The pigs do not eat and are dying. All eyes have turned to Elizabeth Harding who brought the allegations and to the other women who helped condemn Rhiannon Turner. I am loathed to help them, but as the good Christian that I am, I know that I must. Elizabeth Harding's husband Evan Harding has not been seen since that fateful night and has vanished from the village and is presumed dead or has run away from the shame.'

"Coward," said Mari under her breath. "She was pregnant and he just left her." She flipped over the next pages, but they were blank. "No!" she shouted at the journal. "No, no, you can't have ended it there. Ugh! Why didn't I just take the other journals too?"

****

The following day, Mari drove back to the chapel and found Pastor John standing just outside of its doors. There was a soft light from the winter sun shining in the doorway which acted like a spotlight that managed to show off his physique under the blue T-shirt he was wearing. She began to feel even more embarrassed as he spotted her staring at him again.

He smiled as she walked closer. "Another visit? I thought you said in a few days," he said tilting his head to one side. "Or did you come to return the journal you took?"

Mari felt ashamed. She could feel her cheeks redden again. "I'm sorry, I didn't mean to take it, but I couldn't read it all while I was here. The light downstairs isn't bright and it's so faded in some sections. I-I didn't mean to, but at least I did bring it back." Then she stopped. "How did you know?"

"I counted the journals before I left you. When I went back downstairs I saw one was missing, but I knew you'd be back."

"How did you know?"

"Because I knew that only half the information was there. Maybe I should have said that before I was assigned here—well actually when I was told I was coming here—I wanted to do a little research of my own. I was looking for the chapel community books and came across the journals. Treharne does have a colourful history, you know. When I found them, I read them too, although I only scanned through them trying to find something I may not have known about this town. The pastor is buried here with his wife in the graveyard, and you'll find the graves of some of the other names mentioned in the journals."

"What did you mean? You said 'a colourful history?'"

"The hanging of the witches. It's a local story, you know, and told to young children so they'll behave, the legend of the three ferch Ellis sisters. They came from this area so they were executed not far from here, but since that time, the land boundaries have changed and some books that mention it say they were tried and then executed in England, but they weren't. They were hanged here in Wales. They do also say, though, that there was a fourth sister and she escaped."

"You don't believe in that sort of thing?" asked Mari.

"I'm a man of God. We believe in the Divine Truth, not superstitious stories. Whatever went on in this town at the time was hysteria, not witchcraft. All that happened was the execution of three innocent women, not witches."

"So, what stories do you know about the one who escaped?"

"I don't think there are any specifically," he said. Stepping inside the chapel, he gestured for Mari to follow him. "There are a couple of stories, you know how it is over the years. There's one story I do know and that is that one of them may have lived here. And then the other story is that she would come to people at night and steal them away in their dreams. There you go see, just ghost stories handed down from generations. Do you know the town square?"

"Yes, I was there yesterday." Mari nodded.

"Another story. There was a burning there. Legend says that if you go there on the night of when it happened that you can hear her screaming and cursing the village. Thing is, no one really knows when it happened. They always end up as stories for Halloween night."

Mari scowled. "Really?"

"I said they were just stories to scare the children. I don't know when it happened. I just know the stories that it may have."

"It happened on the fourteenth of November, sixteen-eighty-four."

"How do you know that?"

"Joseph Johnson wrote about it in his journal." She reached into her rucksack, took out the journal and handed it back to John. "That's why I'm back. There must be more entries before and after. His journal finishes a week after her death and then there are blank pages."

"As though he lost the will to document anything else after it?" said John sadly.

"Maybe. Or he started a new journal? But I did notice that the other books don't have anything from him after that time either. Nothing until the new Pastor took over and started the records again."

"Do you want to see his grave?" asked John. "The pastor who wrote the journals?"

Mari nodded. "Yes, I would like that very much"

The graveyard was quite large for such a small chapel, she hadn't realised from the front when she first arrived and its garden was kept trimmed and neat. Wild colourful flowers grew in some of the open areas and birds chirped happily away in the overhanging trees. But it wasn't just another typical town graveyard, not anymore. They walked beyond the modern and most recent graves, along a smaller path that banked down to the furthest side of the chapel where John stopped besides a very modest grave. The inscription simply read: 'Here Lies The Body Of The Most Reverend, The Pastor Of Treharne, Joseph Johnson.

Born 1639. Died 1691

RIP'

Next to his grave was inscribed,

'Here Lays Anna Johnson, Wife To The Pastor Of Treharne.

Born 1645. Died 1702.

RIP'

"They weren't that old." Mari said looking down at both graves. She kicked away a few tufts of grass. "Do you know what he died from?"

"No idea," said John. "But people died of all sorts of things back then. And getting into their fifties was an achievement in these parts."

"The small gold crosses in the chapel...other pastors were buried there, why wasn't he?" asked Mari.

"I asked that when I first came here and I think it's to do with his wife, they weren't allowed to be buried in the chapel, so I guess they wanted to be buried next to each other when their time came."

"That's kinda sweet don't you think?" asked Mari sadly, looking down at both graves.

John nodded. "Yes, I suppose it is." He looked around the graveyard. "The mountains over there can be a cruel fortress in the winter months, even in these days. We're lucky that we can get over, around and in some places under it. But back then? They were cut off from other villages and towns over the winter. It was harsh."

"The librarian in the town mentioned that there'd been a flood here two hundred years ago."

"Yes, and it very nearly wiped this town from the map. There's a river over there." John pointed just beyond the graveyard away from the town. "It ran a different direction back then, closer to the village, but it was re-routed about a hundred and fifty years ago to go in a different direction after the flood so it barely comes this way anymore, even after heavy rains, thankfully." He turned toward the town. "I think that's when it started to take shape and it became more of a town. And it's been growing and growing each day. We've had a lot of companies show interest in setting up here."

"Sooo..." she said coyly. "Can I take a look at the other journals?" Mari hoped if she sounded desperate enough, he'd say yes.

"Will you steal them again?"

"Stealing is such a harsh word, John. I simply borrowed the one to read it better and then I brought it back."

"You brought it back because you needed to know more?"

"No. I brought it back because stealing isn't really my thing," Mari said and smiled.

Back in the cellar, Mari brought the whole box down from the shelf again and placed it on the table. There were five journals in all and she opened each one to put them in order. As she sat down, she saw that there was another journal, later than the one she had 'borrowed.'

20th November 1684

'My soul is heavy today. My wife has assured me that I did all I could to save her, but my heart feels black and as guilty as those who condemned her. I know not who Rhiannon Turner really was or what she did, but I know that the potions written in her book cured a sick boy and I cannot believe that she was anything else but a gentlewoman. In writing these journals, I hope that future generations do not condemn this village for its crime. Good folk live here, but they have succumbed to petty jealousies and superstitions.

My only salvation is the child. He was brought to me by the farmer who found him crying for his mother. He will be cared for by the farmer who found him and his goodly wife who has not been blessed with a child. He will be safe from harm and not be persecuted because of his mother. We have agreed that no more shall be said on his matter.'

"Her book?" Mari queried. "Could that have been her grimoire? Oh Mari, stop reading too much into things. It could have just been a recipe book or similar but wouldn't that be something?" She daydreamed. "To find a genuine or to even have proof of an actual grimoire here in Wales?"

****

Mari sat in a study hall at the university in front of a computer and began to type away, 'Witch trials of the 1600s'. Surprisingly, a number of them came up. She narrowed it down. 'Witch trials 1680 to 1700, Wales.' 'Zero results found.' Mari sat up straight and frowned. "But there was definitely one. Why can't you find it?"

"Try, Witchfinder General Judge, advocate trials UK," said a voice from behind, startling her.

Standing there was the gorgeous—and pride of the faculty—Simon Jenkins. Simon was almost six feet tall, with dark hair, dark eyes, gorgeous facial features, a great body and just about everything else that she felt attracted to. Her eyes briefly drifted off into a daydream, their eyes only for each other, touching her... Mari shook herself clear off the daydream. Sure, he was handsome. Yes, everyone wanted to be with him or near him. But on the downside, he was an arrogant big-headed sexist rat that made her feel like a complete failure each time she opened her mouth to speak to him. From what she had heard, he'd slept with most of the girls from the senior years and even some of the female faculty. He'd been in her year when she first attended the university. He cheated on his exam—so rumour had it—and somehow he still managed to achieve such high marks, that he ended up as the talk of the university when he graduated with first class honours. He impressed them all so much that they offered him a job teaching, on the condition that he could just take off when he wanted to do his 'work and research'. It made it all the more unbearable when she returned five years later to take on a new study course. She felt like a failure for having to come and start over again. "Oh hello, Simon, I didn't notice you standing there." To her shame, she could feel herself blushing.

"No, you didn't," he said, smiling. "I called your name at least twice and you were so engrossed in what you were looking at, that I had to come take a look. Are you researching witchcraft? That's a bit of a new one for you. Aren't you usually into some sort of archaeological hunt or on some obscure burial ground somewhere?"

"As it happens," she said, closing down the computer screen, "I've found a very interesting subject right here in Wales."

"Superstition myths and legends do not present themselves with facts very often. If you're hoping to do your Masters on that, you might want to think again," Simon suggested.

"But as you may remember from previous papers written right here in this very university, myths and legends do at times derive themselves from fact. Anyway, I don't think you should be so concerned about my work. How about yours? Are you getting any further in your anthropology theories? Weren't you working toward writing some paper for an American science magazine at one time?" She said it on purpose knowing very well that he had been rejected by them—twice.

"No," he said confidentally. "I've decided to take a different direction. But yours does sound fascinating." He leaned in closer. "Perhaps we could help each other with... research?"

She turned away from him and her smile turned into a frown. "Thanks, but I think I have it covered."

"Rhiannon," he said suddenly. "I read that your chosen subject was a made up witch called Rhiannon."

"Not made up. Very real and I have proof that she was here in Wales and that she was executed here too." She was a little taken aback. "And how did you know what I was doing?"

"I do teach here remember. I always look at students' dissertations. See if I can assist in some way."

"Assist or take over and take credit? No thanks Simon, I'm able to work all this out on my own."

"Well I'm here if you need me."

Mari rolled her eyes. "Yeah thanks, but I'll still pass."

She turned back to the computer as Simon walked away. "Fuck it" she whispered. "Why didn't I think of that?" She typed in 'Witchfinder General Judge advocate trials UK'. And most annoyingly, up came pages and pages of the information she needed.

CHAPTER TWENTY-FOUR

Simon sat in his office and put his feet up on his desk. He had his own personal agenda with Mari's chosen topic. He'd been looking for a particular book that was fabled to exist and buried up in the mountains of Snowdonia and that had belonged to Rhiannon. It had been a pet project of his for a while, but he'd always come up with nothing – well nothing that could help. And Mari had always been very good at finding out information. Women always had a way of fluttering their eyelashes and being privy to certain information that no one had thought about and he wasn't going to let her out of his sights. He didn't care how much sucking up he'd have to do to be with her.

He sat up and switched on his computer and typed the words he suggested to her, 'Witchfinder General Judge advocate trials UK'. Several references came up. The most famous were the trials of the ferch Ellis sisters, but was one of the few entries for Wales. His true passion, however, was for the old Welsh fable about the witch who murdered some men from the area that he grew up in and whose stories had become more gruesome over the years and often told to frighten children, especially around a campfire on Halloween.

Simon's enthusiasm on the subject had started a few years back when his brother decided to delve into their family history. His brother, Jake, had traced their family line all the way down to the sixteenth century and discovered that they were farmers based in Treharne.

They owned a small farm in the foothills of Cadair Idris, which was the mountain range right behind the village.

But his great grandmother painted a different picture to the one that was told to scare children. When he was a small boy, he remembered how this frail wrinkled woman would captivate the family with her tales about a beautiful woman with long dark hair and big blue eyes, who had all the men wanting her attention and all the women jealous. This beautiful woman had magical powers and enslaved a local married man to be her lover. His great grandmother used to say that this powerful witch read from a magical book, a grimoire that mysteriously disappeared after she did. He could never understand why his great grandmother always told the same thing to him about the importance of the story until his brother uncovered one small flaw in their family tree.

In the late 1600s, the Jenkins family surprisingly presented a child to the pastor to be christened. No questions were ever asked by the villagers, no one even knew, not even the midwife, that Mrs Jenkins was pregnant. It seemed that a miracle had happened as Mrs Jenkins had been barren and was now very near her thirty-fifth birthday which was considered old to be delivering her first child. Simon smiled. He'd hit a dead-end looking for traces of the grimoire and Mari had already gotten further in the short time that she'd decided to research this story than he'd done. It was the grimoire he wanted—if it even existed, the magic book that his great grandmother spent most of his life talking about. And he knew that Mari would lead him straight to it with her research on Rhiannon.

Simon picked up his mobile and pushed a button. "Jake... Yeah, hiya... Remember you did some research on the family tree? Do you think you could send me all the notes you have? I might have something to add to it."

****

Mari couldn't put the journals down. Each time she stopped to give herself a break, she found herself thinking about what she'd just read or where she hoped they would take her. She barely touched her food when she began to read the journals again, starting with the entry of the day that Rhiannon arrived that caused such a stir in the village.

January 19th 1684
'The winter has surely rendered us defenseless this year. The snows came two months early and there is no sign of them thawing. The winds blow around us driving the snow further around the mountain passes. I can only pray that our parishioners in the outer farms have forethought the harsh weather and put away as much of their harvest as possible to see them through these cold months. I am unable to visit to offer solace or to give spiritual guidance. I am fortunate that my good lady wife has stocked our larder and that we have enough wood for warm fires, as I feel that we have become prisoners in our own home. Our service on Sunday lends us little respite, but some of the villagers have attempted to reach us. For their sake, we offer The Lords Prayer and a short sermon, which seems to please them.

As I write this, a new arrival has all the tongues wagging. It seems that old Mother Tydfil, who owns the cottage near the stream, has had a new visitor. I can scarcely believe how such a frail young woman can endure the harshness of the mountain pass, but she has arrived. It saddens me to write that shortly after her arrival, her aunt, Mother Tydfil, passed away and was buried within the orchard that she attended by her niece.'

Mari reached over and picked up her tablet. She typed in 'Witchfinder General Judge advocate UK' once again into the search engine and waited for the information to collate together. Several versions of the same tales from that era came through again, but one caught her attention once she scrolled through them all. The information spoke about the court appointed judges that would be dispatched in the absence of the witchfinder and that their role stayed in place up to 1701 when the laws changed. She read a portion of a five page dossier and was intrigued by the different aspects in which the laws were reformed at the time simply to prove women guilty. The false charges were always embellished and the punishment severe. Women accused of using the craft were sentenced to death, by drowning, by stoning or by hanging, as in the case of the ferch Ellis sisters. There was just one documented case that had a different outcome, but as she read on, she saw that the document was incomplete. Mari's research had hit a snag and only the originator of the document could help.

Her excitement was short-lived. The document at the end was credited to Simon Jenkins. "Oh, you have to be kidding!" she shouted into her tablet. "Anyone but him."

Mari knew that the information she needed would come from him and the research that he had started. And as much as she hated the thought, she reached over to her phone and began to text another student. 'Do u have Simon Jenkins' phone number?'

The phone pinged with a message a few minutes later. 'Why on earth would u want to speak to him? He's a bit of a creep, best avoided.'

Mari replied to the text, 'Yes, I know, but he has research notes I need.'

CHAPTER TWENTY-FIVE

Simon felt very pleased with himself as he admired his reflection in the silver spoon he was using to stir his coffee and waited for Mari in the university coffee shop. He knew that sooner or later, she would have come for his help. And if he did help her, she'd have enough confidence in him to let him stick around. Let her do all the work and hope it led to the grimoire. He'd brought over a pile of his notebooks and documents after she sent him a long text explaining what she was looking for. And of course, he was very forthcoming. He sipped his espresso and checked out each female student who walked by, until he saw Mari and stood up to greet her.

"There's no need," she said, partially dismissing him.

"But still, a gentleman is a gentleman." He dipped his head with a slight grin.

"Words I thought I would never hear coming from your mouth," Mari said in a sarcastic tone.

"You have me all wrong," Simon said with a shrug.

"We'll see," said Mari. "The paper I'm working on needs some of—"

Simon interrupted her. "A coffee first. What do you want? My treat."

"No, I don't want anything. I just want to—"

"I insist. A cappuccino? That's what you like, right?"

"Yes," she said looking anxious. "How did you--"

"Martha!" he called over to the woman behind the counter, "Can I get another espresso and a cappuccino?"

The woman nodded. "I'll bring them over."

"Now then," began Simon. "I'm disappointed that the research you're doing has hit a wall already."

"No, not hit a wall. Why didn't you mention yesterday, that you had written a paper on the same things I was researching? You could have saved me some time."

Simon looked at her and hesitated before he answered. "I didn't think it could help."

"There were some things I just couldn't get past and then I began to read a paper that you wrote, or some of it anyway, about judges being appointed in the late 1600s in place of the Witchfinder General?"

Martha brought over the coffees and Simon gave her money. "Keep the pennies Martha, and put them in the charity box."

Martha smiled and nodded as she walked back to serve others.

"Sorry, you were saying?" said Simon.

"You wrote a paper and I was hoping that you would have access or copies of some of the trials of the time."

"The whole thing proved inconclusive. That's why I stopped," insisted Simon.

"From what I've found so far, Rhiannon was tried and convicted, but not in the usual way."

"It's a dead-end, she's just a story," said Simon. He stopped smiling. "The first and last woman to be executed that way in Wales? I couldn't find anything that even mentioned her name. Yes, I found that a judge did affiliate some cases in Wales, but it never said anything about a witch burning. What I found out was that most of these women were either sent to jail or they were shipped off somewhere. Out of sight, out of mind, so to speak. The hangings, stoning or even any burnings were over. Britain didn't want to be associated with the hysteria that was gripping Europe and America." He couldn't let her know his real interest in her project. She was more likely to trust him if she thought he was helping her.

"I need to read those notes because it feels like you have a piece of a story and I have another piece of a story that will then lead to a whole other piece of the story that's out there. And I can only find out if I join the other two pieces together."

"There isn't anything in them that you can't read in any other witch trial."

"But it's not any other witch trial, it could be hers. You act like you want to help me one minute and then you don't the next."

Simon sat back in his seat and looked at Mari. How to convince her to bring him along while pretending he wasn't doing this for anyone else but him? "It's not that I don't want to help." He bit his lip and looked away for a few seconds, hesitant, before he looked back at her and said, "What's in it for me?" Then he noticed two young, attractive, female students walking past them in very revealing shorts and cropped tops. .

"Hi Simon," said the blonde.

"See you later," said the other brunette.

"Yes, hi ladies. Don't be late for class." He looked back and saw Mari roll her eyes. "What!" exclaimed Simon with a grin. "I can't help it if—"

"You know what? I don't care. It's not important," Mari said, shaking her head slightly and rolling her eyes again, "What did you mean exactly? Before, what did you mean?"

"Well..." he started. "I came to an abrupt... end, so to speak, and I never did finish one part of the story that I needed." He sat up and signaled for her to come in closer, "You help me and I'll help you."

"And just how can I help you? You have more information than I have. I've just started."

"Yes, and in that short time you've managed to get hold of Joseph Johnson's journals, whereas I didn't even know they existed. Look, whatever you think of me, I have a paper that is not even finished and that bothers me. Yeah, sure, it still got top marks and it got me a commendation and all that, but the work wasn't complete. We both have different stories to write, but need the same research to do it. I can get hold of a lot of unofficial papers that you will need, and I'm pretty sure with your research skills, you can get other things or work shit out that we both need. But together, we can both get what we want in the end."

"You want us to team up and write a paper together?" said Mari.

"Why do you look so shocked? It's not like we're going to be writing the same exact paper."

"No, but—"

"You're researching a theory about a woman who may or may not have existed and if she existed, she may have been the last woman to be burnt at the stake, and who just happens to be Welsh. I'm sure whatever you find will make an excellent paper. But I need to find an end to my paper and I don't know where to go with it. It could be that in your research, I find what I'm looking for and if I don't, then no harm's been done."

"What would help to finish your paper?" asked Mari.

"Well, I don't know. Something unusual that happened back then. It has to be something that would bring my paper to the forefront and catch the attention of whoever reads it. You know that I've been rejected by those science magazines and I know you think it's hilarious, but it's always been an ambition of mine to have one of my discoveries published. It puts you in a different league with all those other people that we were brought up to admire and what brought us into this subject. To be honest, I don't want to spend my life in this university. So, I need to have a real attention grabber. And I know we'll find one together."

Mari stopped and listened and then gave a small smile as she said, "How about a book that belonged to Rhiannon?"

"What kind of book?" asked Simon.

"I'm not sure, but what if there was proof that Rhiannon owned a grimoire?"

"Well if such a thing existed, then yes, that would be a real find. But there's no proof that there was ever one."

"I think there is."

"How would you know? I mean, there's no real proof on Rhiannon yet." asked Simon.

"Because Joseph Johnson wrote about it," said Mari quickly.

"What? When?"

"It's in his journal. He wrote that he didn't know who or what Rhiannon was, but that the potions written in her book had cured sicknesses in the village. He couldn't believe that she was a witch. I think he refused to believe it, to be honest, because he felt guilty he didn't do anything more to help her."

Simon jumped up excitedly. "That's what I'm looking for! So, I'll help you with anything you need to the ins and outs of a woman called Rhiannon. We'll find out her life, her habits, where she lived, even what she had in her house, just about anything you want to know about her. You'll help me find that artefact?"

Mari sipped her coffee and looked at him, unsure. "Deal," she finally spurted out. "Deal."

CHAPTER TWENTY-SIX

Although her deal with Simon was unexpected, Mari was anxious to get her hands on some of the books and manuscripts that he had and she was happy when he brought over a bag of books the next day. His notebooks were always very complete—dates, names, addresses. Just how he was able to get all of this? she wondered. He had books and books about some of the women, trial notes and documentation given afterwards from the people who were coerced into accusing Gwen ferch Ellis and her sisters of witchcraft. But she'd read all she could about them already.

"There's nothing about any other trials here, where did he find the information, he needed to write all of this?" a frustrated Mari asked herself. She picked up her mobile and punched in his number. "Simon. Where are the trial notes?"

"In the museum," he replied.

"Which museum?"

"The British Museum, where I believe, you used to work?"

"You're kidding, right?" she said with an eye roll.

"No. Do you have any old contacts there?"

Mari paused for a moment. "I didn't leave on good terms with a lot of people there."

"Why doesn't that surprise me?" said Simon quickly.

"Yeah, whatever." Mari dismissed his comment quickly. "So, you have nothing here that can help me, but I've given you all the journals."

"I've given you enough to help you get further than you were yesterday. There's a lot of backstory that is included in those notes that you've probably not even thought of looking through. If you think that you can build a story simply by reading transcripts of a trial online, then go ahead. You don't need to use any of them, or you can let me make a few calls."

****

At 9:30 a.m. Mari found herself with Simon on a train to London. She hadn't asked him to take the whole thing over, but he seemed very insistent that they travel up as soon as possible, to get the trial notes she was after. She walked up the familiar stairs and inside the museum, hoping that she wouldn't see anyone she knew.

"This way," said Simon ushering her through a side door on the ground floor.

"Where are we going? I've never been down in this section before."

"It's an archive room. There are some things that the museum never puts on display, like old records and books dating back centuries. And there are some things here that they don't want to put on display, or even be seen to have. They have a record of virtually every witch trial ever held in this country and a selection of ones from farther away, like the colonies, et cetera. The trial papers you're after are here."

"How d'you know any of this?"

"Because I've seen them," said Simon quickly. "But at the time, they were of no interest to me and what I was after." Just before he opened the door, he stopped and faced her. "Now look, the guy in here is a bit of a creep, but he's harmless. But what am I saying… you used to work here, right? You probably know him."

He's a bit of a creep? Mari had to turn her head slightly to stifle a laugh. Just who did he think he was to some of the women at the uni? "I doubt anyone even knew I existed when I worked here." Mari pouted. "So, let's just find what we need and get out."

The room was huge. It must have covered the entire space from the floor above them. Modern and air conditioned, each section contained five shelves full of books. Some had parchments that had been placed in clear pockets and then filed in alphabetical order and genre order in other books. The books ranged from political references to conspiracies, from ancient documentations listing secret organizations to the infamous witch trials—some never to be made known to the public. All catalogued and added to a complicated system on the main museum database, but kept in case they were needed. Mari sat down in front of one of the computers and punched in dates and the name of the village and then a serial number appeared.

"That's the section you need to find the records," a voice said from behind her. "The numbers tell you what area, what shelf and if my filing is up to date, what order they are on the shelf."

The archive assistant leaned in close over her shoulder. He was a short, dishevelled looking man in his 40s, with receding hair and small framed glasses. His smile made her uneasy and the warning from Simon became crystal clear. She could feel his bad breath on the back of her neck.

"Thank you, I'm sure we'll be OK finding everything we need," said Mari hoping to put him off. But as she rose from her seat and began to move away, he took a step-in front of her and blocked her. He obviously knew nothing about personal space. His gaze went quickly from her face to her chest and then back up to her face and he smiled nervously as she brushed past him and walked toward the section she needed.

Black books with gold and silver embossed lettering lined the shelves. At least fifty in a row and the books were at least five inches thick. She moved along the shelf to find the dates—anywhere between 1650 and 1700 would probably suffice. Mari held her breath when she came across those very dates. The book was larger than the others that measured ten inches by nine inches. This one measured eighteen inches by eleven inches and was even thicker than the others. She looked around and spotted a four-wheeled trolley nearby and brought it over. Carefully, she slid the book to the edge in the hopes of it taking the weight as she carefully edged it out. But it only caused the book to drop and land on the trolley with a massive thud that vibrated the trolley and sent its echo out into the quiet room.

"What was that!" shouted the archive assistant. "What have you done?"

"Nothing!" Mari shouted back. "I just knocked the trolley over," she lied.

She wheeled the book over to the desk, carefully slid it across and sat down. Excitedly, she opened it and began to look for the dates. The writing was illegible at times. Mostly it spoke about animal rustlers, bad debtors and farms being confiscated.

And then it began, the trial of a woman accused of heresy and the craft.

11 November 1684

'On this day was brought before Judge George Harris, the Chief Judge sent to us on behalf of the Witchfinder General, a woman accused of making potions to cure the sick. It was said that Mistress Rhiannon Turner did murder by means of witchcraft four good men from this village—Dafydd Hughes, Mathias Eliot, Lyr Edmond and Ieuen Jones—and then did make potions to relieve ailments as one given to Master Owain Barratt, a ten-year-old boy of good family who was deathly and who, after being given a potion, soon began to speak and eat. His mother, Goody Barratt, has stood witness in the defence of Mistress Turner but the evidence in prosecution given by Goody Harding and Goody Jones cannot be ignored.'

"At last," said Mari. She took out her notebook and began to write as Simon pulled up a chair and sat next to her.

"This is what you were looking for right?" he asked, looking over at the notebook.

"Yes, it is." She took a breath and then said, "I'm sorry."

"For what?"

"I didn't trust you. I thought you were just after those journals and you'd ditch me sooner or later."

"I told you. We both have an interest in this story. If we both see it to the end, we'll get enough information to finish off our own work. It made sense, that was all."

"I know you're desperate to finish it... you must be if you're helping me. I guess I just don't work well with—"

"Look, let's just get on with this" Simon interrupted. "We're going to hit enough brick walls without falling out. Whatever you think of me is irrelevant compared with what we're about to uncover. If our theories are right, we could even rewrite some history."

Mari smiled and nodded. "Maybe not rewrite it too much, but we do get to know something that wasn't known before." She stopped for a moment. "Does that even make sense?"

Simon laughed. "I get what you mean. So you have the transcripts?"

"Yes, I have the start of it. I don't know how long it's going to take to read it all though. I don't think I'm going to finish it today."

"I can help with that." Simon picked up his briefcase and opened it. Reaching inside he brought out a cordless handheld scanner.

"What's that?" asked Mari.

"A digital scanner. We just scan this over each page and it saves it all to a memory card inside, then when we get back we can download the whole lot onto a computer."

Mari hated what was going through her head. She wanted to dislike him so much, but each time she wanted him to fail, he'd come up with something to help them both that she hadn't thought of. And the annoying thing was, she couldn't quite understand why she hated him to start with.

"I know," said Simon. "You're amazed at my genius, right?"

Sitting aghast to his comments, all Mari could do was nod.

"Well don't think me too brilliant. I always carry one of these in my case. The amount of times I had to leave things when I was just getting started was just annoying and time wasting. So I was told about these little tools and I bought one. I'll tell you one thing. This ingenious gadget has saved me so much time." Simon looked around. The archive assistant was nowhere near so began to scan the page. "Just turn the pages you want scanned. It's not allowed so we'll have to be quick."

"You're breaking rules?" asked Mari.

"Do you think I'm the kind of man who sticks to them? How else would I have got any work finished? There's no way they would allow the university to borrow any of these books and even if they did, I'd have a hard time convincing the university of paying for the costs involved. And you'll never finish reading and taking notes today so this is the best way."

"You've done this before?"

"Of course, I have. I said, lots of times. Keep turning the pages."

****

Back on the train they'd managed to find seats with a table. Mari sat opposite Simon as he stared out of the window. Five minutes into their journey and without even looking her way, he asked, "Why are you staring at me?"

"Because you keep surprising me," replied Mari.

He turned to look at her and leaned over the table. "Your trouble is that you don't trust anyone." He reached into his case and pulled out a memory stick. "Here, take this."

"Why are you giving me this?"

"Because it's your research. Whatever you find just run it past me too in case it's something that I can use."

"I don't get you sometimes."

"That's because you think I have an ulterior motive for helping you." He sat back in his seat, held up his hands and began to ramble off a number of cliché quotes, "My hands are clean. I've told you why I'll help you. We'll both get something out of this. Two heads are better than one"—he rolled his eyes—"yadda yadda

yadda..." His voice trailed off. He didn't sound as if he was interested in talking anymore.

Mari wasn't letting it go. "It's because when you were at the university years back you did nothing but steal work from others."

"Is that what you heard?"

"Yes."

Simon carried on looking out of the window. "You heard wrong."

"Then tell me something different. Tell me your side."

Simon looked at her again. His expression had changed, and he seemed hurt about her comment. He leaned across the table and said, "I was a good student. I was thorough and I was like you, I could get information that no one else seemed able to do." He smiled and pointed at her. "Yep, just as good as you are. I found a different edge and proved my theories each time. But I wasn't perfect either. I had... distractions. But whatever I submitted in those exams was mine. I had a room-mate and he wasn't always into all that studying, most of the time we both partied forgetting we were supposed to study too. He would read over my notes when he thought I didn't know and make up his own based on my notes. So one afternoon he came back to the dorm unexpected and caught me in a... what can I say... embarrassing position with a female from the faculty... a married female. And he blackmailed me – and her. I helped him with his course work because he was a lazy fucker and was going to fail and his rather wealthy and influential parents would most definitely cut him off financially if he did. He plagiarised MY own work for his and I took the flack. Thing is, even with his excellent work – and it was excellent because it was mine, I still got higher grades than he did. These days he's happy though. He got some high flying job somewhere in the world that his father bought for him and I don't have to hear from him again."

"But your work was excellent. I mean, I think most students read your work the same as they would some scholar with a higher IQ than Einstein!"

"Yeah thanks for that." He smiled but his face showed regret. "You want to know why I didn't go off into that big bad world and do something else now right?"

"Pretty much, yes."

"Because of all the papers I write and the awards that I get, I have one that isn't finished, you were right when we first spoke, it does bother me and I can't leave it to go do something new. Because even though I do leave the university to go on digs or to authenticate newly found artefacts, the real work, the work that I have been pursuing most of my life can only be done here." He sat back again, raising an eyebrow and said, "And being part of the faculty in a prestigious university like ours can come with a lot of perks. Take today, for example. There's no way we could have called up the British Museum and got permission to read some of their priceless works as quickly if I didn't name drop and also be able to read them all without any supervision."

"Yeah that's true," said Mari. "You know what? I can't wait to read what we scanned!" she said excitedly. "Did you say you'd read it too?"

"No. I said I knew where they were."

"Well I can't wait. Soon as we get back, I'm downloading what we have and making notes."

Margarita Felices

CHAPTER TWENTY-SEVEN

As soon as Simon dropped her off later that night, she began to download each page from the trial books onto her laptop and then she backed each one of them up so she wouldn't lose them. She quickly made a few sandwiches and a mug of tea, placed them next to her desk and began to read from where she left off in London.

11 November 1684
'The accused, Rhiannon Turner, has brought forth her case. That the accusations made by Goody Harding and Goody Jones be false. It was revealed that Rhiannon Turner did fornicate with the husband of Goody Harding and that Mistress Turner is with child and she claims that she only stands accused because of a jealous wife. I have asked the accused of her involvement with the craft, of devil worship, which she has denied. I await the testimony of Goody Barratt and the evidence brought by the Court Prosecutor John Maddox-Hughes that Goody Turner did make a potion to give to the child. Goody Barratt did take the oath to God that she will tell all truths in these proceedings. Maddox-Hughes did ask Goody Barratt if her son Owain was well and she replied that he was. He did ask her about the potion that Mistress Turner did give her. But Goody Barratt will not testify against Mistress Turner. Instead, she made her feelings known in the court that if it were not for the potion, her son would be dead. Maddox-Hughes addressed the court revealing that the village physician had all but called the imminent

death of the child. How did this herbal potion bring the boy back from near death if not be filled with the craft?

Maddox-Hughes has dismissed this witness.

The court was shown what appeared to be ungodly objects taken from the gardens of Mistress Turner. When asked, she told the court that they were not of pagan value and used only to pray to her gods. At this stage, the court was interrupted by Goody Derwena Jones, widow to a man believed to be struck down by a mystery illness to which Mistress Turner stands accused of causing.'

"Oh, not good," said Mari, "They wouldn't have liked those new-worldly type items." She took a bite of her sandwich and swallowed it quickly, had a sip of tea and continued reading.

12 November 1684

'The court has resumed with testimony to the events. Accused Mistress Rhiannon Turner has been brought back into the courthouse. Today, we will hear from the wives and family of the deceased men whose lives were taken and that Mistress Turner stands accused of murdering. It is witnessed that Mistress Turner was known to all of the deceased.

Goody Mary Hughes is the widow of Dafydd Hughes, a local man who had been in good health. Mistress Turner is accused of having a hand in his death by means of witchcraft. Those accusations are to be proven in this court.

Maddox-Hughes has waited to allow Goody Hughes to speak. The woman of frail disposition appears timid and is in fear, unwilling to speak against Mistress Turner.

"He was a good man," Goody Hughes has told us. "He liked to drink but he was a good provider."

On the night in question, Mr. Hughes had come home for his evening meal. Goody Hughes had served his favourite broth and his ale and then she went to bed. His son, Stefan, found him later that night. His corpse-like features. His sunken black eyes looking upwards toward the heavens. Mistress Turner has expressed her innocence and claims she was nowhere near their farmhouse.'

13 November 1684

'As the court reassembles and the accused placed in the witness box, Maddox-Hughes asked Mistress Turner to explain the sudden deaths in the village since she arrived. She could not, but suggested that perhaps they were poisoned by their wives' bad cooking or perhaps they had taken their own lives through unhappiness?

The laughter from the court was silenced after the outburst by Mistress Turner.

With the evidence and accusations taken it was time for Mistress Turner to plead for her innocence. She beseeched the court to listen to the evidence brought against her and see it for what it is. It was nothing more than scaremongering from a jealous wife who was barren and hated her for carrying her husband's child. The accusations made against her are futile and without real true cause. She has not met any of the dead men other than in passing and has not used any sort of craft towards any of the good people of the village. Her potions are made from the local plants grown around them all and used to only help those who would seek comfort from them. She is a woman with child and her treatment and condition should be taken into account. To await our verdict we have committed Mistress Turner to the local jail until she is called.

This evening it has come to the court's attention that Mistress Turner has used her craft to escape from her captors and has absconded to the mountains. Eight men from the village have sworn to bring back the witch. For a witch she must be, to have escaped from a locked prison. She will be sentenced for her crimes this very night and her sentence will now be severe.

The witch has been brought back. Although all that she pleads is for the life of her child who has been born and left near the mountains, she will be tied to the stake and flames will cast her evil soul into hell. She has decided her own fate by showing us how witchcraft can be used. For how else and why, would she run from this village if she truly were innocent? And now the law will take its revenge to the fullest.
On this night, 14 November 1684, Rhiannon Turner is sentenced as a witch, a heretic and a murderer and will be burnt at the stake for her crimes against God and man. With my work here done, I will leave these records to bear witness of the legal proceedings of the courts of this land. ~ Chief Judge George Harris.'

Mari stared into the distance, "That wasn't a very fair trial," she said aloud. Yawning, she looked at her clock and saw that it was 3.30am already and she hadn't got any sleep. "Oh crap," she said, yawning again, "I better get to bed."
The few hours that Mari had left to get some sleep proved difficult. Her mind wandered to the trial and subsequent verdict. She wondered how Rhiannon had

escaped. Where did they find her? And what happened to her baby?

Mari opened her eyes unable to sleep with all the unanswered questions she had. She had only read half a story and there was so much more to read now that the journals made more sense. Joseph Johnson had written a little about Rhiannon before the trial and a little after it. Had he written anything else that could be combined with these trial notes? Was there yet more to be discovered?

CHAPTER TWENTY-EIGHT

Mari's lack of sleep and anxiety kicked in as she rang Simon. "Hello Simon. Look, I need to read one of the journals I gave you. I need it straight away."

"I haven't finished with them yet."

"You can still have them, there's just one I need to read. I need to confirm something that I read from the scanned copies. Can I come over and get it?"

"What, now?" asked Simon sounding surprised.

"Yes. It's almost 8:00 a.m." Mari looked at her watch. "Shouldn't you be on your way to classes by now?"

"I know what time it is and no, I'm not due in any classes this morning, hence the reason for having a lie in."

Mari grimaced. "Oops, sorry. Look, I wouldn't normally, but it's important. I can come over to your place now."

"Yeah, fine," Simon finally agreed. "You know the place."

****

Fifteen minutes later, Mari arrived at his apartment. Another clause in his contract was that he would be allowed to live in one of the plushest rooms on the whole university complex. Mari knocked the door and Simon answered wearing only a towel. His hair was wet and messy as though he'd try to dry it quickly. She tried not to stare at... well, just about any part of his body.

"Sorry, you should have said you were taking a shower," said Mari stepping in through the door. She didn't want to turn around and look at him. She didn't need him to see how surprisingly aroused she was.

"The journals are over there," he said pointing at a table. "Why do you need them so urgently?"

"There's something I needed to read, the parts where... somehow she managed to escape. They imprisoned her before they had decided her sentence and she escaped. That's why they found her guilty. I wonder if she'd stayed whether they would have done that. Anyway, Johnson's journals might have more on that."

"Do you want to look now?"

Mari looked at the near naked Simon. If he could only read her mind right now, "No, do you mind if I take it with me... so I can compare some of the scanned pages to this and see how it matches?"

"No, that's fine. I'll give you a call later and see what you've found out. I might have news of my own."

Mari nodded, sorted through the journals, picked the one she needed and packed it in her bag. "Right then, speak later, OK?" And she quickly walked past his near naked body and out the door.

****

Back in her room, Mari turned each page over carefully. The flooding at the chapel may not have submerged the journals under water, but the damp and black mold had penetrated some of the pages. She squinted to try and make out some of the text and shined her phone torch onto the pages to try to make out the faded writing.

17th November 1684
'A strange occurrence has happened since I began to write today. As I sat in the vestry, I was summoned into the chapel where Sion Evans, Emyr Roberts, Alwyn Creu and James Clwyd had entered and they gave me an unexpected request. They held out a brown cloth bag and said that it had the ash and bones of Rhiannon Turner. They wanted me to keep them here until a ritual could be performed that would bind her soul inside a Buckley jar. They intend to have me recite a Latin prayer in three days.'

"Strange occurrences?" muttered Mari. "These people would see rain falling the wrong way and say it was strange." Mari picked up her tablet and began to type. 'Buckley jars.' On the screen an array of different pots and crockery from over the ages were displayed. She read out loud, "Mass produced crockery and enamel dishes." She sounded disappointed. "Well I suppose they were poor farmers and these were cheap at the time." She read on, 'especially adapted lids to keep produce dry.' "Why would you bury someone in a jar like this?"

She went back to reading the journal.

'A book has been brought to me today. The superstitious villagers have burnt Rhiannon Turner's cottage down to the ground, but within it they have found a wooden chest. Inside and carefully protected, was a brown leather book that contained her potions with strange incantations that I do not understand. It has shamed me to believe that she may have been a witch as they say. The only good that has come from it is that Mr Harding is now free from any harm. I have decided that this book will be buried with her, hidden from all and hope that the good Lord watches over it. If it truly is a book of the craft, I wish no other to unwisely look upon it. I cannot say what the outcome would be if they do. And in opening the book, it may be the lack of good food or water that has made me believe it, but I have seen something in those pages. I swear on my own precious good book, that I have seen the souls that it has possessed. I wish for no other human to see the darkness I have just witnessed.'

Mari's eyes widened and she bit her lip in a half smile. The realisation of something new entered her head. If all of this was true, then somewhere out there was a genuine grimoire. A witch's spell book of incantations, stories, beliefs, a treasure important enough to get Simon the very closure that he needed to finish his work and to get his paper published. And maybe even a further scholarship for both of them! This was not only a research story. This was now going to become an archaeological project too. Mari sat back, amazed. A grimoire? Were they on their way to truly discovering an actual grimoire? Or was it just a book full of harmless herbal potions, like the ones Rhiannon had been giving the people of the village? At least Simon would be pleased.

18th November 1684
'Today, I performed a ceremony that I deemed unholy even if it was brought to us from the Catholic Holy Father himself. The Chief Judge has left us a prayer sent to him from the Pope in Rome. The bones and the ash of the witch lay in the bowels of our chapel. They will be placed in a Buckley jar brought to us from Ewloe and blessed by me here in this holy place. An iron band will be made by the blacksmith and will be bonded around the mouth of the jar to imprison her tortured soul

and it will be coated with tar to seal it tightly. It will then be taken, along with her potions book, and hidden high in a remote part of the mountains that surround this village and where her curse on this village, I pray, will end. I beg to the good Lord to keep our secret safe, for if she were to return, I am sure that hell and fury would also follow with her.'

Mari sat back in the chair. There were a few things that didn't sound right. They were so afraid of this woman that not only did they burn her body, but pretty much everything that she owned and held close was taken away. And then she wasn't even given a proper burial. Her bones were collected, put in a jar and buried somewhere high in the mountain. Mari was so engrossed in what she'd discovered, she hardly heard the knock on her door until it hammered an almighty bang and she jolted in shock.

At the door was Simon. "Well, did it help? Did you find anything else out?"

"Sit," she said smiling. "You're not going to believe what I've put together. It's bits from the scanned copies and the journals."

"You already told me that she escaped," said Simon as he sat in an armchair. "If that's what you're going to say."

"That's an important point, but it's not that." She sat at her desk and looked at her notes. "After she was burnt, lots of weird things started to happen in the village. The villagers were so frightened that they asked for something really bizarre from the Witch Finder and they were sent it. There was a prayer that the pastor had to perform and then they could lock her bones in some jar and bury it high in the mountains."

"That's ironic," said Simon, "seeing as they tried her as a witch and then they recited some prayer. It could have even been a genuine spell but they called it a 'prayer' to justify themselves. Peasants!" He seemed angry.

"I guess they were frightened enough to ignore that and a prayer from a religious source counteracted any they saw as demonic, so in their eyes it wasn't a spell but a prayer. They did the prayer and things began to change in the village. But they were still so frightened of what they thought she was that they buried her and some of her things up in the mountains somewhere."

Simon seemed engrossed in her every word. "Her things? What kind of things?"

"Well this is the best bit," said Mari with an excited smile. "They reckon that they found some sort of book in her cottage before they burnt that down too. I believe the possibilities could even be that she really was a witch and that it was most likely her grimoire, but they obviously didn't know what that was. Although, then again, she could have just been an ordinary woman and it could have just simply been a book with all the potion recipes she made in it... but you know what they were like back then. Anyway, they buried that with her too."

"Did they give a location for her grave?" asked Simon. He looked excited this time and pleased at how much she'd found out.

"No." She pouted. "Of course, they're going to leave that part out. The point was for her never to be found so they were unlikely to make a map, right? But I was thinking about it. It was winter and it would have been really cold and they wouldn't have wanted to trek out too far. This is a village that would have got cut off from the rest of the country so they wouldn't have gone too far up that mountain. The village back then was something like two miles away from the start of the mountains and that was only to the path that lead around it. Farther, if they were climbing up it. They would have had to have passed over farmland so if we start at the point, that was the edge of the village back then—"

"Then we can maybe retrace some of their steps?" interrupted Simon enthusiastically.

"Exactly!"

"Do you think you could narrow it down to where we start?"

Mari shrugged. "Well, that's something we have to find out. But it wasn't a massive place at that time. There had to have been a path going over to the mountains at some point and I doubt very much they were going to go take some impassable route in that weather and make it all the more difficult. The original trails are mostly gone these days. Hikers might still use some of the older ones so we could find a hiking route. There's bound to be some information around. I guess it'll be trial and error for a little bit."

Simon smiled and leapt out of the chair. "I knew you would do it!" He grabbed her hand and pulled her up to him. He picked her up and swung her around holding her close. "I knew you would do it."

****

It surprised Mari when later in the day Simon called over to her bedsit. If he'd just given her some warning, she could have at least tidied up and not had her wet underwear spread about the place. And she would have made herself a little more presentable.

"I have something to show you," he said excitedly. He walked straight past her and into her living room as soon as she opened the door, not waiting for an invitation to enter. He rolled out a map on the table and placed condiment pots on each corner to keep it from rolling closed again. "This is a map of the village as it appeared in the late 1500s."

"Where did you get it?" asked Mari looking down at it.

He eye rolled. "In our very own archives at the university. I was sitting in my office just wondering how we would find an accurate version and I just typed it all in and it gave me a number and well... here it is. It shows boundaries, forests, orchards, even where certain farms were. And it shows a clear pathway to a road alongside the mountain the carriages used to travel on."

"But it doesn't show any paths up the mountains," said Mari, staring at the map.

"Yes, it does." Simon pointed at a section of the mountain. "Back then, there was a pass over the mountain. Heulwen's Pass was used very regularly before the road around it was made. I bet they used the same pathway up the mountain."

"It looks like a steep climb."

"We also have a lot of climbing kit here at the university." Simon raised an eyebrow. "We could quite easily make our way up and have a quick look, see what we find."

Mari smiled and nodded. She was just as anxious as he seemed to be, to get there. "We could get everything together and maybe go tomorrow? You know, as its Saturday and we have no classes."

"Let me sort the kit out today. I'll text you later and let you know whether we're going tomorrow or not."

****

Heulwen's Pass was named after a tragic young woman from the mid-1200s who was lost in the mountains and whose ghost was supposedly seen by travellers that had wandered off the trail and found themselves lost. It was a pathway rarely used anymore after the road was etched out around the mountains to let carriages and carts pass to the other side. Later, in the 1700s, another path was laid farther along and this path was partially lost and not used by anyone other than sheep and farmers or accidentally by walkers wanting a leisurely walk before tackling the mountain.

Simon drove Mari to the edge of a field, the nearest place to the old pathway. It was thankfully a nice clear day, but as every hiker knows, the weather up a mountain, especially one like Snowdon, changed very quickly. Both stepped out of the car dressed in walking boots, light trousers, T-shirts and waterproof jackets. Mari tied hers around her waist. Simon opened the boot and took out two trekking poles, handing one to Mari. "Ready?" he asked.

Mari nodded. "Yes."

But Mari wasn't really prepared for a long hike. An hour or two, three at the most and they would already be back and sitting in the car, planning their next climb. She hoped that the gear he'd packed didn't mean that he was prepared to walk all the way up today.

It hadn't rained for a few weeks so the field that they walked across was firm, but the grass and weeds at times came waist high as they walked through it and to the base of the mountain. Mari looked up. "Hope it's not all the way up."

"Somehow I don't think they would have walked so far up. It was November, the snow had come down already and it must have been bitterly cold. They must have found some cave to hide it in. We'll have to keep a look out for anything in the rocks, a marking or even what looks like a hole that could be an opening to a cave. It could be anywhere and hidden over time."

Up they climbed. The path he'd chosen didn't even look like a path at times. The ground was full of loose stones, grit and dirt. On both sides of the path star moss grew in clumps surrounded by purple foxgloves and small white Snowdon lilies. In some areas there were so many of them that it resembled snow and Mari wondered if this is what Rhiannon would have seen too.

Mari used the pole to help her climb but at times she needed to grip one of the huge boulders just to keep her steady. She didn't want Simon to see that she couldn't cope with the climb in case he decided to leave her and go on his own. Her insoles began to ache as she forced her legs to take the steps of an experienced climber who took at least two steps to her one. She could feel the muscle threads in her calves cry out after each step.

Simon seemed proficient in everything he did. Mari tried to stay close behind him taking as many steps as he did, only he never faltered and she had more than the odd slip. He seemed overly keen to get on this hike.

"Simon!" shouted Mari.

He looked down. "Do you want to stop?"

"No," said Mari, waving him on.

But Simon did stop and stretched his back. "Look just a little farther. It looks like there's a bit of a rest stop a little farther up. Let's get to that and conserve energy. We might still have a climb to do."

Mari turned to look behind her. She hadn't realised that they'd climbed so far up already. "Oh my God," she said trying to focus. Her body rocked a little, unsteady in the altitude. "I hadn't realised…"

"Don't look down!" insisted Simon, "it'll make you light-headed."

"Bit late," said Mari shaking it off. "Let's carry on to the spot you mentioned and rest up."

****

Almost another hour later and Mari just couldn't take another step. They'd already ventured high up into the mountain, farther than she thought they'd go on their first day. "Stop!" she finally shouted up at Simon. "For God's sake, I have to stop. We've been climbing for ages." The large flat rock to her right looked so inviting, covered with overgrown foliage and fauna. She sat down to catch her breath. Kicking away some of the overgrowth, she didn't notice a small mark chiselled into the rock, an upside down triad with a line going through the centre of it, until she was about to sit on it

"Wait, what's that?" Simon pointed at the rock and licked his fingers. He knelt down beside her and began to rub around it.

"What is it?" she asked leaping from the seat to look.

"It's a marc gwrach," he said, smiling.

"What's that?"

"It's a mark that locals would put to warn anyone close by that there was a hex here. We must be very close to something and we don't even know it. Keep an eye out for anything unusual around here. It may be a little farther up, but we're close now."

Mari looked up and then around. "There's not much left we can climb. The rest of it looks like mountaineering not walking."

Simon nodded. "Yeah, you're right. I didn't bring enough carabiners and harnesses for that sort of climb."

He sat next to her and took a deep breath and then nudged her elbow with his, "I don't suppose you do any rock climbing, right?"

"Do I look as if I do?" asked Mari smirking.

Simon smiled and shook his head slowly. "You know, I imagined that we would come up here and immediately find a cave that's been hidden and…well it's an archaeologists dream, right? To find some hidden treasure and show it off to the rest of the world."

"Is that what we're looking for? Treasure?"

"Isn't that really why we're here? I guess, not in the precious jewels sense of the word, but maybe something equally valuable." Simon sighed. "But we've either passed it without realising it, or there was nothing here to start with or we've…"

Mari screamed. "Oh my God what the fuck are those?" and watched as two small rodent like creatures scurried into some bushes.

Simon rose to his feet quickly and kicked away at the greenery and just there, was an opening in the ground, buried over from years of debris and plants. It was the entrance to a cavern shaft with just enough of a gap to let in small animals.

"What is it!" shouted Mari.

"I don't know. Give me your torch."

Simon pointed the light down into the cavern. "I can't see much." He kicked away at the ground and it opened up more. "I'm going down there."

"Are you nuts?" asked Mari pulling him back. "You have no idea what's down there or how far you'd fall."

"We're up a mountain in Wales. What could possibly be down there?"

"OK, well you don't know how far down it goes then. We should come back later with someone. Maybe even mountain rescue or some trekkies or someone."

"And what if it's just a cave with nothing? Do you want to explain why we got the entire mountain rescue team up here? Or—" he winked, "what if it's the cave we've been looking for and you've just given away its location for others to explore instead of us?"

Mari pouted. "Guess not. But I can't hold your weight if you go down there."

Simon looked around and then opened his rucksack. He took out a climbing hook and attached it to his rope and secured it around the boulder with a Belay device so that he could control the speed of his descent. Then he dropped the other end of the rope down the hole. "You won't have to and there's only one way to find out what's down there. I'll go first, and if it's nothing I'll come straight back up. If it's something, then you come down. So... are you game Mari? Because I am." He kicked away at more of the ground dirt and when the opening got big enough for his body to fit through, he began to descend.

Grit came away from the shaft walls as Simon descended. He blew away dust that landed on his mouth until there was no wall to abseil down from and the shaft opened up into a vast open dome-like chamber. He switched on his torch and aimed it at the ground. Just a little farther and he'd be at the bottom of it.

Landing with a bit of a thud he waited for the dust to settle before calling up. "Pull the rope up, tie it around yourself and then come down."

Mari looked down into the hole. "What's it like down there?"

"Dusty," said Simon patting himself down. "But the ground is soft in some parts, like sand. Get down here." He looked around as his eyes adjusted to the little light and switched on his torch to take a better look around. "Come down. I'll catch you toward the end so you don't fall." He shined the torch light around the floor area and highlighted old wooden torches discarded on the ground. "Seems whoever came down here last left torches. I'll light them while you make your way down." He picked up the first and brought out a lighter. Surprisingly the first torch lit straight away, and then he lit the second and wedged that between some rocks and moved on to a fourth and then a fifth until all were propped up to light up the cavern.

Mari pulled up the rope, tied it around her waist and took a breath before entering the hole backwards. Grit and dust fell below, some on Simon until he moved away from it, falling over on some of the rocky debris on the floor in the process. She didn't land with the thud that Simon had, but he made sure to catch her before her feet touched the ground. Holding each other they stared into each other's eyes until, "OK, let's take a look around," Simon said, pulling away.

Mari turned full circle taking in the vastness of the cavern. "It's dark. I can't see anything." She switched on her torch.

"Let your eyes adjust to the torches. No one's been down here in centuries, but something's happened down here."

"How can you tell?" asked Mari.

Simon picked up the rocks near their feet. "These have been chiselled away from the walls. You can see the marks from a blade."

"What were they looking for?"

"I don't know. Have your eyes adjusted yet?"

"Yes, a little," said Mari. She slowly shined her torch onto the walls and looked around the cavern. "It's bigger than I expected."

"This was definitely used for something. They would have had to have come the same way down, there's no other entrance. Well, none that I can see yet."

Mari took a few steps towards a cave wall and squinted at the patterns that she could see. "There are markings here. They feel like they've been scratched into the walls." She brought her torch closer to light the wall. "Are those crosses?" asked Mari.

Simon came closer, and felt along the scratched wall. "They look like Christian symbols, but how bizarre."

"Why bizarre?" asked Mari.

"Well, it's not what you'd expect to find, that's all."

"Were you hoping for caveman drawings?" Mari asked with a smile.

"Sarcasm is not becoming to you Mari." He said abruptly, "And yes, maybe."

"So," Mari began, "we have Christian symbols in a cavern that seemed to be hidden in a mountain. Maybe someone fell into it and got bored."

"No, they are not the usual symbols. There is writing under each one, but it's worn away. See if there are any others around."

Mari took a slow walk around the cavern, shining the torch onto the walls, "There's another one over here, and the markings are clearer."

Simon almost ran to her. He pressed his fingers over the markings. "Latin. Shine the torch right at it. I'll see if I can make any of it out." He brushed away at some of the dust to look at the symbols, "Something something ... ...holy... something something... blessed... this says protected... holy church... and buried? This isn't just some sort of graffiti, it's a prayer. See if you can spot it anywhere else while I try to read more," said Simon excitedly.

Mari tripped over a few rocks and had to climb over another pile to see another symbol etched into the rock. "This one has a different symbol, and it's not a cross."

Simon hurried toward, that one too. "It's a papal symbol... An early version. But how...? I don't get it. Why is this down here?"

"Maybe this was used as a church back then?" said Mari.

"Yes, and they all came in through the roof to attend Sunday service!" he said, returning her earlier piece of sarcasm.

"Hey! No need to get shitty sarcastic with me! You're not the only one who can read these symbols. For example, this word here, like the ones over there, does not say protected, it says 'protected from.' They are protecting themselves against... well I don't know what... but this isn't just an ordinary cavern, this is something else."

"Look at this." said Simon. He had already found another etching in the rocks on the other side of her and was studying it.

"What have you seen?" asked Mari, joining him.

"Protection from again..." Simon smiled. "Yes, fine," he said with a huff, "You were right. It's 'from' but a protection from what?"

Mari sat on the pile of rocks and looked around the full scale of the chamber. There certainly wasn't any other entrance, but a lot of debris. "Let's look at this logically."

Simon turned to face her.

"There's an awful lot of chiselled marks in this cave, rocks that you say had blade patterns on, so why is there so much of it here and why? It didn't get thrown down here from up there or we would have seen broken rocks up there too. And they would have fallen differently." She stood up and began to walk around. "It's almost as if they chipped away in here to build something. They didn't take it out, they left it. There are markings all around the walls that are carved so they would stay here permanently."

"What are getting at?" asked Simon.

"That they were hiding something in here. The symbols are meant to keep something in."

"How do you figure that out from just looking at these rocks?" And then Simon suddenly sprang to life, his quiet demeanour gone. "They were hiding something!" he finally said. "They took away part of the cave walls and rebuilt it."

"Except that these walls look like originals."

"They are dusty and covered in plant life. It could be hidden behind all sorts of other rock piles."

Mari was already on the case. She ran her hands and thumped parts, hoping to find some sort of hidden passage.

"What are you doing?" asked Simon.

"It always works," said Mari not stopping. "Haven't you ever seen it in films? People tap panels and find things, why should it be different with rocks?"

Simon shrugged. He began to do the same until they met each other on the other side. "Well there goes that theory," said Mari with a wry smile. "Any other suggestions?"

Simon sat on the rocks that Mari had previously sat on and looked around the cave. It was the pile of earth and mixed rocks and stones not far from him. "What if they just piled the stones back up against the wall?" he said, pointing. "What if they simply chipped away at the wall, made a hole, put whatever they were hiding into it and then filled it back up with dirt and then piled whatever was left up against it?"

"One way to find out," said Mari on her knees digging at it. "Are you going to help or just sit there?"

It took a good twenty minutes to move the mound, gravel, earth, rocks and then one bigger boulder-shaped rock that took all their strength to move just a little and, behind it all, a pile of smaller stones came away from a cavity in the wall as soon as the mound was gone. Simon was about to reach inside it when Mari stopped him. "Are you nuts? You don't know what's in there."

"Again, you're going to say that? You said that up there and now we're down here and nothing happened." He looked at her face. Her eyebrows were raised and her eyes pleaded for him to listen to her. "Fine," he said with another huff. Shining the torch inside, it seemed to go in deeper than he thought. "I can't see anything. I'm going to have to reach in."

"Oh God, I can't watch this," said Mari squirming, half watching, half hiding behind her hands.

Simon reached in, gave his body a jolt and screamed. Mari jumped and fell back onto her backside while giving out a half-hearted yell. "What? What is it?"

Simon took out his hand and waved it in the air, laughing, and in so doing almost fell over himself.

"Bastard!" shouted Mari. "That's not even funny."

"No, it's not funny, it's hilarious," said Simon laughing. "I mean, really, take a look around this cave, have you even seen anything alive yet? D'you really believe that anything could be living inside these walls?" He reached in again and feeling the hard sides of a wooden box, tapped on it. "There is something at the other end, though. I'm trying to grab at it."

The sounds of dragging echoed in the cavern. "What is it?" asked Mari.

Simon brought out his arm and started to break away more of the cavity. "Help me break through this, there's something hidden back there."

Mari helped him break away at the dirt and grit, and then Simon reached in again.

Out came an old square wooden box. Two metal locks wrapped themselves around the box. Simon looked down and around him. He picked up the large rock nearest his foot and bashed away at it until it gave way. Inside was a large object wrapped in an old piece of black linen. He carefully lifted it out of the box to unwrap it. It was a book. He opened the first page and saw the drawings and incantations and then closed it again. Simon smiled as he held the book in his hands and stood up. He stretched out his arms swinging the book around like you would a small child. "Do you know what this is?" he asked, excited. But before Mari could answer he said, "A grimoire! It's an actual fucking grimoire." He dropped to his knees hugging it, everything he'd been searching for, all these years, at last! He looked at Mari who'd joined him on the ground. And before he knew what he was doing, he kissed her.

Who knows how long they'd laid there on the soft dirt wrapped in each other's arms and covered only by their jackets. Simon started to get dressed, reaching for his jeans and boots. "We have to get out of here, before it gets too dark to go back down the mountain."

Mari pulled up the jacket that covered her and stretched, yawning. "Would that be a bad thing? To be stuck here until morning?"

"We'll freeze our arses off if we do." He put on his boots and looked up at the cavern entrance. At least the rope was still secure. He pulled on it and then grabbed his rucksack as Mari was getting dressed. She hadn't even noticed that he'd put the book they'd found earlier inside it and that he'd already started to climb up.

Mari looked up at Simon as he neared the top and clambered out of the cavern. Occasionally she would have to look away when dust and small stones rained down on her as she got dressed. "OK, hurry up. I don't want to stay down here too long either."

But Simon didn't answer. Instead, he pulled up the rope until she couldn't see the ends of it.

"Hey!" Mari shouted up. "What are you doing? What's the hold up?"

At last Simon peered down the hole. "You know," he started, "I was really hoping you'd see through this whole thing before now... and you were close. I thought you saw through me at the start."

"What? What are you on about?"

"Do you really think it was an accident we got together?"

"Simon, please stop playing about. Get me out."

"I never really wanted it to end like this. I really like you, but I've been looking for this book my whole life. And now, thanks to you, I have it. My grandmother was very thorough when she told me the stories about this book but there were parts missing that I couldn't work out." Simon looked down at Mari. "This book is everything. It's why I helped you. And I knew you'd lead me to it eventually. You don't even know how good you are at finding things, first day out too. I knew it years ago when I first met you and I was going to ask you then, but before I knew it, you were gone. Imagine my surprise when I knew you were back. By then, I'd done a lot more research of my own and the funny thing is, I didn't need any of it. I just needed you. But I didn't know how to convince you to help me, until—"

"But we just—" Mari screamed up.

"Yes, I know and that was fun."

"You used me?"

"Of course, I did, but you used me too. The museum? Getting you access to those trial books? You knew that I'd be able to do that for you. Now look... I'm sure you'll find a way out of there soon, you're a resourceful girl. Or maybe someone will even hear you screaming. But I need a big enough gap between you and me —a sort of head start —to do what I have to."

"Which is what?"

"Do you have any idea what this book is? I mean, it's a book with all sorts of magic, even an alchemist chant. Everything I'm going to need is in this book and how to prepare it is all here."

"Are you fucking nuts?"

"There." He sighed. "Now that's the sort of girl I'd really like to have known. You can be a bad girl when you want to be, Mari. Shame it wasn't earlier. I might not have been tempted to just... leave you to it."

Then there was silence.

****

"Simon!" Mari shouted up. "Simon, are you still there?" Mari looked around the cavern. The light above was fading and it was starting to get cold, she had to work fast. She saw her jacket still on the floor where they'd both laid picked it up and put it on. She looked around the cavern, there didn't seem to be anything that she could use to throw up, like a makeshift hook and with anything that resembled rope. She stepped on a pile of stones and stretched up to try and reach the edges of the shaft they abseiled down from, but it was still too high to reach and pull herself up.

She collected some rocks and piled them up on top of each other. The others already there made the pile higher and she hoped she'd be able to climb on them to get closer to the edge of the shaft and somehow pull herself up and then out. But it still wasn't high enough, so she continued to drag over as many as she could carry to build her platform.

It was only after removing some other stones piled up against another wall that the rest came tumbling down around her. She skipped out of the way just in time, but it still managed to trip her and make her fall to the ground.

When the dust settled, she noticed that behind the rubble was another carved away chamber.

Mari looked closer and saw that it contained a brown earthenware pot. She stared at it for the longest time before she got nearer and peered through the debris, clearing it away to bring it out. She carefully pulled the jar from its hiding place and held it in her hands, staring at it with complete amazement. She slowly took a step backwards and lost her footing sending her to the floor. The jar flew through the air and crash landed behind her. "Oh piss it!" she yelled out.

A high-pitched noise made her stop moving in fright. The contents from the pot that were scattered on the floor began to glow. White smoke filled the cavern, and all this while, Mari was still slumped on the floor with her mouth open as a ghostly form began to take shape. The smoke thinned out and a woman appeared in front of her. A ghostly apparition with pale skin, long black hair and wearing a long blue dress. Mari's heart pumped hard. What was it? She felt light-headed, in shock at the image that was forming in front of her. She opened her mouth to speak.

"What is this place?" the woman spoke first.

"It's a cave... well, a cavern."

The woman stood in front of Mari and looked down at her, her image solid no longer less transparent. "What year is this?" she asked quickly. "What year?"

Mari just stared, unable to speak until the woman extended her hand and helped Mari to her feet. Mari trembled. The woman's hands were icy cold. "W-Who are you? Where did you come from?"

"Who am I?" The woman inhaled and looked over to the broken pieces of the pot on the ground. She looked back at Mari and said, "You have freed me, and I am grateful. My name is Rhiannon—"

"Turner?" gasped Mari and then quickly covered her mouth with her hand.

"Yes, Turner. How did you know?" Rhiannon seemed surprised.

"But you're... I mean you're..."

Rhiannon looked around the cavern, quietly and said, "A witch?" She smiled broadly.

"I was going more for... dead." Mari shrugged. "But whatever."

"What year is this? What time are we?" Rhiannon asked again.

"It's twenty-nineteen," said Mari still staring at her.

Rhiannon faltered for a moment, taking a step back, and appeared shocked at the discovery. "Four hundred... f-four...?"

"Are you all right?" asked Mari. "Do you need to sit down?"

Rhiannon looked around, "There doesn't seem to be much to sit on."

Mari smiled, almost laughing "No, I guess not."

"Why are you down here alone?" asked Rhiannon.

"I didn't come here alone. But I was left here." Mari pouted. "A man I trusted led me here and then dumped me."

"Even over the ages, the treachery of man never changes. They are all the same," Rhiannon said sadly. She took a step forward and Mari took a step back in fright. "You needn't be frightened of me."

"Well, it's not everyday someone magically appears from nowhere in front of me. I'm allowed to be a little nervous," said Mari.

Rhiannon nodded. "Yes, I suppose it is uncommon."

"I've read about you. The journals described you as a witch…"

"Journals? I am written into journals? How quaint."

"Yes, well they are a little vague but what they call you, well…an evil witch—"

"Witch, yes," interrupted Rhiannon sharply. "Evil no. Well, I may have taken the souls of men to place at the altar of Mother Morrighan."

"So, you did kill them as it said in the trial notes?"

Rhiannon came closer. "I don't expect you to understand." She looked around again. "I have little strength, but I feel the need to leave this tomb."

Mari looked up. "Well unless you have a ladder or a rope, it's not happening. I was piling those rocks closer to the opening so I could try and climb up."

"Oh child," Rhiannon said smiling. "Did we not just agree as to what I was?" Rhiannon closed her eyes and grabbed Mari's arm. *"Rym goleuni, cwyd fi i'th gyfarch"* 'Powers of light, ascend me to greet you', and before Mari knew it, Rhiannon had lifted them both up and onto the ledge above, and to the mouth of the cavern. Rhiannon stumbled, almost falling back as their feet touched the ground. She staggered over to the large rock that Mari had previously rested on and reached down to steady herself and then sat on it. But as she touched the rock, she screamed out, "It burnt me!" and fell onto the ground.

"It has a mark carved into it," said Mari. "We noticed it before we went down into the cavern."

"I'm still weak," said Rhiannon. She took a breath and looked up to the skies. "But it feels so good to breathe in this air once more. My soul has been trapped down in that cavern and now that I am free, I need to see how much things have changed. Does Treharne still stand, or has the goddess answered my prayers and wiped it from this earth?"

"No, it still stands… I mean it's still there," said Mari brushing off the dust. "It's a town now, though, and a bit bigger, I guess, from when you knew it."

Rhiannon looked down the mountain. "Do you think that many generations still live there… even those families from my time?"

"I don't know."

"Let's find out," Rhiannon said softly.

"Why?" asked Mari.

"No reason. Just an urge to begin righting wrongs."

Just as Mari was about to speak, Rhiannon looked at her, smiled… and then she disappeared.

****

Slowly, Rhiannon began to walk down the streets of Treharne. She stared up at the streetlights, and walked around them, holding up her arm to feel the heat. But she felt nothing. She gazed into the shop windows and at the people who hurried past her as if she wasn't there. But the noises of each passing car made her turn quickly in different directions. And her lack of concentration sent her into the road where headlights came toward her. She raised her hand quickly. *"I'r mynydd ac at ddiogelwch."* 'To the mountain and safety.' She disappeared seconds before the car made contact with her.

Rhiannon stood in front of Mari again. She was out of breath, but not from running it appeared, more from fear. "What is that place? That is not Treharne."

"It is. It's just a different time now, it's moved on."

"I can't see the road to my cottage. I didn't recognise anything."

"Well, none of that is going to be there. I doubt any of the roads that you knew exist today. Your cottage doesn't exist anymore, it was burnt down not long after you were…" She stopped talking.

Rhiannon's eyes widened. "Murdered by those villagers? Burnt alive with no mercy?" She walked over to Mari. "Are you from that village?"

Mari shook her head, unable to speak straight away. "No, I don't live here, I'm from Cardiff. I'm a student and I found a book one day that mentioned a woman burnt at the stake here. I'm writing a paper for my university course and I found journals in a chapel that told a story," she babbled quickly.

"I don't understand you."

Mari's pulse was racing. "Look, this all seems crazy. But maybe we both need to sit and talk about our stories. I know a little about you."

"How could you know anything about me?" Rhiannon said defiantly.

"It was written down... In the journals that were kept in the chapel. The pastor was there with you, and he wrote it all down."

"Joseph Johnson? I remember he came forth while I burnt. The only one who stood in front of them all." Rhiannon's voice rose. "He did not again once I began to cry out as the flames tore away my skin. He hid like the others, cowards in shame." The skies clouded over and the moon that had been visible was now hidden and a slight breeze began to pick up.

Mari looked up as it got darker and felt the chill of the wind as it began to howl around her. "What are you doing?"

"I am regaining my strength. What else did it say?"

Mari held back. She didn't want to tell Rhiannon everything. "I read the trial notes too."

"Yes, the trial where I was convicted with no defender to help me. I stood accused of being a witch."

"But you are one," said Mari quickly and then realising that she'd spoken too quickly.

"I never harmed any of them. I cured their sicknesses," Rhiannon responded in her defence.

"And the men? It said that you killed those men."

Rhiannon stared at Mari. "Yes, I did. And I will tell you why I chose those men, but not today. I feel a kinship between you and me. I have much to learn about this world and you will teach me."

"What if I don't want to?" Mari asked gingerly. "What can you possibly want to prove now?"

"I can still suck out the soul of any man. And I will do so unless you help me."

"What if I don't care what you do?" Mari asked, trying to sound convincing.

"Then I say you lie and I don't believe that you want to do that, especially to me. Isn't there much you want to learn from me?"

Mari huffed. "Help you with what then, exactly?" she asked.

Rhiannon smiled. She turned to face the town and looking down over it she uttered, "I have a score to settle."

CHAPTER TWENTY-NINE

Simon entered the wooden lodge he rented and placed the book on the table. He sat on one of the kitchen chairs and just stared at the book. He couldn't believe that he actually had the grimoire that his grandmother had spoken to him about—pretty much all his life—when talking about the Welsh witch who had cursed a village. But there it was. He wasn't sure if he should even touch it, open it again or be looking at it so much. Archaeologists spend years researching and digging to find that priceless artefact and he spent less than a month riding on the coattails of a woman who had no clue why he was really with her. Granted, she'd done most of the work and he'd come and snatched it from her, but wasn't that the norm? If this wasn't some sort of sign that the book was destined to be his, then he didn't know what it was. Lucky for him, all Mari was looking for was a pile of bones and proof of a woman who was the last to be accused of being a witch. *Good luck with that,* he thought with a smile and an eye roll. His gaze moved him closer and closer to the book, so much so that his breath bounced off it and he felt it back on his face. Then he sat upright, lifted up the cover and began to read the first page. It was more than just a spell book. It was a fully loaded, touched by blood, grimoire.

Grimoires didn't just react to a spell. They also reacted to the one casting. It took a certain kind of someone with the ability to even be able to pronounce some of the words that were in old Welsh. He always knew he had some abilities. They'd been passed down through the generations. His grandmother used to tell him stories about her father. That he could predict certain weather conditions ahead of them actually happening. And his father could do the same. His grandmother used to say that predicting the weather was just one of his gifts. That only certain members of their family had special gifts of their own. The Jenkins family had always been known for their gifts. He'd always wished he was psychic. Truth was, he didn't know what he was. He didn't know what his gift was—if he had one at all. Until one day, not long after his brother had completed the family tree project of his, he finally found out what his gift was. He could literally speak any language. Old, new...didn't matter. He could read, write or speak any known language. He'd kept it to himself for years until he became interested in ancient artefacts and archaeology. It meant he was always one step ahead of those looking for ancient treasures because while they interpreted wall symbols or hieroglyphics, he was already on his way to finding the tomb or the artefact. If he concentrated hard enough, he could move items and of course, he could also predict the weather. And to think that he let Mari believe that she had the upper hand with the Latin inscriptions on the cave walls. He'd almost laughed out loud at the time. He didn't know how he'd kept such a straight face!

The book opened, he gazed at the pages within the grimoire that were beautifully decorated with colourful scrolls and flowers on the outer edges on some pages and words framing the pages and written very elegantly in old Welsh on some others. He gently brushed his fingers over the pages and then turned a page over. His eyes skimmed over each word, and his smile widened as he translated a few sentences in his head. Each glorious page turn delighted him more. Chants and spells for all sorts of things. To cure diseases and illnesses, grow roots from the ground with the flick of a finger, change appearance, summon an alchemist, control spirits and one that stood out the most, possessing of souls.

****

Rhiannon walked along the main street of the town again. The noise from the traffic and from the people continued to overwhelm her as she walked on in the hopes of finding some landmark that would tell her where she was. Just one landmark to let her know where she had once walked. Not even the stars above could guide her to where her cottage used to stand. She stopped at a bench near a park, sat down and placed her head in her hands. All she had to do was concentrate and try to remember. The mountains weren't that far behind her, so her cottage had to have been close by. But the whispers from the town whirled around in her head and grew louder, but she couldn't make out any of the sounds, it made it hard for her to concentrate.

With her eyes closed, the only familiar sound was that of the chapel bells as it summoned its worshippers that evening. She stood and walked toward the sound and found that some of the landscape had opened up and began to look familiar. She remembered the times she used to walk into the village with her arms bare or with just a small shawl and command the stares of the men and the scowls of the women. As she neared the chapel, she felt a cold chill. A fear entered her that she hadn't experienced before and she found herself in the town square. It had changed over the four hundred years since she'd left it. And the reason for the fear she felt inside was quite clear now. This was where she met her death. This was where she cried out for mercy and was shown none. Now she had a better understanding of where she was. Not a few yards in front of her, she remembered the shop where she bought her supplies. It was the place where she first met Evan. Over the other side of the road and on the next block, was the house of the midwife and where she learnt that she was with child. To the bottom right of the same street, stood the jail where they'd held her before she tried to run for the mountains.

And then she stood still, a shiver ascended up her spine and she began to shake.

Not even realising it, the spot where she now stood, was where they'd tied her up and lifted her body on the stake so that the flames rose higher and covered her. She stared over to the chapel that was now silent. She was going to bring her curse down on this town with a reign of fire and death. She would start with the chapel. She would destroy the very building that those Christians held in such regard. Those good Christian folk who should have saved her, but didn't. She walked at a quickened pace toward it and opened the gate only to be halted by a heat that made her stop. She stepped forward, looked toward the chapel and slowly raised her arm up. She stretched out her fingers and felt the invisible force that surrounded the holy place that she could not penetrate.

Rhiannon pinched her lips as she forcefully turned around and walked away. From the chapel she knew the directions to her cottage. She walked through some of the darkened streets to avoid stares from people and then stopped. Now, it was a piece of land, unused, unkempt and different from the land that she had lovingly brought to life.

"No!" she shouted in disappointment. She looked up at the skies. "Oh, Mother Morrighan, I have nothing here." She looked at the mountain. From this point she had tried to run from the villagers who chased her, and a memory seeped into her head, a dark and heart-breaking memory.

At first there came a small cry. Then came the tears and the pain deep in her heart so unimaginable that she fell on all fours onto the ground, sobbing. She remembered her child and the heartless way in which they had left it to die. She remembered her pleas of help, that her child was an innocent. They left it in the cold for the wolves. And soon anger replaced her tears. She promised them all that she would make them pay and she wasn't going to care what year this was. She closed her eyes and began to concentrate. She just had to take herself back to that time, to those responsible, and bring the aura of their souls back to the village, to present day and to her. She tilted her head up slowly and began to sniff the air. She could smell the sweet aura of its countless generations, each one blending with other bloodlines down the ages until... Rhiannon lifted her head and smiled. "Emyr Roberts," she said softly. The bloodline of Emyr Roberts was the first to show itself. "You sat on the council at my trial. You passed judgement on me and let me burn. Today, as I willed it then, I will end your bloodline."

****

In a new and upcoming part of the town, James Roberts lived alone in a very modest newly built apartment. His investments had proved very lucrative and he returned to his hometown of Treharne the year before after working and living in Cardiff for a few years. He hoped that he could find equally profitable deals in the northern part of Wales. He had already started to reap some of his success and to bring in new investors.

He sipped a glass of wine and watched, puzzled, as the lighting in his apartment flickered on and off. Then he walked into his bedroom, took off his clothes, stepped into the shower and began to bathe.

****

Rhiannon closed her eyes. *"Nid oes gan amser bresenoldeb ac mae eneidiau hynafol y rheini a'm cyhuddodd wedi dangos eu tylwyth i mi. Rwyf i, a gondemniwyd â thân, yn dychwelyd i ddial am fy marwolaeth â thân. Boed i'r fflamau ymledu ymhell gan losgi cnawd fel y llosgodd fy nghnawd i, a boed i'th enaid borthi f'un innau â'th farwolaeth."* 'Time has no presence and the ancient souls of those who accused me have shown me their kin. I, who was condemned with fire return to avenge my death with my fire. May the flames reach deep, burning away flesh as it did mine and may your soul feed mine with your death.' When she opened her eyes again, she was standing in his bathroom.

The water falling from the showerhead stopped and he looked up at it. He tapped the showerhead and then tapped it again even harder, groaning when still nothing came out, until flames shot out of it. He staggered back trying to fan the flames away from him, but only succeeded in spreading them further around his body. He clawed at the cubicle glass door trying to get it open but it was sealed tight and he couldn't get out. He pounded the glass but it wouldn't break.

His agonising screams could be heard throughout the apartment complex and it alerted his neighbour who came to his front door. He banged the door loudly and pushed at it several times to break in and enter.

Rhiannon watched as the burnt naked body slumped down in the shower cubicle. The flames turned back to running water splashing over a smoldering charred corpse and washed burnt flesh into the drain when the front door came crashing open. Her job done, Rhiannon disappeared before she was seen.

****

Mari was so shocked to see Rhiannon just appear in her room that she almost tripped backwards. Instead, all she did was fall on the sofa behind her. In shock, she uttered, "W-What? How?"

Rhiannon tutted, "I'm a witch, remember?"

"Why are you here? Why are you back here with me?"

"You left Treharne." Rhiannon pouted.

"Of course, I did. What was I supposed to do, go looking for you? You disappeared. I was going to go back there tomorrow. I needed a few things from here."

Rhiannon walked around the room and looked at the objects on the shelf, the books, the paintings on the wall. She finally turned to face Mari. "We are linked. When a witch wants to join with herself, she thinks about the centre in her own soul, a place of safety. When I thought about you just now, I came here. I don't know why. But I think perhaps it may be because it was you who freed me? I haven't worked it out yet."

Mari's eyes followed Rhiannon around the room, but she didn't utter a word.

"Where are we?" asked Rhiannon.

"Aberystwyth," said Mari.

"I have passed through this town before, but many years before I lived in Treharne." She turned to face Mari. "You want to know about me?" asked Rhiannon smiling. "I can feel it. Don't be frightened of me. I wish others harm, but not you. So, what is it you wish to know?"

A little hesitant Mari began, "I'm not sure anymore. I just didn't ever believe that I'd find out directly from you."

"And you are still afraid even though I tell you I wouldn't harm you?"

"I guess so. I-I'm just…"

Rhiannon took a breath. "Just ask. Begin and I shall answer. I am grateful to you for releasing me."

Mari nodded. "There is so little written about the witches in Wales." She stopped for a moment. "I was researching and found your name by accident."

Rhiannon looked surprised by the revelation. "I didn't think my name would go into any history books, or even there be any mention of my fate."

"Yes, your fate," said Mari quickly. "What really happened to you?"

Rhiannon sat down, her smile gone. Looking over to Mari, she began, "I have passed through this life using my craft. From village to village, while the people there grew old, I did not, thanks to Mother Morrighan."

"Who?"

"Our Pagan Goddess who I honoured and gave gifts to. Each gift bought me time, and that kept me young."

"What kind of gift?" said a curious Mari.

"Souls. I would take souls and keep them in a small glass jar. When I needed the life back in this body, I would take them to her altar and ask for the time they would have had left on this earth to be given to me."

"You killed them?"

"Yes," Rhiannon confirmed. "I killed those men. But I did them a mercy."

"Killing is killing, no excuses."

Rhiannon tutted and shook her head. "One man I remember, Dafydd Hughes. He was a brute of a man and his wife, small and timid. He beat her every chance he could. I saw it one day walking to the store. He slapped her and she fell, and not one of those so-called Christians ran to help her. And I remember that she spoke out against me at my trial after I helped her."

"You did kill her husband?"

"I did and I regret nothing. Of course, if I'd known she would side with Elizabeth, I would have left him to beat her some more." Rhiannon laughed, bit her lip, and then added, "But I took out his soul and offered it to Mother Morrighan who gave me the rest of his years. You still think me wicked?"

"Two wrongs don't make a right is the saying these days," Mari said, wagging her finger at Rhiannon.

Rhiannon sighed. "It was a saying back then too." She winked. "Always hated it. What they haven't written about, I suspect, is that I also saved some of them from the sickness and one from being alone."

"You're trying to justify ending their lives sooner than it should have."

"At least three of those men were sick and no amount of potions was going to save them. One was in such pain... and I saved him from that pain. I did possess his soul, but I did not gain years from it." She looked at Mari's unconvinced face. "You would put an animal out of its misery, right?"

"It's not the same thing and you know it."

"It is the same," argued Rhiannon, "and it is done." She waved her hand in the air. "All in the past and you can choose to accept that I did them no real harm or you can believe that it was unjust, it matters not!" Rhiannon pouted and folded her arms.

"How many did you take?" asked Mari. "Over the years. The truth, I want the truth."

"Hard to say. Hundreds, thousands perhaps over the centuries. I lost count and did not wish to know."

"Why men? Why didn't you take the souls of women? Why was it only the men that you took?"

"Their souls are stronger. Women's souls carry too much emotion and sorrow, whereas those of men didn't carry those feelings at all," she answered casually. "The hearts of women are always broken by a man. I could not bear to keep their sorrow within me. So I took the souls of the men, and I never thought twice about it."

"I read the court notes from your trial. But it didn't really give that much information. It said you were arrogant and against the teachings of the Lord?"

Rhiannon scowled and clenching her teeth, she looked over to Mari. "You would be arrogant in a trial where they accuse you with no defence. Each day I would plead for the rights to a fair trial and none were given. I was accused of the craft when all I did was give aid to those few that needed it."

"But you were really using the craft and you had killed those men, so even if you didn't like your trial, you were guilty. Whether they were bad men or not, you took their lives from them and you're dismissing that as if you've done nothing wrong."

"I can't expect you to understand. It's our way. I am not the first witch to live this way and let me tell you that there were some who were much worse than me. Children being lured away and eaten, does that not make what I did less wicked?"

"I think it puts you all in the same boat."

"Boat?" Rhiannon tilted her head slightly, confused by the terminology. "Let me retell you a little of my story for now and see who should be judged most harshly. I was brought forward to trial accused only because of a jealous wife! She poisoned their minds against me. I was not feared by those in the village until she planted that evil seed in their heads. They had no idea what I truly was, but while the trial continued, she made sure everyone thought the same."

"Why did she hate you so much?"

Rhiannon took a breath and was about to answer. She looked distant, her eyes moistened as if about to cry, but stopping short of it. "Evan," she finally said. "Evan Harding was my lover and his wife, Elizabeth... was the one who accused me of using the craft. I don't even think she wanted it to go as far as it did, but once those accusations came, she played them until the end. And I was with child..." Rhiannon began to cry. "And she couldn't bear the fact that she was barren and my child was her husband's."

"I read that. You were pregnant and they executed you both."

"No," said Rhiannon, shaking her head. "I ran. I ran toward the mountains where we could be safe. But my child came early and before I could reach it. The villagers... they caught me and dragged me back. My child was birthed as they dragged me and they left it... they cut off the cord and I could hear the cries... I don't even know what I had." She put her head in her hands and sobbed. Through her tears she said, "But I will make them all pay for what they did to me and to my child."

And Rhiannon disappeared—again.

****

Mari quickly packed her laptop, clothes, notes—anything that she needed. She had to return to Treharne because she had, in a way, released Rhiannon's wrath and she had to find a way to make things right.

She rented a small bed-sit in the town near the chapel, bought food, a newspaper and then sat down in front of a small gas fire. Just as she was about to re-read the journals, the newspaper headlines got her attention. The day before, a man had died a bizarre death in his own bathroom. He'd been burnt alive. Mari knew that only one person could have been responsible for something so strange. A noise behind her made her jump out of her chair, dropping her sandwich and the newspaper onto the floor. Standing there was Rhiannon.

"What have you done?" insisted Mari.

"I cursed this village. I am making them all pay." Rhiannon was defiant.

"Four hundred years ago!" yelled Mari. "Those people back then killed you. And I get you're extremely pissed off, but the people here, now? They didn't do it. For God's sake…these people are descendants, they are not them."

"They are to me!" Rhiannon was angry and stood face to face with Mari. "I don't have to explain myself to you."

"Then why are you back here? Why have you come to me again?"

"We are tied together. You released me and I am centred to you."

"Then I command you to stop!" snapped Mari.

Rhiannon started to snigger and then gave a full belly laugh and walked away from her. "You command me?" She turned to face her. "You?" she pointed and laughed again. "You?"

"Yes, me. If I released you, then you have to do as I say."

"It doesn't work like that."

"Then there's something you need from me," said Mari. "That's it, isn't it? You need something from me."

Rhiannon pouted and then sighed in a slight agreement. "Yes, you're right." She seemed nervous as she paced around the room. "A book. I had a book that is known as a grimoire. It was in my cottage. But now I have no cottage. I need you to find it."

"No," said Mari quickly. "You've killed a man already. Why do you need it? You seem to be doing just fine without it."

"The book is part of me. I will always have one part of me here and the other… where I was. I need you to find it."

"No," insisted Mari. "You have to stop wanting to kill people and then I might help. Until then, it's no."

Rhiannon was angry. Marching over to Mari she raised her hand and extended her index finger.

"What are you doing?" asked Mari.

Rhiannon pointed again. "I don't understand," she said looking shocked. "You should be on your knees in pain."

Mari raised an eyebrow. "Are you threatening me? I'm trying to understand you and you want to hurt me? And here you are trying to convince me that you're only trying to right what was done to you."

Rhiannon walked around the room, as though she couldn't understand it. She raised her finger, pointed and disintegrated a vase on a shelf.

"Hey!" shouted Mari. "That's not even mine!"

"My powers still work," Rhiannon whispered. She pointed at Mari again. And again, nothing.

"Maybe as I was the one who found you, your powers can't be used against me?" said Mari folding her arms with a defiant smile.

Rhiannon walked over to the window, with a slight smile and a raised eyebrow she said. "There are other ways." She pointed at the man who was walking across the road. "See that man over there?"

Mari stood beside her and shrugged. Then she watched in horror as the man doubled over in pain. He dropped to his knees then on his back, screaming, and clutching at his stomach in excruciating pain.

"If with one finger I can bring you all to your knees, imagine what I can do to this whole town with one hand." Rhiannon smiled as she released the man from his pain.

Mari watched as the man staggered off, catching his breath and holding onto the wall to help him keep upright, until she lost sight of him.

"I won't..." Mari said boldly, "help you."

Rhiannon looked out of the window again. The street was empty now, and then a car drove by. Rhiannon pointed and the car drove straight into a lamp post and burst into flames.

Mari stepped away from the window. "What are you trying to prove!" she shouted. "Why did you have to do that?"

"So that you can see what I can do. I need my book."

Mari watched the light as it flickered from the flames below and lit up the street. She heard shouts from people who'd started to run to it, trying to put it out, trying to get the occupants out.

"I promise that I will wipe this town from existence if you do not find it," said Rhiannon.

"Simon has it," Mari finally blurted out, "We found it that day in the cavern. But he left with it and I don't know where he is now."

"Then you better find him... before I set this town alight."

****

Mari sat back in her armchair. She didn't have a clue of where to start looking. He'd left her in that cavern and she didn't know where he could be by now. It was while thinking that she saw the jacket he'd left in the cavern. She picked it up and started to search through the pockets. There was nothing in the outside ones. The inside left pocket was empty but the one on the right had a receipt for a rental cabin just outside the town and not too far. At least it was a start.

When she arrived at the door, she heard music from inside, the lights were on low and she broke its ambience by pounding on the front door.

"What!" a voice yelled from inside and then the door was forcefully opened. His smirk just made her angrier. "Mari! Nice to see you managed to climb out." But before she could tell him what she thought of him, he turned his back on her and went back inside. She followed him, slamming the door behind her.

"Your complete bastard!" Mari shouted. "You left me."

"Of course, I did." He poured himself a drink and lifted up a glass to see if she wanted one too.

Mari shook her head.

"I knew it. As soon as I started reading your past work that you'd be the person I needed to find the grimoire."

Mari took a breath. "You used me?"

"Look," he said downing his drink. "Your research into ancient folklore is outstanding. Imagine my surprise when I learnt that you were looking into the very same folklore that I had been studying for some time."

Mari crossed her arms. She was listening, but under it all, she wanted to break the bottle over his head. "Why didn't you just ask or say what your intensions really were?"

"And risk you finding the book without me and taking it for yourself once you knew its worth? Or worse, taking it to a museum for them to put in a glass case? I don't think so."

"Was it that important that you had to use me the way you did? I swear she was right about men."

"Who was right about men?" asked Simon taking another sip of his drink.

Mari bit her lip. "Well, here's the thing." She walked over to the bottle and poured herself a drink. "There I am, piling up rocks under the entrance so I can climb out, when I come across this unusual jar."

Simon eye rolled and then looked at his watch. "Is this going to take long? Places to go, books to read, you know?"

Mari took a breath. "Well, let's just say, you found what *you* wanted and I found what I wanted. Thing is, the *my* thing is going to burn this town to the ground and kill people unless I get the your thing back to her," she said widening her eyes and tilting her head to the side. "Oh sorry, did I not mention that I seem to have brought the *my* thing back from the dead? And she's a bit pissed off."

"Shut up!" said Simon sarcastically. "Oh wait, I get it. You're spinning me a story thinking I'll foolishly believe it, and then you'll just grab the book that I found for yourself."

"OK, firstly, this isn't a made up story and we both found that book, you just managed to get your pants on quicker than me and secondly, she wants her book back and sooner rather than later, she's going to come and find you and she's just going to take it whether you like it or not." She downed the drink and added, "Did I say she was a witch? She was the one who got me out of that cavern, and Simon, I wouldn't piss about, I'd let her have the book."

Simon's grin was annoying Mari each time he did it, he was so close to laughing at her. "Tell you what. You go tell your witch to come and see me and we'll talk it over."

"You don't believe me do you?" said Mari.

"Not for a minute."

"Fine. Well now I know where you are, I'll invite her along to persuade you properly." She turned on her heels and walked out the door.

Mari walked to the door as Simon shouted, "Witch? As if."

****

Rhiannon looked up at the bright blue sky and smiled. She closed her eyes and imagined the same feeling from the same sun on her face from the last time ever she'd stood on the same spot four hundred years ago. But to her it didn't feel as though all that time had passed. It felt as if she'd gone to sleep one night and woke up the next day.

Other than the chapel, the square was the only other part of the original village that remained. Perhaps that was what drew her to that spot each time—the place of her death. The place she'd last seen her Evan and the place where she cursed them all. She opened her eyes and raising her hand to cover the sun, quietly she uttered, *'O'r goleuni sy'n gwneud ein byd yn ddisglair. I'r tywyllwch sy'n ei guddio. Boed i'r goleuni ar y dref hon gael ei guddio nes i'r felltith gael ei chyflawni.* 'From the light that brightens our world. To the darkness that hides it. Let the light upon this town be hidden until the curse has been done. And dark clouds crossed the sun to cast a shadow over the town and shroud it in darkness.'

Cars screeched to a halt at the sudden darkness and it took people by surprise. People in the streets looked up to see the clouds and realised that they weren't moving along to bring the light back. People began to run in different directions, pushing into each other as part curiosity and part panic descended on the streets.

Rhiannon stood in the square and felt the aura of the generations that had passed through it and she hated them all. In the town square the old fountain still spewed out water through the same raised stone vases and angels into the ground water basin. She remembered how she would stop and take a drink from it when she would come into the village. She looked to her right and saw the ghostly images of the ladies who used to stop at that corner. Some who used to say hello but others who would look at her and then whisper to the others all huddled together and then laughing, the ladies that held Elizabeth in such high esteem. There was nothing more fulfilling she remembered, than walking through the middle of them knowing that she could turn them all to dust at the mere flick of her finger. How she wished she had done just that.

She walked around the fountain letting her hand hang loosely in the water while she remembered Evan and the time they had together. She wished for his arms to be wrapped around her again, to hear his voice, and to see his smile.

The man who came to talk to her didn't see it coming. Why would he? He stood so close to Rhiannon that she could smell the alcohol on his breath.

"What ya doing?" he asked.

"Remembering," said Rhiannon.

"Pretty one like you shouldn't be alone. I don't know how it got so dark. But I know a cosy little bar we could go get a drink." And he grabbed her arm.

Rhiannon pulled away, while the man took a step closer. "You look like you want company. Why don't you let me give you what you need?" insisted the man.

Rhiannon smiled. "I'll tell you what." she started. "Why don't you take a walk to that wall over there and show me how much you want to please me?" She stared deeply into his eyes and the man looked dazed as he walked over to the wall.

It started off as a small knock into the brick wall with his forehead. Then it became greater, more forceful. By the fifth hit, his head had already opened up but he didn't stop.

Rhiannon walked away as the man carried on, only casually looking back to see him finally fall to the ground with most of his head spread over the wall and the floor.

The lamplights on the main street had switched on, as if it had realised that the night had arrived but was only 3:00 p.m. Rhiannon stopped opposite a brightly lit shop and sent a flaming fireball through the window, which exploded inside. The doors opened and the screams from people running out of the shop and away from the flames made Rhiannon shrug and simply walk away.

The back of the building sent debris over the streets behind it and it followed with the igniting of the building next door. Soon both buildings were nothing but flames and heat. The fire engines screamed down the road and unraveled their hoses to try and put it out and firemen then ran inside to contain it from within and rescue any forms of life still inside.

Rhiannon walked around to the next street and then down the alleyway to stand behind a man as he smoked his cigarette behind the restaurant he worked in. He didn't even seem curious as to what was happening in the heavens, or that the fire engine sirens were blasting from every end of the town. He was more concerned with keeping his cigarette lit. He never flinched until he felt a presence behind him and he turned around to see her standing there and then with a surprised look, he took a step back. "W--what --- you scared the shit out of me! What do you want? You can't be behind here... and I ain't got any drugs or money if that's what you're after."

Rhiannon looked into his eyes, the same brown eyes that stared at her in the courtroom and who uttered not a word in her defence. Those eyes had condemned her and now she was going to make him suffer. "You are Alwyn Creu," said Rhiannon.

"No, I'm not," said the man. "I'm a Creu yeah, but not Alwyn. I don't know any Alwyn. I'm Mike."

"I see his eyes looking at me!" shouted Rhiannon. She raised her arm and pointed at him. "You, who accused me and signed my death."

The man took a drag from the cigarette and threw it down on the floor. He stepped on it to put it out. "Look lady, I don't know who you're looking for, but it ain't me. So, I've finished my break now and I'm going back in to work."

Rhiannon stepped forward and touched his forehead with her finger. *"Mil o ddarnau gwydr a'r holl ddarnau bach yn rhy finiog ond eto'n ddigon mawr i dorri'n gynifer o ddarnau mân. Torrodd dy dylwyth ddarnau ohonof i felly fe rwygaf dithau'n ddarnau. Na foed iti waedu nac anadlu mwy."* 'A thousand shards of glass, all the little pieces too sharp but big enough to cut into so many little pieces Your kin cut the heart out of me and I will you rip you apart. Bleed and breathe no more.'

And the man stood straight up, unable to move until Rhiannon moved her hand towards a broken bottle that was lying on the floor and pointed at it. The man stooped down and picked it up. Turning back to her he seemed trancelike, expressionless as he began to stab himself in the face with it. The pieces of the bottle shattered away with each stab and some of them lodged in his skin. With each movement the pieces ripped away at his flesh. Over and over the broken bottle shattered a little more as he then began to jab the sharp ends into his chest, then his neck, and into his face again. Blood poured from the wounds onto the floor, until his face was completely removed and he collapsed landing on his own blood on the floor.

Rhiannon walked away—and another bloodline gone.

****

Mari heard loud noises coming from outside and looked out of the window. It was already dark. How could that be? She looked at her watch. It was only 3:00 p.m. "Rhiannon," she said to herself. She sat back down and called up all the research sites she could remember from her time at the British Museum. Whenever she wanted to get authenticity for an item she would be able to trace things back sufficiently enough to be able to date certain objects.

Although she had left the museum several months before, she was relieved to see that her permission status had still been retained in the research tool. She needed to know more about the villagers if she was to save any chance of saving any dependants.

She glanced over to the newspaper on her desk and read the updated story about James Roberts and then of the two bizarre deaths that had happened only in the last few days. Mari just couldn't get rid of the thought that it was all related to Rhiannon's vengeance threat. James Roberts' family had been in this village since the thirteenth century. At the time of Rhiannon's death, his five times great grandfather was Emyr Roberts, one of the trial members. He was also one of the men who came to see Joseph Johnson that night to perform the spell that captured Rhiannon's soul into the jar.

The second man whose death was being treated as a drink enthused suicide, was named as Nicholas Bell. The newspaper described him as recently coming to live there. He wasn't connected to the town at all but it seemed odd that a man, who had just left the local bar in a happy state, would bash his head in for no reason against the wall right in the centre of the town.

The latest death was Michael Creu. He worked in a diner and had lived in the town all his life. His family had been in that town since the twelfth century and would have definitely been there when Rhiannon had been there. Was he related to Alwyn Creu, one of the jurors?

CHAPTER THIRTY

Mari ran into the chapel and slammed the door behind her.

"Hello again," said a voice from behind. It was the pastor she'd met when she first came there, John. "You look like you're being chased by the devil. What's wrong?"

Mari slowed down her breathing and attempted to speak. "I am in a way." She walked down the aisle toward John. "I think I may need some help from"— she pointed upwards to the heavens—"if he can."

"What's the matter?"

"Remember I came here to research a story about the last woman to be burnt in Wales?"

"I remember you stole another of the journals. Do you still have it?" asked John.

"I didn't steal it," said Mari ruffling her brow. "I borrowed it and yes, I still have it. But that's not why I need help. Do you know about the strange deaths that have been happening these past few days?"

"Yes of course. We're holding one of the funerals here when it's time."

"Well I know who's responsible and I don't know how to stop her."

"Her? If you have any information, you must go to the police."

"I doubt they will be able to help with this. It's not the usual crime scenes."

"You're not making sense."

"Rhiannon!" said Mari quickly. "It's Rhiannon, the witch I was researching. She's back and she's taking revenge on the generations that burnt her at the stake and who killed her baby."

John gave her a puzzled look as though he was face to face with a mad woman. "Rhiannon, a person who has been dead for over four hundred years? Are you sure you're feeling all right?"

"It's crazy, right? I would say the same if it were in reverse. So, let me tell you the whole story and see whether you feel the same way afterwards. Because I need some sort of help and I don't know where else to turn."

Mari felt frustrated that he didn't believe her, she didn't have the time but she knew she had to do something to convince him so she stretched over, grabbed his hand, walked him over to the window and opened the blinds.

John looked out and then down at his watch and then back outside into the darkness.

"It's 3.30 in the afternoon, John, explain that," said Mari. "So, shall I start from the very beginning or go into what happened yesterday and today and what's going to happen tomorrow if she gets her way?"

John looked out of the window again and nodded. "The beginning," he said finally.

Mari sat John in one of the pews and she began to recount the story. "Well, you know I came here to get some research for university and we found the journals. After I 'borrowed' them, a uni professor, expressed an interest in my work. You see, he'd been researching about an occult book that his grandmother used to talk to him about while growing up and that she always said was hidden away somewhere up the mountain and he thought we could join forces." She stopped for a moment to catch her breath and then in an almost whisper she added, "Although he did leave some of that out at the time." She cleared her throat and began again, "Anyway, he had contacts in the British Museum and we got permission to read the minutes from the witch trials here in Wales. One of the trials was about Rhiannon, but there wasn't very much information. It was very sketchy, but I managed to piece some things together. With those records and the notes from the journals and also the parish records, we were able to find where she would have been buried. So, this professor and I took a trip up the mountain. At first it was really about getting our bearings and to take a look around rather than a full excavation. Well, so I thought. And never in a million years did I think that we would find a cavern on our first trip and then what was inside it."

"What was in there?" asked John.

"We had to be lowered down into it. The professor brought a load of hiking gear, I wondered why at the time… I should have known. Anyway, when you go down into it, it has a small shaft at the beginning of it and then it opens up into a big cavern. We go down into it and took a look around. Someone had definitely been in there over the years. First thing we saw were the symbols carved into the walls. We translated most of it and then we noticed a manmade wall. We took it down to see what was behind it. I remember his face when he brought out a box and we eagerly got it opened. There it was. The very thing he'd been looking for. It was right there, first time out looking for it. Like it wanted to be found and we… we were caught up in the moment and"—she looked down at her hands and clenched her fists—"and it doesn't matter." She looked around the chapel and tutted as she faced John. "I didn't even see it coming. He used the rope we brought to get back up to the top, took the book with him and left me down in that cavern."

"He left you alone?"

"Yes."

"Well, he sounds like a real bastard to leave you down there," said John in a shocked voice.

"Hey, I thought your kind couldn't use language like that?"

"We're very modern. We can do a lot of things that were frowned upon once. Now carry on... you were saying?"

"Well... I figured it would be dark soon so I had to hurry and try to get out of there. I thought that if I piled a lot of rocks under the opening that I might be able to climb up it and then get out."

"Good plan."

"Yeah, I thought so too, except that they don't always stay in the type of pile that lets you climb on. So I kept bringing over rocks and piling them higher and higher and then I began to move a pile of rocks a little farther away from where I was and that pile came down around me. I had to jump around to avoid them hitting me. And that's when I saw it—there was another chamber cut into the wall and it had cleared away when those rocks fell—a jar in amongst the rubble. There was an old pot with an iron ring around the neck, but it had corroded over the years through damp and mould and it just crumbled away leaving the stopper in it. I picked the jar out and studied it. And then I lost my footing on the loose rocks, slipped and sent the pot flying up in the air. It crashed to the floor... and released her."

"Released?"

"I don't know what else to call it. It broke and she appeared. And she's been creating havoc ever since.

Thing is, because I released her, she's sort of tied to me. And I don't know what else to do."

But John continued to look skeptical. "It's just that—"

Mari stood up. "I knew you wouldn't believe me. Modern pastor, eh? Well, you don't know shit. I've seen things that would throw all your theories about life out the window, so if all you can do is roll your eyes at me as if I was ill or insane, then I may as well find a way of getting rid of her myself."

"I didn't mean"

"It doesn't matter what you meant. All I know is that the way of getting her back to wherever she came from, is hidden in this chapel. And whether you believe me or not, I have to start looking."

"But I gave you the journals, I have nothing else," said John.

"Yes, you do. The pastor when Rhiannon was alive, Joseph Johnson, I think he may have been buried with a book that had a prayer or a spell. It's an incantation that will bind her again. She's going to burn this town down to the ground, but not before she kills even more descendants of the people who got her convicted back then. You can look up the list of the men at her trial, because so far two of their descendants have died. She's killed another guy too I'm sure of it, for no good reason and I'm pretty sure she started the fires in town. Oh, and did I mention she's also blackmailing me to help her?"

"How is she doing that?"

"She has just one agenda, and that's revenge. She wants my help to find her book and if I don't, she's going to hurt people."

"Her book?"

"Her grimoire. It's a witch's magic book. She's already shown me that she can hurt people when she wants, and it's not something I want on my conscience, so I need her gone."

John didn't say a word. He stared at her for the longest time and Mari couldn't work out if he believed her, was humouring her, or was about to throw her out of the chapel. "Look, I'm not saying I don't believe everything you've just said. But it's hard for me to just accept. We don't believe in the supernatural, you have to understand that."

"If we open his grave and it's in there, it'll prove to you that I'm not insane, and what I'm telling you is the truth."

"You'll need special permission if you want to open his grave anyway. I can't do that for you and there's no guarantees that what you're looking for is even with him. Or even exists. And it'll still take a few days to organise," said John. "I'll have to ring the Bishop and he can—."

"We don't have the time," interrupted Mari. "All I need is a shovel… and a lookout," she joked.

****

It was the part that Mari enjoyed the most when she used to go out on archaeological digs. Whenever they found a tomb, she would make sure that she was front and centre when it was opened.

Luckily for them, the graves of Pastor Johnson and his wife, were toward the side of the chapel and away from the main populated areas, because this would have taken some explaining. It also helped that it was dark and people had other things on their minds than to worry about two people with a shovel in the middle of a graveyard.

Mari couldn't have had a bigger smile as she and John shovelled another pile of dirt up and out of the grave. "You can't imagine how hyped up I am," she said looking over at him. "I was the same in Rome two years ago. We found a door hidden in the ancient ruins and once we broke through, we found a massive chamber, right under the original ruins. I was lucky enough to be there the time they found a stone coffin..." A thud made her stop talking. The earth thinned and the shovel and a wooden coffin connected. She stared down, then at John as he cleaned off the earth and debris that still covered the coffin.

John took out a small bottle from inside his jacket pocket and started to drop Holy Water onto the coffin. "Father, I ask you to please anoint our dear departed as we..." He stopped. "How do I even bless this? 'Dear Father in Heaven, we're about to dig up your pastor, and we're very sorry'?"

Mari did all she could to stop a snigger. "I have no idea. How about, 'Here lies Joseph Johnson. We're sorry to wake him'?"

John poured the rest of the water over the coffin. "I guess that will have to do."

An oak coffin lay rotting beneath them. Carefully, John removed more of the debris until the whole length of the coffin was exposed for the first time in almost four hundred years.

"Wow!" said Mari. "I can't believe what good condition this coffin is in after four hundred years. By rights, it should be falling apart as we get near it. I can only imagine what state he's in if this is anything to go by."

"I don't even want to imagine how many laws we're breaking right now," started John, "let alone the religious ones. And I'm only doing this because you were... well, so insistent and I wanted to help you."

"Look, if we don't find something to stop Rhiannon, you can kiss this town goodbye and even more of the trial descendants are going to die. And if there's no book here then we know what he wrote was most likely hysteria from the time. But if there is something here, then it'll prove to you that I'm not insane and making all this up."

John nodded and picked up a crowbar. He hit the side of the coffin and forced it up, breaking parts of the lid until the whole piece came away.

Joseph Johnson was buried in his chapel robes. Some of the bones were intact, but most of his skull had disintegrated over time. But it was the book that Joseph Johnson had in his hands that made Mari give a little shriek. The answer to all of this was in there, she just knew it. She pointed down to it and said, "Told you. Look, it's there!"

Carefully, they lifted the book out of his bony fingers and Mari blew away the dust. The book was covered in fine cotton and sealed after that in leather and sewn together. Clearly, Joseph Johnson wanted to keep this book intact for the future. She lifted up the book and placed it on the side as they both climbed out of the grave. She gently examined the book before opening it. "It's another journal. Let's go inside and see what we can read from it. I hope it's not too damaged or faded."

Inside the chapel, they sat in the front pews while Mari carefully opened the book and scanned over the pages.

"But why would he have it buried with him and not keep it with the others?" asked John.

"Because this one has more than just an account of what was happening, this one has the exact details, warts and all," Mari said with a smile. "Look at this entry dated January 9th 1685." She began to read aloud,

'I did not ask nor wanted to speculate as to why this happened. When Farmer Parry and Mrs Parry came to me to bless their child, I did not ask how this once barren woman was now blessed with a son. But as soon as I saw him, I could not disguise the fact that this was the offspring of the woman who wept for her child as they burnt her body. The same woman that I helped to bind her soul for all eternity. The child had her blue eyes as he looked at me, as if he knew what had been done here and could see into my heart and the guilt that I carried. But he was still an innocent and I did not see it necessary to question why they had taken the child into their home, but hoped that the good Lord would pardon my involvement in the crime with the salvation of the child when my time of reckoning arrived. Therefore, on the ninth day of January 1685, I, Joseph Johnson, christened, Llyr Wyn Parry into the Christian world, knowing that he would be safe from any harm and I will take the secret of his mother to the grave. I have given my blessing to them raising the child and persuaded them that perhaps it would be wise to not elaborate where the child originally came from. But to let them inform the villagers that Mrs Parry had given birth, not knowing she was with child until the event happened and with the heavy snows it made it impossible for her to visit the midwife."

"Oh my God, her child didn't die!" exclaimed Mari.

"What?" asked John.

"Rhiannon. She said she was going to make them all pay for what they did to her and her child. But he didn't die. A farmer took him... a farmer!"

"Will that make a difference to her? Will it stop her?"

"I don't know. But perhaps it will make her refocus because somewhere out there is her blood. What if her flesh and blood is walking around? We have to find a lineage. We need to tell her."

"But what if it backfires?" asked John. "What if she finds her great-great grandson and does something to him?"

"Like what?"

"I don't know, she could want him to join her or enchant him and he could be more a prisoner than her family."

She thought for a moment and then stood up and gave John the book. "Look, you keep reading this. Somewhere in this book it has to say how they put her soul into the jar. And I'll see if the moment is ever right to tell her."

"Will it work today though, the prayer?" asked John.

"I don't know. But I don't have anything else to work with. We don't know if this would have worked if she was alive too, so we have to find it. There's more in this journal than we know right now. And any little bit of information that we can use is better than nothing, because if they did bind her soul by using what's in this book, only a pastor can do it." She looked at John and smiled. "That means you."

****

A little later Mari's mobile phone rang, and John was on the other end. "I did a genealogy check and it was simple to track down the farmers' family."

Mari gripped the phone tightly and then sat down. "You've found them?"

"I found some information that might be of use. They stayed in Treharne until the mid-eighteen hundreds. Then they moved to London, but they came back to Wales a few years later. It doesn't say why. There are records in London showing when they joined that chapel. It's a central research base that most clergy can look through. You just type in a name and a town and all its residents with that name, pop up."

"Is the family still here?"

"No, any relatives moved away a long time ago. But some of them are buried here, in the churchyard, in fact. But before you say anything – no, we're not going to be digging them up."

Mari groaned. "Is comedy part of the modern clergy?"

A brief pause from John and then, "It's an entrance exam."

Mari smirked at his humour. "We were so close."

"No, it's fine. You see, there is a small connected family left. In fact, there's a descendent living not too far from here. He's a university professor and you might even know him. He works in the same place that you're studying in."

Mari gasped, almost dropping the phone. "Oh God, please tell me it's not him. He practically told me his story and I took no notice."

"You know him?" asked John quickly.

"You remember I told you that I came here with a colleague, a professor?"

"You told me he was a shady person. He left you in that cave."

"Well, yes, he is and he did. His name is Simon Jenkins...oh crap, I didn't even think about the names." She eye rolled. "I'm so stupid!"

"You couldn't have known. Jenkins is a popular name in these parts."

"I should have seen the similarities. When we first started this, he told me that he'd been researching a different story, but that both stories were sort of intertwined. That's why he was going out of his way to help me, because we would end up helping each other. He was right, but I'm wondering if he even knows how much he is linked to her."

"He's a descendent of Rhiannon," said John, "the great-great and so on, grandson of her son Llyr. The baby she thought was dead."

"I could kick myself," said Mari tutting. "On the plus side, we may have a bargaining tool to use against her."

"Are you going to tell her?"

"I don't know yet. I might just tell her that her baby didn't die, but I won't tell her anything more than that. Damn it all," said Mari frustrated,

"Are you going to tell him?" asked John. "He needs to know where he came from."

"I don't know. Perhaps." She stamped her foot. "Damn it!" she said shaking her head. This was too unbelievable. "He was right here and he has no clue who he really is in all of this. And it's because he doesn't know, that I really do need to find him. Before she kills him for stealing the grimoire and then we're all truly fucked." Mari bit her lip. "Oops, sorry vicar."

John laughed. "Pastor." And in a cliché biblical voice he said, "You are forgiven, my child."

****

Mari jumped back when she hung up on John and saw Rhiannon standing there. "Fuck!" she said touching her chest. "You really do have to start letting me know when you're just going to appear." She hoped Rhiannon hadn't heard her conversation.

"Don't you feel me yet?" asked Rhiannon. "We are linked. I can always feel where you are."

"Well I'm not a witch, am I?"

"That is very true." Rhiannon nodded in agreement. "But it doesn't matter, I have felt my grimoire and I need to go and get it. And you will come with me."

"I guess I have no choice. You'll probably hurt someone if I don't."

"See, there is a little witch in you. You've started to read my mind." Rhiannon joked. "You may want to close your eyes."

"Why?"

Mari and Rhiannon stood outside Simon's cabin. "How did we get here?" asked Mari. She looked over to the familiar cabin. "Why are we here?"

"Because it's in there. My book. And he's reading from it. But it won't take too long."

"What won't take too long?" asked Mari.

"The book will kill him. It belongs to me"—Rhiannon leaned in closer to Mari —"and it's very loyal to me."

Mari rushed through the door to see Simon standing near the table. He was reading but not from the grimoire as she had expected.

"Don't read from the book anymore!" she screamed.

Rhiannon took a step forward. "Is this the man who left you in the cavern and who now dares to read from my book?"

"Yes," said Mari, "but don't even bother about him. I couldn't care less about him. Give her the book, Simon, before she lights up the rest of this town."

Simon closed the book and stood up.

Slowly he turned to face them and Rhiannon gasped out loud. "Evan?" she finally whispered stretching out her arm toward him.

Simon looked amused. "You are Rhiannon I suppose?" He looked over to Mari, "Really? Is this the best you can come up with? Where did you find someone to dress up and pretend in this town?"

"Simon, I swear this is not made up."

"So, 'Rhiannon,' how is this going to go down?" Simon mocked.

But Rhiannon couldn't speak. She turned to Mari. "What trick is this? How could you even—"

"I swear I don't know what—"

"It's him," interrupted Rhiannon, "but it's not him. How could this be?"

"I don't understand what you mean," insisted Mari.

"Tis his eyes, his mouth, and I see some of Evan in his face."

"I swear I have no idea what you're talking about."

But Rhiannon was overcome. She took another step forward, stretched out her hand as if wanting to touch Simon's face, and then pulled it away. Tears began to fall down her face. She turned to look over at Mari. "I cannot," she said sadly. "My heart still grieves and this man stands before me as my Evan once did. I'm sorry, I-I cannot bear this sorrow."

And Rhiannon was gone.

Simon stared at the space where Rhiannon once stood. "What the fuck?"

"You have no idea." Mari sighed. "She wants the book back. You have to give it to me so I can take it to her."

"No!" Simon said sternly. "Theatricals. I don't know how you did that, but I don't really care. And now you need to leave."

An explosion turned their attention to outside. "Oh my God, she's doing it again!" Mari shouted at Simon.

"It's in the back!" said Simon with a sense of urgency. "Let me go and get it."

Mari waited for him to return. After a few minutes, Mari called out, "Simon? Simon?" She went into the room that he'd walked into. Mari hung her head. The curtains from the open window flapped in the breeze. "Oh, for fucks sake, Simon, you total twat!"

Simon had slipped out the back of the cabin.

CHAPTER THIRTY-ONE

Rhiannon stood in the main square again. She couldn't stop the tears from falling as she remembered back to how it used to be. The stone hexagon shaped fountain was still in the same place as it was when she was there. The water still flowed through it, but it looked all wrong, it was now surrounded by the lights and the noise. The village was so quiet back then. The only light came from torches outside of homes or from the moon. But the breeze that brushed past her face was still the same. That same mountain air that touched her face as she stood tied to the burning stake. Rhiannon couldn't control it any longer, tears turned to anger. She raised both arms and arched her hands. Sparks shot out, sending fireworks above her. Then she whipped them like illuminated ribbons toward the building in front of her and where once stood the store where she'd first met Evan and Elizabeth. The roof exploded and sent it high into the sky. Rhiannon sighed deeply and a smile returned to her face. That was better. Another flick of her hand and the building on the other side of the road, now a small bank, but what used to be the site of the inn, went up in flames.

She virtually glided through the darkened side street. From where she had started her walk, she could just about map out where her cottage used to be. She was curious to see what stood there now.

She began to recall parts of the village. The path she was taking was also there when she walked to the village and back again. Funny how some things were lost and others remained. An explosion made her turn and laugh. If only those puritans could see what she was doing today. Of course she was a witch, but she wasn't a bad one. They could have all benefitted from her powers if they'd only given her a chance. She should have turned them all to ash when she could. She stroked her stomach; she would have made a good mother. And a good wife to Evan, if he'd left that shrew of a wife. She carried on walking to a clearing and saw that just beyond would have stood her cottage. Today it was empty. Nothing but a grassy area. The orchard was gone too. The only thing that remained familiar to her was the mountains that she'd tried to reach before they came for her.

Rhiannon clenched her fist in anger. It may have been four hundred years ago, but to her, the memory was still as fresh. With a sneer she turned, stretched out her arm, pointed to a small semi-derelict building and blew it up.

****

The chapel shook with the last explosion as Mari ran inside to see John rushing to the door. "I expected you sooner."

"He did it to me again," said Mari sounding angry and pissed off.

"Who?"

"Simon. He said he was going to get the book so I could give it to Rhiannon, but he climbed out of a window and he's gone again. And she's going to destroy this whole town if we don't find that spell."

John shook his head. "I'd find it a lot easier if you called it a prayer like Joseph did. I can only imagine his horror at having to prepare for this prayer knowing what they had all done to her and what they were now making him do."

"It's like they believed there was a difference, eh? They killed Rhiannon because they said she was a witch and then here they were in this very chapel, asking their pastor to perform something that, let's face it, wasn't anything short of witchcraft themselves."

John flicked through the pages again to find the chant. "It's in Latin."

"We know that," said Mari joining him again. "Can you do it?"

"I can try. I have the items that are needed. We need another jar, something to hold her soul in."

Mari looked around and in the corner, under one of the other statues, was a silver box. "How about that over there?" she pointed.

"That's an heirloom, been in this chapel for centuries." John insisted with a frown.

"It looks strong and the best part is that it's most likely soaked in all that holy prayer that's gone on over the years. Better than any holy water, although we'll be using lots of that too." She walked over to inspect the box closer. "It even has a lock! We can seal it tight. It's silver all the way around. It's perfect."

"Not real silver, just coated."

"It's perfect," Mari said again. "You find the 'prayer' and get all the things you need for it. I'm going to find her and bring her here."

"Where will you find her?" asked John.

"She seems to find me," Mari said and smiled. "But I have the feeling she's going home, so that's where I'm going first. I know the area where her cottage used to stand so she might not be too far from that. But somehow, I'll find her." She pointed at her head.

"Apparently, we're linked so we can both read each other's minds and I'm having a problem with that."

****

Mari wasn't wrong. On the outskirts of the town was an open field. Over the years, the town had tried to build on the land, but for some reason, the buildings never proved to be very stable. It seemed that the only things that wouldn't wither and die around that area were flowers, roses, marigolds and violets, just like the ones that surrounded Rhiannon's cottage.

As she approached the grassy area, and even though it was dark, she could just make out a figure sat on one of the benches. To Mari, Rhiannon always seemed to be in complete control. She was headfast and determined to get her revenge, but this evening Mari saw a woman who seemed beaten and alone.

"I knew I'd find you," said Mari. "I didn't know how, I just did."

Rhiannon raised her head and touched her forehead. "That little bit of witch, eh?" She gave a little smile that soon disappeared. "My cottage was here. Right over there." She pointed to a nearby plot of land with nothing on it except a few small remnants of a ruined old wall. "Over there was an orchard. The fruit that grew there made the best jams and pies and it extended far back beyond the boundary. And behind it there were a few acres of fields that ended up near the mountain path." She sighed and stared out. "I can remember it all as if it were yesterday. My garden was full of vegetables and flowers. I grew them and never used the craft on them— well maybe not as often as I could have." She smiled as she looked up at Mari again. "I couldn't use it too often really… it would have given away what I was."

"But they found out anyway," said Mari sitting beside her.

"They only found out because of a jealous wife, not because I used the craft, and they didn't even have proof, just her ramblings and insinuations. I finally found a village that I could settle and rest in. I made potions from the herbs in my garden and gave it to those that their physician said would die. I saved them."

"And you fell in love? I can relate..." Mari said softly. "It doesn't always go the way you want it to."

"Evan," Rhiannon said in a whispered voice. She closed her eyes and smiled. "I loved him so much." She faced Mari, "I didn't set out to do that when I came here. I never ever in all my years come close to loving a mortal, it took me by surprise. We met in the general store one day and then he passed by the cottage on his horse as I was attempting to lift a tree trunk from the garden. He helped remove it. Then he came to help with my garden and it was nice at first to have some company. I gave up a lot of my magic for him so I wouldn't be discovered, so we could stay together," said Rhiannon sadly and almost tearfully she added, "And then he watched me burn. They all watched me burn. And you think that I should have compassion for those who live now?"

"But it's not their fault that their family did that."

"I could have had a family. I could have finally been happy. Do you know how many generations you can live, but be alone? My child could have lived to breathe the air, to grow and to love. But instead, my newborn was dragged through the dirt and left for the wolves. I hate them all!" she screamed. "My revenge is long overdue."

"It doesn't make it right Rhiannon, surely you know that. Those that did this to you should have been punished back then."

"Hatred follows down the bloodline. I cursed this village and I will destroy it as they did me."

"And then what?" asked Mari, standing to face Rhiannon. "What good will it do? Will it bring back the life you had? Will it bring back Evan? Will it make your soul rest?"

Rhiannon shrugged. "You know, it just might."

"You're wrong. It was a dark time back then for women who made potions," said Mari. "It was no different in other parts of the world, the amount of hysteria brought about by vengeful people. But it's a different time now." She hoped that some reasoning would change Rhiannon's mind. "In America, not long after you, they had a terrible time accusing women of witchcraft. The Salem Witch Trials are famous and people study the whole era."

Rhiannon smiled. "Things have moved on a lot since I left."

Mari smiled. "You blow hot and cold. One minute I sympathise with you and the next—"

"I still have things I need to do," interrupted Rhiannon.

"But those people don't exist anymore." insisted Mari. "See, that's why there's no need to do what you're doing. You have to stop. You have to give—"

Rhiannon interrupted Mari again. "I have to do what I have to do. And you have to do what you have to do. But I will do as my curse was set. And there is nothing you can do." She looked at Mari, her face stern. "And I wouldn't even try if I were you."

"Why? What is it that you can do to me? Because you've already tested that and it didn't work remember? You managed to destroy a few pieces of china in my apartment."

Rhiannon sighed. "You are right, I cannot harm you. I am bound to you for releasing me."

Mari smiled - a small victory perhaps.

Rhiannon shrugged and nodded. "But don't think that I cannot harm those around you." She raised her eyebrows and smiled. "There are always other ways to hurt you."

"What if I could tell you a few things, especially this one thing that you will not believe of what happened to some of those that you knew?" asked Mari quickly. "Those that harmed you."

"Like what? Can you tell me what happened to my Evan? Did he have a good life after I was taken? Did he live a long life without me?"

"He disappeared."

"What? How?" asked Rhiannon, and the softness in her voice had returned.

"There is no record of him after your death. I've searched every register of every town and there is no mention of him. The journals that Joseph Johnson wrote said that he'd gone. He disappeared that night and was never seen again. Joseph Johnson suspected that he took off into the mountains and died or was eaten by wolves or something, but he never came back. Or he could have just changed his name, not wishing to be part of what happened here."

"I saw him through the flames as I cried out. It would have been the last thing I saw, if it wasn't for his shrew of a wife Elizabeth. Tell me, do you know what happened to her?"

"I do, yes. She's buried in the chapel cemetery. I can take you to her if you want to see her grave."

"Did she die a most painful death?" Rhiannon scowled. "I hope that she did."

"Well, I'm not too sure, because the entry in the journals didn't really say too much, but she did die of a disease that seemed to eat away at her throat. These days, we call it throat cancer and I guess back then without drugs, yes, it would have been excruciatingly painful."

"Would you think it was as painful as feeling your own flesh burn off you? Or having the smell of your hair enter your throat to choke you as it charred?" asked Rhiannon.

"Well I'm not too sure. But I believe it would have been a very painful death and she wasn't very old either. There isn't much written about too many people in this town from back then."

"Then I can at least have some comfort that it happened that way to her."

"I can just show you her grave." said Mari quickly. "Do you want to see it?"

"Yes," said Rhiannon standing up quickly. "Yes. I would. Let me dance upon her grave."

Mari hoped that by getting Rhiannon to follow her, she could get her inside the chapel and then John could recite the prayer and trap Rhiannon. As they got closer, Mari saw John look out of the window and just as they were about to step through the gate, Rhiannon stopped.

"I cannot," she said, catching her breath.

"It's just over there." Mari pointed. "You wanted to see it," Mari insisted.

"I do want to see it. I just can't pass through the gates, I couldn't before. It's consecrated ground and I am prevented from entering." She looked up at the chapel. "This was the first thing I wanted to burn down when I came down from the mountain, but I'm glad I wasn't able to. The pastor was very good to me and he was the only one who stood up and asked them to stop on that night."

"It was his journals that led me to you. He was plagued with guilt after it happened."

"It wasn't his doing. He may not have tried very hard, but at least he did try."

"I have something to tell you," began Mari. "He didn't just speak up for you he—"

"I've wasted enough time!" Rhiannon interrupted her sternly. "It is time to put an end to all of this."

And then she was gone.

"Damn her," said Mari as she walked through the iron railings. She entered the chapel to find John at the altar, surrounded by candles, incense, a silver cross, the box, holy water and the book, opened at the verse.

John had his eyes closed, his arm outstretched as he began to speak from the book, *"De profundis tenebrarum, et quaerite in anima—"*

"Stop!" shouted Mari. "Stop, stop she's not even with me."

Mari hurried down the aisle toward John. "What happened?" he shouted, "I saw you both talking outside."

"It's consecrated ground. Because of the prayer that trapped her, she can't enter anywhere like this. We'll have to do it somewhere else."

"But it says to do this on consecrated ground. How can we do it if she can't enter?"

"I don't know" said Mari. "I really don't know."

"Did you tell Simon who he was?"

"No," said Mari. She sat beside him. "I was going to and then I thought I should tell Rhiannon first. But she stopped me just as I was going to tell her everything and he's gone too, so the secret is still that."

"What was the logic in telling her first? He has the grimoire and if he knew how they were related, he might just stop and help us get rid of her. Being related, he may have inherited some sort of... I don't know... magic down the line?"

"Or knowing him, he'd use it to gain her trust and make it a hell of a lot worse for all of us here," Mari said, raising an eyebrow.

"We can't sit on this information. She's gaining revenge on people who had nothing to do with all of those back then."

"Don't you think I know that?" snapped Mari.

"*If* she knew that her heir was alive, she might just stop."

"It's not just about the baby," said Mari. "It's about everything. She was murdered in such a horrific way. That memory is as clear to her as if it were yesterday." Mari paused and took a deep breath, "Because to her it was yesterday."

John placed his head in his hands and brushed his hair back. He stood up and faced Mari. "If we don't share this information, she's going to keep killing and burning down this town. Instead of sympathising with her for what they did to her, let's remind her that they are all dead now and that she has family in this present day, and then pray to God that it's enough until we find a way to really stop her."

Mari stood and faced John. "I have to find Simon. He needs to know the truth, whatever happens."

CHAPTER THIRTY-TWO

Rhiannon knew just where to go next. Being linked to Mari wasn't all that bad, after all. Simon had headed back to the cabin and barely had time to get up from his chair before Rhiannon forcefully opened the door and entered the room.

"Rhiannon, I assume?" asked Simon getting up from the floor. "Mari told me all about you, but I didn't believe her."

Rhiannon came closer. "Yes, you have similar eyes, but I see nothing else. You have my grimoire?"

"I do," said Simon. "But before I let you know where I've hidden it, I need a few" —he paused— "'assurances' that I will be rewarded."

"You dare ask that of me!" shouted Rhiannon. "Do you not know what I can do to you?"

"I do, but the problem with that is that you'll never find your book if you do anything to me." He grinned and walked around Rhiannon. "So, here's the deal."

Rhiannon stood stunned by his request, but silently she listened.

"My grandmother used to tell me about you. Although I think the stories about your beauty were greatly misguided."

Rhiannon eye rolled. "I do not need to hear your compliments."

"Fine," replied Simon. "Here's the deal. I can take you to your grimoire right now. But I want a few things answered before I tell you what my reward should be."

"Just talk!" said Rhiannon, frustrated. "In four hundred years, men have not changed, always wanting something, never wanting to give—"

Simon interrupted. "OK, well I want to know this one thing first. You are a powerful witch, why do you need the grimoire? What's in it that you need?"

Rhiannon faltered for a moment. "You think my grimoire is nothing but a book of magic. You can find a spell and all that you dream of will come to you. But the grimoire can do much more. In it lay the souls that I took. Those that can be placed at the altar of Mother Morrighan and I can have their years. I do not wish to go back into the darkness. And it also has a spell that I can use to reunite souls and I wish that very much."

"But the book does have spells to do other things, right?"

"Of course, but it depends on what you want and why you want to use it. Spells do not cast if the energy around you is false."

"What does that mean?" asked Simon quickly.

"You really are a foolish mortal." Rhiannon grinned.

"And you're a foolish witch without a grimoire, begging some foolish mortal for it back!" snapped Simon. "So, here's what I propose. I want you to cast a spell so that my powers are heightened. You can't feel them because the grimoire has most of your magic too. But I've read some of it. I know what happens to witches who haven't used their full power from the grimoire for a while. I want you to get my powers to full potential and then I want you to cast so that I can do more."

"Foolish *and* greedy," said Rhiannon turning to face Simon. She took out a small bottle from her pocket and held it tight in her hand.

"What does it matter to you if I'm able to cast too? You'll be gone with your resurrected lover and what I do in this world won't be relevant to you," Simon added.

"Because the world doesn't need your kind of magic." Rhiannon raised her hand and pointed.

Simon froze. He stretched out his palm. "Stop! Whatever you're going to do, stop and think. I've hidden it somewhere and you'll never find it. Without me, it's gone forever."

Rhiannon began with a whisper. *"Hen felltithion a drosglwyddwyd i mi. Tyrd â'i enaid a'i gorff ataf. Boed i eiriau natur rwymo'r dyn hwn nes bydd un arall yn ei ystyried yn deilwng.* Ancient curses passed to me. Bring forth his soul and his body. Let the words of nature bind this man until another think him worthy."

A green glow surrounded Simon, paralysing him. The light wrapped itself around him, swirling around his legs and rising to his head. It entered into him via his mouth and his eyes turned green before exiting through his nostrils. Rhiannon opened the bottle and Simon turned into a vapour, his body form disappeared and he entered it.

"A man is a man is a man," said Rhiannon rocking her head from side to side. She brought the bottle closer to her face. "You never change and perhaps someday you will realise that I'm not a witch who bargains."

Rhiannon looked around the room. Just where had this foolish man hidden her grimoire? She opened the drawers of the Welsh dresser, the cupboards, and then went into the bedroom. She looked through the bookshelves, throwing the books onto the floor and overturning all that was in her way.

She calmed herself down, took in a deep breath and closed her eyes. If the grimoire was close, she hoped that she would sense it. But nothing came to her.

She screamed, trying to concentrate, to centralise herself, but the noises of the town filled her head. This century was too noisy. She forcefully knocked herself into the wall as if willing her soul to remember how it felt to be near it. "You have to feel it, Rhiannon!" she shouted. "It's here, you know it's here!"

Mari ran through the open door to see Rhiannon holding a small bottle in her hand. "Where is he?" she shouted. "What have you done?"

Rhiannon looked pleased at her little capture as she lifted the bottle and gave it a shake. "Why do you still care about him? He's done nothing but fight against you. He left you in the cavern after he bedded you and then he took the book—my book. And the stupid man wanted to make a bargain with me. Me! Nothing has changed even in this century. They are still all the same."

"Not all the same!" screamed Mari. "You put him in a bottle?"

Rhiannon gave her widest grin yet. "My greatest pleasure since my awakening."

Mari shook her head. "Listen, I found out something important today that you should know."

Rhiannon shrugged. "About what?"

"Your child, he didn't die," Mari blurted it out. "He didn't die."

Rhiannon's smile disappeared. "I do not understand your humour, it is cruel and it is cold."

"I'm not joking. Your child. Yours and Evan's. He didn't die that night."

"He?" Rhiannon walked over to Mari, and glared into her eyes. Face to face, she added, "How could you know what it was? My child was torn away from me and left for the wolves to feast on!" She threw the bottle onto a chair where it bounced once and then teetered on the edge. "My child was left in the dirt, with my blood still over it."

Mari kept one eye on Rhiannon and the other watched as the bottle rolled off the chair onto the floor. It didn't break, but she had to make sure that Rhiannon wouldn't get it again. "Your child didn't die, Rhiannon, he lived. It was a boy. You had a little boy."

"No, I heard the cries as they dragged me away," insisted Rhiannon.

"He was found. He didn't die. I can help you. I can help trace the line down the years."

Rhiannon was silent. She stopped looking at Mari and just stared into the distance. Mari took her chance and kicked the bottle under the table.

"The farmer?" asked Rhiannon turning around quickly. "He came out of the darkness as I was running. I thought he left us when he saw the villagers surround me. I never thought that…" She looked at Mari. "Did he find him? Did he take him?" Rhiannon's face changed to relief, happiness, almost excited. Her smile widened for the first time since she had been awakened.

"They named him 'Llyr.' It was written in the journal that they buried with Joseph Johnson."

"But how did you find it?" asked Rhiannon.

"We dug him up," said Mari raising an eyebrow. "We dug him up so now you don't have any reason to keep killing or destroying this town."

Rhiannon stepped closer. "Oh, but I do. Either way, they burnt the flesh from this body."

Mari groaned. "Four hundred years ago! These people who are related are only that—related. It's not them."

"I don't care." Rhiannon smiled. "They took my life."

"You took theirs," Mari insisted. "Don't tell me those men whose souls you captured, deserved it."

"What if I told you they did? What if I told you that each and every one had done something bad in their life or something bad was happening to them that made their souls cry out to me and that is why they were picked. One beat his wife, another was in pain and he was suffering and he kept his illness from his family. I ended it, so none would suffer."

"I'd still say it was wrong."

"Well to you perhaps, but to them I gave peace and to me it gave me years that I could have used."

"You did it for you!" insisted Mari.

"Of course. And for Mother Morrighan, the more souls I gave her, the happier she was and would grant me new life."

"If you stop hurting people, I'll help you find anyone that is your family. I promise."

"I can find them myself." Rhiannon scowled.

"And how are you going to do that? You didn't even know you had one until just now. And what if you've already started to hurt them and you didn't even know? Have you even thought that what you're doing might have them caught up in it? You won't find them without me and I won't help you unless you promise to stop destroying this town."

Rhiannon was suddenly face to face with Mari again. "You dare threaten me? The things I could do with a wave of my little finger. Are you not afraid?"

"Terrified," replied Mari, "but I can't let you keep hurting people."

Rhiannon stared into Mari's eyes, and with a scowl she disappeared.

Mari's phone rang. "Hello?"

"I think I've found something else," said John.

"I'm on my way to you now," answered Mari

****

John flicked through the journal again. He read and then re-read the passage from Joseph Johnson.

'Today, four members of the village came to see me in this chapel. Sion Evans, Emyr Roberts, Alwyn Creu and James Clwyd, have told me of the curse upon this village and that they have obtained a prayer…'

John stopped reading, "The men that died this week, their surnames were Roberts and Creu. She's seeking them all out one by one," he said out loud and returned to read the rest of the book.

"…of their own, that has to be performed and then to bind the bones of Rhiannon Turner so that her curse can be lifted and imprison her soul forever. I admit that I am uneasy performing such a task. But they are insistent that only I can perform it. And that I don't have much time to prepare for it. To me, it seems ironic that they have burnt a suspected witch and yet they are asking me to recite a prayer that is not, in my eyes, holy. Even if it came from the Pope himself, this is not an earthly prayer they ask me to perform. But I feel that if I do not grant their wishes, consequences may befall my family… even to this chapel and also to me. I have agreed to their demand and will study this Latin prayer and perform the ceremony as instructed.'

John turned the pages over and there was written a Latin verse,

'Ex tenebris lumen fulgere exusta sit anima, imo surgere.

In cordibus nostris per caritatem, quae tenet, maneat necesse est quae a vita non abscondam.
Uires uentum tenet per ignes occidit animam.
Fructum dedit potestátem ligándi anima ex omnibus Rhiannon Turner aeternum et cetera, non ex malo corde eius transtulit ea quae in hoc mundo.
Nos tenebris anima sua in abyssum inferni detrusisset, et ossa illius in hydria beatus.
Dominus custodiet animam tuam Dominus solus ne ea profugus usque ad iram judicare saeculum per ignem.
By the dark and the light, let the soul that burnt bright rise up from deep within.

By the love that holds our hearts, by the life that needs not hide.

By the wind that holds our strengths and the fires that killed the soul.

Bring forth the power to bind thy sister and the soul of Rhiannon Turner for all eternity and let not her heart rest from the evil that she has brought into this world.

We cast her dark soul into the abyss of hell and her bones into the blessed jar.

Let only the Lord they God guard her restless soul until the wrath of judgement be upon us.'

'The deed is done and whether this has worked or not, I see that a peace has come back to this village. The very next day, the heavy air that engulfed us all has been lifted and if this was a prayer to revoke her curse, it has worked. Her bones have been sealed inside a Buckley jar that belonged to James Clwyd and four of the villagers—Sion Evans, Emyr Roberts and Alwyn Creu—have taken the jar and some of the possessions found in Rhiannon's cottage up into the mountains where it will be buried forever. This will be the last entry in this journal. It will be hidden and buried with me on the day of my death. I pray to the Lord that she is never found, for her wrath will be severe on this village. - Joseph Johnson 16th November 1684.'

John sat back and sighed. Just what had he gotten himself into? The chapel door slammed behind Mari as she entered and almost threw him out of the seat in shock.

"Sorry," said Mari as she approached. "I didn't mean to scare you. What have you found?"

"You were right. The villagers did go to Joseph and ask for his help. The verse that they were given could only be recited by a pastor and in a holy place. He wrote it all down and so that no one else would use it, he hid this journal by having them bury it with him."

"That's great!" said Mari smiling. "But why aren't you happy?"

"Two things. First is the one thing that stands out the most with all of this. This so-called prayer was—" He faltered for a moment.

"Was what?" asked Mari.

"Well when it was recited, she was already dead at the time," said John, "So is this prayer supposed to kill her? What if it doesn't?"

"I think more than anything it's to capture her soul, her essence of life. Without that, she is as good as dead. What's the second?"

"Consecrated ground. She couldn't enter it, remember? We have to do it here."

"I know, but we'll have to think of that when the time comes. She's going to continue to kill people who are related to the ones that burnt her and we can't let her carry on doing that. And she's punishing this town for something that happened hundreds of years ago by doing what they did to her, setting fire to it. Do you want her to continue?"

"No," said John, "of course I don't."

"Then let's keep reading and find out what we'll need to do this prayer and where we can perform it away from here. Because if we don't, this town is going to be gone and so are the other family members of those who killed her."

****

Mari didn't know where to start. She didn't know the town at all, apart from her accommodation, the church and the cabin. She walked around the streets. It all resembled a scene from a film. Sirens on vehicles blasted past her, the smoke from the now extinguished buildings lingered in the air, giving little respite to the smell, cars heading in different directions screeching to a halt every now and again and the skies were still dark. Mari tried to think of just where Rhiannon would go and hide. And a mental picture entered her head. Rhiannon was sitting in an open space.

Mari closed her eyes and could see the surroundings. It was a park not far from the cabin that she'd passed on several occasions. She hurried toward it.

The open air was a blessing from the smell of the burning buildings behind her. As she neared the play area, she saw the back of a figure on one of the swings. Rhiannon was there alone with her head leaning on the chains.

"You've found me again," she said. "Still linked."

"Is all of that your doing?" asked Mari standing in front of her. "The fires?"

"It is." Rhiannon didn't move, didn't even look up.

"Why!" shouted Mari. "Don't you think what you've done so far is enough? Can't you just accept that you are here now and they are gone?"

"I wish I could say yes to you. But I can't. My heart is vengeful and I cannot stop. My soul has been in the darkness for centuries and I must fulfil my curse, it is the way."

"Well you can't exist this way!" Mari yelled at her again. "Look at me."

Rhiannon looked up at her and Mari saw that she'd been crying.

"This place used to be my life." Rhiannon began, she looked around the play area, "This is nice here. The children can play and be free."

"I bet it was idyllic back then, when you were here."

"It was," Rhiannon smiled half-hearted, but still a smile. "I don't care to tell you how I acquired my cottage. It was mine and I loved it. I had several of the men from the village pass by my gates often waiting for an invitation, but I only ever let Evan enter. His cruel wife, his barren jealous wife, she..." Rhiannon's tears returned. She abruptly stood up and faced Mari. "That wife couldn't keep her mouth shut. She started with a few rumours told to those hags in the village and then it all happened from there. They were wicked days. A child of nature would never survive if accused of the craft and she knew that."

"Is that what you are? A child of nature?"

"I am whatever you wish to call it."

"Did Evan care what you were?"

"He didn't know. But he sided with his wife until the day I was to be sentenced and he came to free me from the prison."

"He came to help you? That's how you escaped? I did wonder. Then, why were you captured and punished, but he wasn't?"

"He didn't come with me and you forget, I was charged with bewitching him, so everything that he did, everything he said, was against his will, which made him innocent of everything. And even though he was happy to lie in my bed, he was steadfast to his marriage and that meant that he would not leave his wife. But he had such guilt, because he knew he'd broken the vow he was so adamant in keeping. I feel that he understood helping in my escape would free his heart of that guilt."

"I wonder if it did help him?" asked Mari.

"I hope he suffered as I did," Rhiannon said harshly.

"I guess we'll never know, but if he did die, he was never buried next to his wife. He could be anywhere, he could have even died up on that mountain you were trying to get to."

"Good, let his soul be restless," Rhiannon replied, but then added sadly, "but I loved him. I really did love him and I know he loved me too. If I could just have one moment with him again… I would… My grimoire would do that, you know." She closed her eyes and breathed in the evening air. Her eyes opened widely again as she proclaimed, "But I cannot forget that he watched me burn and did nothing. That they all watched me burn. And you think that I should have compassion for those who live now?"

"Yes I do, because it's not their fault that their families did that to you."

"I could have had a family too. I could have finally been happy instead of being fearful and running away from everyone. Do you know what it's like to be chased from village to village? To live in fear that someday your gift will be discovered and used to aid wars? My sisters have fallen into that trap. If you do as they ask of you, you live. If you don't, you...don't." She paused and sniffed at the fragrant air that passed her. "My child could have lived with me to breathe the air, to grow and to love. But instead my newborn was dragged through the dirt and left for another to raise. My revenge is long overdue."

"It was wrong, I get it, but what you're doing doesn't make it right either Rhiannon, surely you know that. Those that did this to you should have been punished back then. Don't punish anyone now for the sins of their ancestors."

Rhiannon stayed silent for a moment then looked up. "I promised while tied and burning on that stake that I would wipe them all out and I have to adhere to my promise. And if it is the kin of their blood, then that will be punishment enough." And then she disappeared.

Mari groaned. "Crap, I hate it when she does that." She took out her phone and called John.

"What's happened?" he asked

"She put Simon in a bottle."

"She did what?"

"She put him in a small bottle. But on the plus side, she didn't find the grimoire."

"How do you know?"

"She said Simon tried to do some sort of deal with her."

"He sounds like a real prince. Where is he now?" asked John.

"I left him in his cabin. He wasn't going anywhere. I kicked him under the chair."

"Harsh." John laughed.

"He deserved it. I'm going to get him now."

"So, what's our next move?"

"Well, Simon would have hidden it somewhere close. It's got to be at the cabin somewhere so I'm going back to look for it. I'll talk to you later." And she cut the call off.

****

The door was open when Mari reached Simon's cabin. She looked around the room, walked over to the armchair and got on her knees to look under it. The bottle was just within her grasp so she reached in and brought it out. She picked it up and looked closely at the flickering bright green light inside of it. "Oh God, Simon, she really did put you in a bottle?" The flame flickered higher in the bottle. Mari stifled a laugh. "Well it serves you right if it is you." She continued, "Did you really think you could hide the book from her? You can be so thick sometimes." Mari held the bottle in her hands. Did she really want to release Simon? Could he ever be trusted? She gave the bottle a little shake. "That's for leaving me in that cavern," she said smiling. The glow inside it turned a lighter green and then came back to the brighter deeper green. "Oops, sorry." She shrugged. "Didn't actually think you'd feel that, but then...I was hoping you would." And she gave it another, smaller shake.

She placed the bottle on the table and stared at it. "So how do I get you out?" Mari stroked her chin. "Pretty sure the book would let me know if only I knew where you'd hidden it." She looked around the room. "You're shit at hiding anything, so let's see if I can find it before Rhiannon comes back." Just before Mari started her search, her mobile phone rang.

It was John again. "Where are you?" he asked.

"I'm in the cabin that Simon was using. I thought I'd come back and see if I could find the book. It has to be around here."

"Maybe Rhiannon has already taken it?" said John.

"No, she would have said. And we would definitely know. It's here somewhere. I just have to figure out where."

"Do you need any help?" asked John.

"Yes, I think I do."

****

John arrived less than half an hour later. "So where have you looked?"

"This main room, the three bedrooms, the cupboards, under the bed...you name it, I've looked for it."

"Maybe you need a fresh pair of eyes to go over everything," said John sighing as he looked around. "Shall I start in here? Shall we just both start in here and double check all the drawers and cupboards?"

Mari nodded and they both got to work, opening deep drawers and slamming them shut. Cupboards were emptied of their contents and some of it was thrown over the floor. Paintings were lifted from against the walls in case any secret nooks were hidden behind them, but nothing.

"OK," said John, "let's start in that bedroom and work our way across."

Mari lifted the mattress off the double bed and brushed her hands over the base of the bed. She looked under it, feeling for anything that could have been hidden under the base. John checked the wardrobes—in them, on them, and behind them. The chest of drawers had a few of Simon's clothes in them, but nothing else. Then they moved onto the second bedroom and did the same, and again for the third. Mari looked in the bathroom, behind the toilet cistern, inside the toilet cistern and even behind the wash hand basin.

As she left the bathroom, John left the third bedroom. "Anything?" he asked.

"No, nothing. It can't be here, where else would he go?"

"Come on," said John. "Let's sit down in the kitchen for a minute and rethink where we can go next. I'll even put the kettle on." He smiled.

Mari sat at the kitchen table and looked around at the mess. "Should we clean up before we go?" she asked.

John switched off the kettle and looked around. "Maybe we can say it's Simon's mess?" He grinned.

Mari started with a small laugh. "And you a pastor, telling lies." From which then erupted a full belly laugh. "Maybe we could shake it out of him." She pointed at the bottle that still sat on the table top.

John handed her a mug of tea and sat down. He looked around the room, grimacing at the mess. "They're not bad, these cabins."

"Yeah, they look OK, if you like that sort of thing."

"I remember when this land was derelict. In the past they used it to store grain from the farms in the area. I used to play in and out of the old sheds with my friends."

Mari looked puzzled. "You're from this area? I didn't know."

"I moved away when I was eighteen, did a bit of travelling and then decided to get into the clergy."

"How did that happen?" asked Mari.

"I don't know, it just did. When I was qualified, they gave me this assignment and I was fine with it. I was coming home, after all."

Mari stopped mid sip. "Yeah, I bet that was a surprise, to end up back where you started." Then she stopped talking. "Hang on, this whole area? This whole area was industrial?"

"Yes, but more agricultural. This was farming country remember, but that seems to have declined over the years and new office buildings have taken the place of what was here before," said John. "They cleared it out and filled in a lot of it and then this whole area became a holiday complex."

"Filled in?"

"Yes, the grain was stored underground..." And then the penny dropped as they both stared at each other open-mouthed.

"He's found somewhere underground," said Mari excitedly. She jumped out of the chair. "OK, there has to be some sort of opening." She started to stamp her feet. "It has to be here somewhere. It's not a big space."

The flooring was wooden and varnished. Each panel locked into the other. None of them seemed out of place. The living room area was the same as were the bedrooms. "Damn it!" said Mari. "I was starting to get excited. There isn't anything like that in here."

"In here maybe not"—John pointed outside—"but outside?"

"You are a genius!" cried Mari and quickly opened the door. "It has to be somewhere close, if there is something like that. He'd want to keep an eye on it so it shouldn't be far."

The grounds were covered in fallen leaves. The beauty of having the cabins built near the woodlands at the start of autumn. Mari kicked away piles of leaves from the front while John did the same at the side of the cabin. Frustrated, she groaned. "There's nothing out here either. Where the hell did he…" and then she heard a hollow thud as she took another step. Smiling as John came close, she cleared the dirt away to reveal a small trapdoor.

The wooden door opened with a slight creek. "I have a torch in my car," said John leaving Mari to peer down into the darkness. "Let me go get it."

When he returned, they shone the light down into the dark cellar and onto stairs, and then they began to descend down them.

As in many underground rooms, the cold dampness surrounded them as they found their footing. John pointed the torch at the walls and the floors to see the size of the room. "I don't think this was ever a storage room," he said, breaking the silence. "It looks more like somewhere they'd hang meat to dry out. Maybe there was a cottage above us years back?"

"Can you see anything?" asked Mari.

"No, nothing that…" A crash made him stop.

"What was that!" screamed Mari.

John shone the light ahead and saw that he'd bumped into a small table and chair. "I bumped into a table." He walked around it, shining the light over it and then under it. "There's something under it," he added. "Hold this." He handed Mari the torch and dragged a wooden crate out from under it. He lifted the lid and inside was a carefully wrapped package.

"You know," Mari said, "if you weren't a pastor, you'd make a great archaeologist."

CHAPTER THIRTY-THREE

Mari and John sat in the living room of the cabin. She flicked through the pages of the grimoire. Because it was sensitive and ancient like any historic parchment, she gently turned over each page as she briefly scanned each one. Mari gave a loud sigh. "I don't understand any of it."

"Let me look," said John taking the book into his hands. "It looks like Latin, and maybe some ancient Welsh, both of which I can read." He looked up at an impressed Mari. "OK, maybe I can read some of it a little, but even the odd word here and there is better than nothing."

Both looked down at the pages and scanned for clues. The book was completely filled with incantations, but no hints in removing the spell that held Simon in the bottle.

"I'm not even sure he deserves to be let loose on this world," said Mari pouting.

"No one deserves to be imprisoned for no good reason, either."

"Well you would say that," said Mari quickly.

"Why?" asked John.

"Well being a pastor and all that. You're into this whole forgiveness thing."

"Then what are we doing here?" John closed the book and looked at Mari. "Do you think the things that Simon has done makes it all right for him to spend his life...have his soul captured in goodness knows where? And then for us to be looking for a way to imprison Rhiannon's soul too?"

"Well, if you put it like that, I guess not."

John opened the book again. "Good, now this section here might be what we're looking for. I can make out a few words but it speaks of capturing, gaining souls and then the words 'continens' and 'utrem' which are Latin for bottle or container. Perhaps we'd be better off with help from a translation book?"

Mari took out her phone., "Or an app?" She let her phone scan over the page. A minute or two later, a rough translation made her smile. John stood and held out his hand while Mari held the book open. Reciting the words over the bottle that was on the floor, he uttered,

"Sphaera lux tua donec penitus consumantur de terra. Sunt geminae cum eorum corpus aer et invenietis in domum lagenam tuam quam redemisti sua proven valet. Hanc ego nunc ostendo vobis ipsis non intrare, et impietatis servituti redacti ad verba haec locuta est mortale liberabo te in hunc mundum. Thy aura shall be consumed by the light of the earth. Thy body shall twin with the air and shall find home in thine bottle until thou has proven their worth. I command your very being to enter this chamber and be enslaved until these words are spoken to free you back into this mortal world."

With a flash of light and smoke, Simon appeared on the floor. "What happened?" he asked rubbing his head.

"Rhiannon happened," said Mari. "I told you not to read from her book."

"What did she do to me?"

"She put you in a bottle. She was going to suck out your soul for a snack later." Mari said smiling, almost laughing. "Personally, I wanted to keep you in there, but then John here has a conscience."

"Well thank you," said Simon. "I knew you didn't really hate me."

"See?" she said to John. "The arrogance?" She turned to Simon. "Oh, I really do hate you. Don't let this little rescue fool you," she said, pointing her finger at him, "But I didn't do it for you. I did it because, annoyingly, we need you." She threw him his coat. "Looks like she hates you as much as I do. But she doesn't know who you really are and I need to use you to let her know who you are so we can send her back."

"Who I really am?" asked Simon, appearing confused.

She stared at Simon as John approached him. "And you're going to help us or I swear on all my Bibles that I will find a way of putting you back in that bottle myself."

"Calm down, preacher man," said Simon raising his hands up. "I'm good. You lead the way and like the holy sheep, I'll follow."

****

A little while later, Mari sat in the cabin with Simon. They hadn't uttered a word to each other in an hour. John had returned to the chapel, taking the grimoire with him. He wanted to check a few facts out on the computer and church records he had, and it would be safer in a sanctified place, safe from Rhiannon. The wind began to pick up outside as Mari sipped her cup of tea and stared outside. The moon was out and there were so many stars. She missed all of that living in the city with the light pollution obscuring the magical sights of the universe.

Simon stood to the side of the table flicking his way through a travel magazine when the front door exploded, sending them both to the floor for cover. Smoke filled the room.

Rhiannon walked through the smoke and into the room. She looked surprised to see Simon standing there and raised her hand. "Did I not capture your soul?" With her index finger she pointed and was just about to speak when Mari shot up in front of him.

"No, you can't kill him!"

"Was he not the one who betrayed you?" asked Rhiannon without any emotion. "Why do you want to save him? Did he not defile you, use you? Did he not leave you in the cavern?"

"Yes, he did all those things. He's not a nice person, I know that," Mari answered with a shrug.

Simon looked at Mari as though amazed at her outburst. It was the first time his gaze had left Rhiannon. "I had a reason for everything that I did. It might not have been a good one to you, but it was important to me."

"Stay silent!" screamed Rhiannon.

"There's something you should know," said Mari.

Rhiannon lowered her arm. "What do I need to know?"

"It's about your child."

Rhiannon raised her arm again and pointed at Simon. "You're lying because you want to save him. Tell me what you know and I may spare him."

"He was taken by the farmer."

"You have told me that already." Rhiannon's hand began to shake. "If you have nothing else—"

"They raised him and he lived to a good age," interrupted Mari. "And then he had his own family who then they had a family. Some of them still live. Rhiannon, you *still* have family."

"And what does this person have to do with my family?" asked Rhiannon. She stepped closer to Simon, gazed into his eyes and then she must have seen it.

Rhiannon covered her mouth in shock. "He does haves my Evan's eyes. I saw it before, but didn't want to think of it." She gave Mari a look of utter shock.

"Yes, he might be the biggest shit of the century, but this man, the one you were just about to turn into dust, is your great, great, great, something or other, grandson."

The silence was quickly broken by John as he barged into the room. It took Rhiannon so by surprise that she didn't even retaliate when he doused her in holy water. *"In hac aqua Adiuro te.* With this water, I bind you."

Rhiannon covered her face, screamed and disappeared.

"Damn it!" said Mari. "Now what do we do?"

"I was thinking," said John. "You said she can feel the aura coming from the book so what if we use that to trap her?"

"Excuse me *padre,*" said Simon, "but how do you expect to do that? You know, her being a witch and all, that can obliterate you with a single wave of the finger?"

John didn't appear amused by Simon and seemed about to answer when Mari interrupted. "He's right though, how would we even do that?"

"We go to the cavern where she was left. We can put the book in a circle with the markings that were used to bind her. She will feel the book, but she won't be able to touch it. If we play this right, we can do the same for her. She may walk right into the bigger circle."

"And then what?" asked Simon.

"Then we read the same passage that Joseph Johnson had to read and hope that it does the same thing?" answered Mari.

"Exactly," John replied.

CHAPTER THIRTY-FOUR

John drew a circle big enough to surround the grimoire that he had wrapped in an altar cloth. He looked at the symbols in Joseph Johnson's book and began to sketch them out on the ground. Once they were done, he placed the unwrapped grimoire inside it and began to do the same with a bigger circle.

Mari studied the cavern as John drew a large pentagram on the floor and placed a few rocks that he brought from the graveyard, at each point. He poured a little holy water over them and blessed them.

Simon put his arm around her. "Ahh, remember the last time we were here? Together?" he asked, making sure that John could hear. "We were in each other's arms, just the two of us, naked."

Mari pushed him away, "Yes, I remember. See that pile of rocks over there? They're the ones I tried to use to climb out after you dumped me here! They're the same ones I might use to bash your pathetic head in if you even speak to me or touch me in any way while we're down here."

John smiled and carried on drawing the outline of the pentagram. He looked at the printed pages in his hand, laid them down around the pentagram and placed some smaller pieces of paper in the five wedges. "I think we're all set."

"How do we do this?" asked Simon. "How do we bring her here?"

"The grimoire," said Mari, "It'll do that."

John was hesitant. "Are you sure? I really don't want anything that'll end up helping her."

"I don't know why I even know that it will," Mari said with a confused look, "But I do. Sooner or later, she'll be here."

John uncovered the book in the middle of the circle and symbols and stepped back. It was a good few minutes before he uttered again, "Are you sure this'll work?" He poured a drop of holy water on the book and a scream filled the cavern. Smoke surrounded them all and Rhiannon appeared right in front of them.

She stared at each one, a long, glaring look as if she was trying to read their thoughts and was taken aback when she could not. She stood up, took a step toward the grimoire and saw the symbols on the ground. "Do you think these markings will hold me?" She took another step closer. "I will take my book and then I will be free. My reasons for staying in this town are gone. The bloodlines from those in the past are gone—extinguished. And the world beckons. I have a great need to see the rest of this world."

"We will not let you leave here!" shouted John. "Your time on this earth is over, Rhiannon Turner. You will be cast back into a chamber where your soul shall rest forever."

Rhiannon smiled. "Really? Is that what you think you're going to do? Do you think this pretty drawing will hold me here?"

"Maybe not without some help," said John. "But the stones from my chapel graveyard will. The holy water and prayers that I did on them, will. And the symbols that they carved into the walls to keep you here will. The only thing here keeping you safe right now is this pentagram. Everything outside it will turn you to a pile of dust."

Rhiannon saw Simon as he tried to stay out of her line of sight. "You are my kin. The things I could show you. There is magic in our family, the craft. I can show you the craft. All you ever dreamt about, all can be yours."

Mari shot a look at Simon and he took a step farther back into the shadows, silent, hiding.

Rhiannon's smile had all but disappeared. She looked at Mari. "Don't let him do this. You know what they all did to me. My revenge was justified."

"No, it wasn't," said Mari. "After all that I said to you about those people, you did it anyways. You killed some that weren't even related and you set half of this town on fire!"

"They set me on fire!" shouted Rhiannon. "So I did the same to them."

"They did in your time, but not the men you've killed here, in our time. Did you not realise what you were doing was wrong?"

"They murdered me and took my child."

"Your child was taken by the farmer who found him. Your son lived to a good age, brought up in a loving home."

Mari placed her hand on John's shoulder and turned him to face her. "You didn't tell me everything, did you? I can feel that there's something you're not telling me."

"Tis the magic we have between us," said Rhiannon. "I will share it all if you release me. I have no desire to stay here. No desire to hurt any of you. Or anyone else. I just want you to set me free."

John's gaze left Rhiannon and he focused on Mari. "Yes, I left a few parts out."

"Which parts?" Mari asked.

"I told you I was looking into the family. The church records in the crypt had more information and a few online sites had the rest of it."

"Yes, but you told me it was Simon who was a descendent."

"Well he is," John said slowly, "but there may have been just a small… absolutely necessary… omission of the whole truth."

"How much of an omission?" Mari queried.

John looked over at Simon who was already well hidden in the shadows and clearly did not want to be part of any of the proceedings.

John began to walk around the circle. He took a breath and faced them all. "Rhiannon, your son really was taken by the farmer as we have said. He lived a good life and had his own family. He and his wife had six children, and some left the village and went their own ways. The ones who stayed behind had families too." He paused. "I could go on but the truth is, when you follow the line down the generations, you get to Simon, and a few others, including me. I am a descendent of Rhiannon Turner and Evan Harding. I am of your blood."

Mari gasped.

Rhiannon's eyes widened as she glared at Mari and then at John. She pointed to Simon. "But he has the same…" She looked deep into John's eyes and asked "How can this be? How can it be that you both have his eyes?"

"Your bloodline had a very interesting outcome. One of your son's children had a son. And that son had twin boys, would you believe? Those siblings left this village and I guess they started their own bloodlines." John turned to face Simon. "But it looks like he and I are related." He looked back at Rhiannon, "We are your kin, both of us."

Off guard, she took a step toward him, just a small step outside of the centre circle of the pentagram and it sent her flying backwards with a hard bump to the ground and sent a bright silver snap of lightning into the floor that sent sand, earth and small stones into the air. With a growl, she glided onto her feet, stretched out her hands, closed her eyes and was about to speak.

John began to utter the prayer that he'd found, in a louder, more commanding voice. *"Hoc enim abjecti infernalis adversarii. Hoc igitur maledictus pythonissam propulsamus tibi. Creatura diaboli hostis hac sancta. Et humiliare sub potenti manu anima tua, et projiciamus a nobis Dominum Deum nostrum corpus tuum. Anima tua occultam esse a mundo salus est ad nos, et nos cedamus amori in Deum. O Domine, libera nos ab hac creatura suo, et populo terræ. O Domine libera animam meam hanc se ipso die rogamus vos. Animabus nostris custodire ab hoc malo et salvum satanas. Nos rogamus te per Deum. Nos rogamus vos in sanctis est. Nos te rogamus ac tenebras. Domine exaudi orationem meam et ait ad illam ut in custodia.* We cast out this infernal adversary. This cursed witch, we repel you. This creature of the devil, the enemy of this holy church. You will humble yourself under the mighty hand of our Lord our God and cast your soul from your body. Thy soul to be kept hidden from the world until salvation is upon us and we be judged by God. O Lord, deliver this creature away from our earth and its people. O Lord deliver her soul this very day we beseech you. Keep our souls safe from this evil of Satan. We beseech you under God. We beseech you under his holy word. We beseech you to the darkness. Lord, hear our prayer that it may be answered with her imprisonment."

Rhiannon fell silent, unable to speak. Auras from the chant met in the middle, an eerie fight of energy, one white, one blue. The cave lit up and the shadows disappeared. Simon stepped toward the grimoire and was pushed back by Mari. "Are you nuts? Let it finish first."

The intensity of the energy grew bigger as John continued to chant, "Nos rogamus te per Deum. Nos rogamus vos in sanctis est. Nos te rogamus ac tenebras. Domine exaudi orationem meam et ait ad illam ut in custodia. We beseech you under God. We beseech you under his holy word. We beseech you to the darkness. Lord hear our prayer that it may be answered with her imprisonment." His voice grew louder as Rhiannon was beaten back and eventually fell to the ground, exhausted.

"You are truly my descendent," she said finally, in defeat.

"I'm nothing to you and you are nothing but a reference in a book," John replied. *"Nos rogamus te per Deum. Nos rogamus vos in sanctis est. Nos te rogamus ac tenebras. Domine exaudi orationem meam et ait ad illam ut in custodia.* We beseech you under God. We beseech you under his holy word. We beseech you to the darkness. Lord hear our prayer that it may be answered with her imprisonment."

Rhiannon screamed out, "Today you think that. But soon our bloodlines will reveal what you are!" She looked over at Simon. "What you both are." She gazed over to Mari and to John and smiled. "You will take care of my family. I know you will. I see something between you both. I had that with Evan." She looked at John again. "It is time to go. Before I go, I would like to hold you in my arms as I would have my own son." She stretched out her arms and John didn't falter. For one brief moment, he forgot who she was, his compassion came forward and he took a step forward until Mari pulled him back

"Are you fucking insane?" she shouted.

Rhiannon screamed, "I should have killed you the minute I was released!"

"You couldn't, remember? We're linked."

"I could have broken the link if I'd thought hard enough, but you were my path to the outside." She lowered her head and began to utter a new chant. *"Mewn bywyd rwy'n rhydd...* In life I am free..."

Debris from the cavern began to lift and swirl around them. Simon ducked as a rock came within inches of his head.

John began his chant again, louder than before, interrupting Rhiannon into silence once more. *"Nos rogamus te per Deum. Nos rogamus vos in sanctis est. Nos te rogamus ac tenebras. Domine exaudi orationem meam et ait ad illam ut in custodia.* We beseech you under God. We beseech you under his holy word. We beseech you to the darkness. Lord hear our prayer that it may be answered with her imprisonment."

Mari joined in and they both sent a force of energy into the pentagram. *"Nos rogamus te per Deum. Nos rogamus vos in sanctis est. Nos te rogamus ac tenebras. Domine exaudi orationem meam et ait ad illam ut in custodia.* We beseech you under God. We beseech you under his holy word. We beseech you to the darkness. Lord hear our prayer that it may be answered with her imprisonment."

Rhiannon held it off with her outstretched hand until it began to burn into her palm. She screamed and lowered her hand as the bolt of energy hit her in the forehead and paralysed her.

"Open the box!" John shouted at Mari.

Mari scrambled around the floor looking for the silver box that they'd seen in the chapel and opened it.

"Throw it into the circle!" shouted John.

As the box landed on the ground, Rhiannon's form began to shine and become translucent. From the ground up, her body began to suck itself into the box and a strange fog began to settle inside it. Rhiannon began to scream, "Mari please, I can't go back! Why would you do this?" She stared at Mari and then at Simon. "He used you. You told me he had used you to find my grimoire."

"You still don't understand, do you?" Mari asked. "Compared to what you've done, what he did means nothing."

And then Rhiannon was gone.

Mari stepped inside the circle, closed the box and clicked on the small lock. "What now?" Mari asked, shrugging.

"Now we bury her in the crypt. We can find a place there that will be undisturbed. A place where no one will look because they'll not know there's something there to look for. We'll find a small corner, dig a hole, place her in it and then bury it again, even if I have to put a paving slab over it. If I bless it, it becomes consecrated and even if she was brought back again, she couldn't leave or this time she'll burn again."

"And the book?" asked Mari. "What do we do with it?"

"Let's put it back where it came from. It was safe there," said John.

Simon looked up to the cavern entrance. "It's getting light again," he said.

"That's because the curse is broken," said Mari. "Everything will get back to normal."

"It doesn't bring back the people she killed," said John, stepping away from the box.

A pang of guilt hit Mari. "But where's her justice?" she asked, turning to John quickly. "You know, all she really wanted was to live with the man she loved and have her baby. Those people took it all away. What she did was wrong I suppose, but—"

John placed his arm around Mari. "Those times were different. We've learnt from them, perhaps that's her justice and she just didn't realise it."

Mari pushed his arm off her shoulders. "Well, it's not good enough."

"You act as if she was an innocent. Didn't she kill in her time too?" argued John.

"She told me everything. The man whose soul she took would beat his wife, the others were sick and near dying, she saved a little boy but no one took that into consideration."

"That's not the case for the ones that she's killed in this town since her return. She wanted revenge and she got it, but now her time is over. You can either help with what we do next, or leave. Either way, this is how it has to be done."

Mari stood, unsure of why she felt angry. "Let's just get this finished."

Margarita Felices

CHAPTER THIRTY-FIVE

The grave of Joseph Johnson had remained undisturbed until John and Mari found clues to the whereabouts of a special book that had been buried with him. They spent one frantic afternoon digging in the dark and hoped that God forgave them—and Joseph Johnson too—but the need was too great.

John opened the coffin again, placed the book back in the skeletal hands of the pastor and closed what was left of the lid. He climbed back on to the top and blessed the body with holy water, adjusted the satin stole around his neck and kissed it. "Lord, we send our departed messenger back to you. We hope that he understands why we did what we did, and that he can now rest in peace—again." And he kissed the stole again.

Mari looked down before filling the shovel with earth to cover the coffin. Only when both had finished, did they turn to walk back into the chapel.

On the altar lay a box, ten inches by ten inches and five inches deep. Made of a light lead, the box contained the silver antique box. Rhiannon's aura was wrapped in an altar cloth that John had soaked in holy water. They were taking no chances that she could escape.

John picked up the box and carried it through the side door while Mari carried two shovels and then they both walked down the steps to the crypt.

The corner of a crypt in a chapel seemed like a sorry end to Rhiannon's story, thought Mari. When she started her research weeks before, she never envisaged that it would turn out like this. She had felt such a connection to Rhiannon. The trial notes broke her heart as she read of the injustice. If only Rhiannon had accepted the way things were these days, she was sure that she could have lived in some sort of normality and learnt so much. But here Mari was, spade in hand, digging another hole to bury a secret.

With a heavy heart, Mari placed the box in the hole and turned away while John covered it with dirt and then replaced the slab they'd forced up.

"You're still not happy about doing this are you?" asked John.

"No. No, I'm not. Listen," she said looking at him. "I get it. She was misguided in her revenge. But would you have let her stay if she hadn't killed anyone?"

"I don't know," John replied. He kicked around some dust from the area to make it less obvious they had been there and slid across an old stone plant pot that had been there since before he arrived. "It's your compassion for her story that grieves you more. She was a woman whose life was cut short and it is a terrible tragedy, but then so was what she did on her return."

"There was always a little sadness in her voice. Like part of her didn't want to do any of this, but she was driven by her promise that sort of ate away at her. But then, she'd remember it all, get angry and that's when she couldn't stop."

"And that's why we had to do, what we did. If we'd let her go, what do you think she would have done in our world? Adapted? She would have created havoc." He put the shovel up against the wall. "Where's Simon?"

"He's back in the cabin. This guy falls on his feet each time. He contacted a university in the States and told them about his 'witch' research and theories. They invited him to write a paper and visit to do a few touring lectures. He's finalizing everything now."

"But most of the research is yours," said John.

"He's promised to give me full credit this time," said Mari, smiling.

"Do you believe him?"

Mari smiled and scrunched up her nose. "No, not really, but we can only hope. What he doesn't know is that I've already emailed my notes to our university and they've been catalogued, so if he tries to use any of my research, he will get a nasty surprise."

"Sneaky," John said with a huge grin. "And the grimoire? What's happening to that?"

"It's safe. It's going to our university to be studied. Simon is taking some notes and pictures of it so he can use some of it for his paper. We have no idea of its power, so it needs to be studied. I'm hoping to head up the team that will do that. I'm also going to rewrite some of the stories surrounding Rhiannon and make sure that we're not too severe on her story."

"And you trust him to do only that? Just to take notes?"

"No of course not, so after we finish here, we'll be making a move."

"You're leaving?" John looked disappointed.

"Well yes, there's nothing to keep me here." She looked up at John. "Is there? Is there anything to keep me here?"

John leaned in close and kissed her. "Aberystwyth is not that far away."

Mari smiled and bit her lip. "No, it's not."

And kissed him back.

CHAPTER THIRTY-SIX

Mari didn't know what she was going to say to Simon. The whole point of their journey together was to research and write a paper in the hopes of becoming recognized in the field of ancient studies. And in particular, to one area that had been overlooked making the information that was available, inaccurate. But she had decided that she could write the paper without him being around. Her newly formed relationship with a pastor would just make him a distraction if he stayed. She was going to tell him that he should take that position in the USA and that they should write and edit the paper online instead.

The cabin seemed suspiciously quiet as she approached. She ran inside, "Simon?" she shouted, but no answer. She checked the kitchen and the bathroom, and then his bedroom. The wardrobe doors were open and the top drawer was empty of clothing. Simon had gone. "Bastard!" she shouted. "I should have left you in that fucking bottle." She looked around the living room and the grimoire was gone too. A small envelope on the table caught her attention.

"Oh, please tell me you've not..." said Mari opening it.

'Well by now," the letter began, "you'll have realised that I've gone and taken the book with me. It was never destined to be studied. Never meant to be dissected by scholars who didn't have the first clue as to what it really was and how it could be used by one whose bloodline once wrote in it. What you found out about my family was right (although the pastor part was a surprise). My grandmother always said we were related to a witch, and that we had powers. Rhiannon told me that the grimoire would help enhance whatever I had. So, by the time you read this, I'll be on a plane going somewhere. There's no point in looking because you see, I know how to use this book...and I will be using it!

I really did enjoy our time together—especially in the cavern. And if you hadn't been so distracted with your pastor, you might have noticed some of the clues I gave you that might have given my true intensions away. Fortunately for me that you didn't. So, until we meet again (although I hope it's never), I will say goodbye. Simon.'

"Shit, shit, shit!" screamed Mari. "Will I never learn?" She took out her mobile and scrolled, looking for a number. "John? The cabin's empty, he's gone."

"Who? Simon?" replied John.

"Yes, of course Simon..." said Mari with an eye roll.

"But he agreed that you were both going to write that paper together and have the university study the grimoire?"

"Yes, yes I know that..." Mari tutted.

"What are you going to do now?"

"I suppose I'm going to have to go after him..." said Mari taking a deep breath, "I can't let him use it and you know he'll try. What Rhiannon said about the book and what it's holding inside, it's not just a spell book and he mustn't be allowed to keep it. He doesn't really know what he's got hold of, what it can really do."

"Where are you going to start?" asked John.

"I don't know yet... but I was wondering... do you fancy a little road trip?"

ABOUT THE AUTHOR

MARGARITA FELICES

I live in Cardiff, Wales. It's home to castles, mountains, rugby, Doctor Who and Torchwood, with my partner and three little mad dogs and I work for a well-known TV broadcasting company.

I love living in Cardiff because even after all of its modernisations, there are still remnants of an old Victorian (and older) city.

When I can, I go out to the coast and take photographs. We have a lovely castle in the centre of Cardiff and a fairytale one just on the outskirts, so when I feel I can't write anything, I take a ramble to those locations and it clears my head.

I have a TV production background. I used to be a professional photographer and decided to move into the TV world. I started off working on our local news programmes and then moved on to Arts, Factual, Drama, back to Factual, back to Drama (Torchwood, Dr Who and a few regional shows) – a fascinating journey!

Now I work for the BBC National Orchestra or Wales and we produce some of the music for well known TV shows, Doctor Who for example! I've learnt so much from working there about Marketing and Promotions. It's been an absolute blessing when looking for ways to promote my work.

I suppose it was inevitable that someday I would begin to write novels.

My teachers at school used to limit me to no more than ten pages. I was a reporter on the school magazine and later became its Editor. When I left school, I paid my way through college by writing short stories for magazines. I later moved on to scriptwriting and came third in a BBC writing competition.

I am Gothic; I love the fashion, the architecture and the music. The club in my novel Judgement of Souls 3 is real. While writing it I got all of my club material and clientele ideas from there. I wouldn't have finished that section without it.

My first full length novel, Judgement of Souls 3: Kiss at Dawn was the first story written for the trilogy. I realized before it was finished that there was a great backstory that had to be told. So, after JOS3 was published I began to write Judgement of Souls 2: Call of the Righteous that concentrated on a 300 year history of my vampires and their search for the missing Book of Cain and it also introduced The Righteous, a secret organization started by the Church to find and kill all supernatural and paranormal beings.

Of course, there always has to be a start to a story and Judgement of Souls: Origin, was created and proved to be the hardest book to write. It involved a lot of Crusader history but I'm not a stranger to research. JOS2 involved over 300 years of mortal history including the French Revolution – did you know that a vampire started it?

I have also visited most of the locations from JOS2 and JOS3 that I use in those novels so I have first-hand knowledge of every street, every corner or building that I place my characters in. It's been extremely fascinating.

For JOS3 I visited one of the main synagogues in London to talk about the Hebrew Bible that I use 'loosely' in the trilogy and it's worked out really well.

I've written a few short stories too that I am very proud of... they have been such fun to write and my latest, The Decoys is about two women who are duped by two very handsome thieves to take a very valuable necklace out of the country – but in this case, who's fooling who?

And of course, I have to mention Ordinary Wins that's had some great reviews. It's about how ordinary women can win and find their dream – which in this case just happens to be a famous drummer in a rock band.

JOIN the JOS Facebook pages.
Come on by and join the fangs... vV""Vv
http://www.facebook.com/JudgementOfSouls3TheKissAtDawn

https://www.facebook.com/Margarita-Felices-1406676682975558/

Follow me on Twitter: @felicm60

Follow me on Instagram:
https://instagram.com/felicm60/

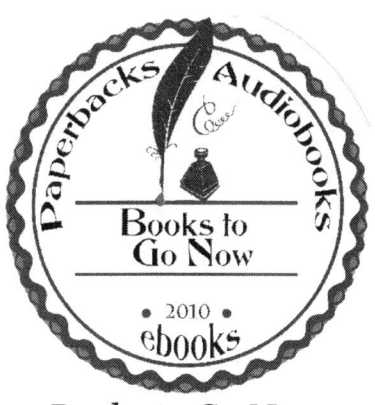

Books to Go Now

You can find more stories such as this at www.bookstogonow.com

If you enjoyed this Books to Go Now story, please leave a review for the author on the review site where you purchased the eBook. Thanks!

We pride ourselves with representing great stories at low prices. We want to take you into the digital age, offering a market that will allow you to grow along with us in our journey through the new frontier of digital publishing.

Some of our favorite award-winning authors have joined us. We welcome readers and writers into our community.

We want to make sure that as a reader, you are supplied with never-ending great stories. As a company, Books to Go Now, wants its readers and writers supplied with positive experiences and encouragement, so they will return again and again.

We want to hear from you. Our readers and writers are the cornerstone of our company. If there is something you would like to say or a genre that you would like to see, please email us at inquiry@bookstogonow.com

Printed in Poland
by Amazon Fulfillment
Poland Sp. z o.o., Wrocław